The

Submissive

The Submissive

TARA SUE ME

 NEW AMERICAN LIBRARY

New American Library
Published by the Penguin Group
Penguin Group (USA) Inc., 375 Hudson Street,
New York, New York 10014, USA

USA | Canada | UK | Ireland | Australia | New Zealand | India | South Africa | China

Penguin Books Ltd., Registered Offices: 80 Strand, London WC2R 0RL, England
For more information about the Penguin Group visit penguin.com.

First published by New American Library,
a division of Penguin Group (USA) Inc.

First Printing, June 2013

Copyright © Tara Sue Me, 2013

REGISTERED TRADEMARK—MARCA REGISTRADA

New American Library Trade Paperback ISBN:978-0-451-46622-8

Printed in the United States of America
1   3   5   7   9   10   8   6   4   2

Set in Perpetua
Designed by Sabrina Bowers

To MsKathy, I'm forever grateful for the gift of your friendship
and
To Mr. Sue Me, thank you for your unwavering support and for never saying, "You wrote what?"

The
Submissive

Chapter One

"Ms. King," the receptionist said. "Mr. West will see you now."

I stood, wondered for the twenty-fifth time what I was doing, and went to open the door leading to the office I'd traveled across town to enter. On the other side was my darkest fantasy, and by stepping inside, I'd be making it a reality.

I was proud of the fact my hands didn't shake as the door opened and I walked into his office.

Step one: done.

Nathaniel West sat at a large mahogany desk, typing on a computer. He didn't look up or slow his strokes. I might as well not even have entered, but I dropped my eyes just in case.

I stood still while I waited. Face looking at the floor, hands at my sides, feet spread to the exact width of my shoulders.

Outside the sun had set, but the lamp on Nathaniel's desk gave a muted light.

Had it been ten minutes? Twenty?

He was still typing.

I counted my breaths. My heart finally slowed from the rocket speed it'd been racing at before I entered the office.

Another ten minutes passed.

Or maybe thirty.

He stopped typing.

"Abigail King," he said.

I started slightly, but kept my head down.

Step two: done.

I heard him pick up a stack of papers and tap them into a pile. Ridiculous. From what I knew of Nathaniel West, they would have already been in a neat pile. It was another test.

He pushed his chair back, wheels rolling over the hardwood floor the only sound in the quiet room. He walked with measured, even steps until I felt him behind me.

A hand lifted my hair away from my neck, and warm breath tickled my ear. "You have no references."

No, I didn't. Just a crazy fantasy. Should I tell him? No. I should remain silent. My heart beat faster.

"I would have you know," he continued, "that I'm not interested in training a submissive. My submissives have always been fully trained."

Crazy. I was crazy to be here. But it was what I wanted. To be under a man's control.

No. Not any man. *This* man's control.

"Are you sure this is what you want, Abigail?" He wrapped my hair around his fist and gave a gentle tug. "You need to be sure."

My throat was dry, and I was fairly certain he heard my heart beating, but I stood where I was.

He chuckled and returned to his desk.

"Look at me, Abigail."

I'd seen his picture before. Everyone knew Nathaniel West, owner and CEO of West Industries.

The pictures didn't do the man justice. His skin was lightly tanned and set off the deep green of his eyes. His thick dark hair begged you to run your fingers through it. To grab on it and pull his lips to your own.

His fingers tapped rhythmically on his desk. Long, strong fingers. I felt my knees go weak just thinking about what those fingers could do.

Across from me, Nathaniel gave the faintest of smiles, and I made myself remember where I was. And why.

He spoke again. "I'm not interested in why you decided to submit your application. If I select you and you are agreeable to my terms, your past won't matter." He picked up the papers I recognized as my application and ruffled through them. "I know what I need to."

I recalled filling out the application—the checklists, the blood tests he'd required, the confirmation of the birth control I was on. Likewise, before today's meeting, I'd been sent his information for review. I knew his blood type, his test results, his hard limits, and the things he enjoyed doing with, and to, play partners.

We stood in silence for several long minutes.

"You have no training," he said. "But you're very good."

Silence again as he stood and walked to the large window behind his desk. It was completely dark, and I saw his reflection in the glass. Our eyes met, and I looked down.

"I rather like you, Abigail King. Although I don't recall telling you to look away."

I hoped I hadn't messed up beyond redemption and looked back up.

"Yes, I think a weekend test is in order." He turned from the window and loosened his tie. "If you agree, you will come to my estate this Friday night at six exactly. I'll have a car pick you up. We'll have dinner and take it from there."

He placed his tie on the couch to his right and unbuttoned the top button of his shirt. "I have certain expectations of my submissives. You are to get at least eight hours of sleep every

Sunday through Thursday night. You will eat a balanced diet—
I will have a meal plan e-mailed to you. You will also run one
mile, three times a week. Twice a week you will engage in
strength and endurance training at my gym. A membership will
be created for you starting tomorrow. Do you have any concerns
about any of this?"

Another test. I didn't say anything.

He smiled. "You may speak freely."

Finally. I licked my lips. "I'm not the most . . . athletic, Mr.
West. I'm not much of a runner."

"You must learn not to let your weakness rule you, Abigail."
He walked to his desk and wrote something down. "Three times
a week you will also attend yoga classes. They have these at the
gym. Anything else?"

I shook my head.

"Very well. I will see you Friday night." He held out some papers to me. "These will have everything you need to know."

I took the papers. And waited.

He smiled again. "You are excused."

Chapter Two

The door to the apartment next to mine opened as I walked by. My best friend, Felicia Kelly, stepped out into the hallway. Felicia and I had been friends forever, having grown up together in the same small Indiana town. Throughout elementary and middle school we sat side by side, thanks to the alphabetical seating arrangements. After high school graduation, we attended the same college in New York, where we quickly learned that if we wanted to remain best friends, we should live as neighbors and not roommates.

Though I loved her like the sister I'd never had, she could at times be bossy and overbearing. Likewise, my need for regular quiet time drove her mad. And, apparently, so had my meeting with Nathaniel.

"Abby King!" Her hands were on her hips. "Did you have your phone off? You went to see that West guy, didn't you?"

I just smiled at her.

"Honestly, Abby," she said. "I don't know why I even bother."

"I know. Tell me, why do you bother?" I asked as she followed me inside. Settling down on the couch, I started reading the papers Nathaniel had given me. "By the way, I won't be here this weekend."

Felicia gave a loud sigh. "You went. I knew you would. Once

you get an idea in your head, you just move right on ahead. You don't even think about the outcome."

I continued reading.

"You think you're so smart. Well, what do you think the library will say about this? What will your father think?"

My father still lived in Indiana, and though we weren't close, I was certain he'd have a definite opinion about my visit to Nathaniel's office. A very negative opinion. Regardless, there was no way anyone was going to discuss my sex life with him.

I set the papers down. "You're not saying a word to my dad, and my personal life isn't the library's business. Got it?"

Felicia sat down and examined her nails. "I don't got anything." She grabbed the papers. "What are these?"

"Give those back." I yanked the papers from her.

"Really," she said. "If you want to be dominated so badly, I know several men who would be more than willing to oblige."

"I'm not interested in your ex-boyfriends."

"So you're going to march into a strange man's house and let him do who-knows-what to you?"

"It's not like that."

She walked over to my laptop and turned it on. "So what is it like, exactly?" She leaned back in her chair while the screen booted up. "Being a rich man's mistress?"

"I'm not his mistress. I'm his submissive. Make yourself at home, by the way. Please, feel free to use my laptop."

She typed frantically on the keyboard. "Right. Submissive. That's *so* much better."

"It is. Everyone knows that the submissive holds all the power in the relationship." Felicia hadn't done the research I had.

"Does Nathaniel West know that?" She had pulled up Google and was searching Nathaniel's name. Fine. Let her find him.

All at once, his handsome face filled the screen. He was looking at us with those piercing green eyes. One arm was wrapped around a beautiful blonde at his side.

Mine, the stupid side of my brain said.

This Friday night through Sunday afternoon, the more responsible side countered.

"Who's she?" Felicia asked.

"My predecessor, I suppose," I mumbled, returning to reality. I was an idiot. To think he'd want me after he'd had *that.*

"You've got some pretty high stilettos to fill, girlfriend."

I only nodded. Felicia noticed, of course.

"Damn it, Abby. You don't even wear stilettos."

I sighed. "I know."

Felicia shook her head and clicked the next link. I looked away, not needing to see another shot of the blond goddess.

"Hello, baby," she said. "Now, I'd let *him* dominate me anytime."

I looked up to see a picture of another handsome man. *Jackson Clark, New York quarterback*, the caption said.

"You didn't tell me he was related to a professional football player."

I didn't know. But it'd do no good to tell Felicia any of this—she was no longer paying me any attention.

"I wonder if Jackson is married," she mumbled, clicking on links to bring up more information on his family. "Doesn't look like it. Hmm, maybe we can pull up more details on the blond chick."

"Don't you have anything better to do?"

"Nope," she said. "Nothing to do but sit here and make your life miserable."

"Show yourself out," I said, walking into my bedroom. She could spend all night digging up whatever she wanted on Nathaniel—I had reading to do.

I took the papers Nathaniel had given me and curled up on my bed, tucking my legs up under me. The first page had his address and contact information. His estate was a two-hour drive from the city, and I wondered if he had another property closer to town. He had also given me the security code to get through his gate and his cell phone number should I need anything.

Or in case you come to your senses, that annoying smart part of my brain chimed in.

The second page had the details of my gym membership and the exercise program I would have to follow. I swallowed the unease that thoughts of running brought up. More details followed on the strength and endurance classes he wanted me to take. At the bottom, in very neat cursive, was the name and number of the yoga instructor.

Page three informed me I'd have no need to bring any bags with me on Friday. Nathaniel would provide all the toiletries and clothing I needed. Interesting, that. But what else did I expect? It also contained the same instructions he'd given me earlier—eight hours of sleep, balanced meals—nothing new there.

Page four listed Nathaniel's favorite meals. Good thing I could cook. I'd look closer at those later.

Page five.

Let's just say page five left me hot, bothered, and waiting for Friday.

Chapter Three

Nathaniel West was thirty-four years old. His parents had died in a car accident when he was ten. Linda Clark, his aunt, had raised him after that.

Nathaniel had taken over his father's company at the age of twenty-nine. He'd taken what was already a profitable business and made it even more so.

I'd known about him for ages. Knew of him in that society-page way those in the lower classes know of the upper class. The papers painted him as a hard-ass. A real bastard. But I liked to think I knew a bit more about the real man.

Six years ago, when I was twenty-six, my mother had gotten into a really bad situation over credit card debt, following her divorce with Dad. She owed so much, the bank threatened foreclosure on her house. They would have been well within their rights to do so. But Nathaniel West had saved the day.

He was on the bank's board of directors and convinced them to allow Mom a way to save her house and get out of debt. She died of heart disease two years later, but for those two years, every time his name was mentioned in the papers or on the news, she would retell the story of how he'd helped her. I knew he wasn't the hard-ass the world thought he was.

And when I heard about his more . . . delicate tastes, my

fantasies started. And kept on. And kept on, until I knew I had to do something about them.

Which was why I found myself pulling into the driveway of his estate in a chauffeur-driven car at 5:45 that Friday evening. No luggage. No bags. Just my purse and cell phone.

A large golden retriever stood at the front door. He was a beautiful dog, with intense eyes that watched as I got out and made my way to the house.

"Good boy," I said, holding my hand out. I wasn't overly fond of dogs, but if Nathaniel had one, I needed to grow used to him.

The dog whined, walked toward me, and pushed his nose into my hand.

"Good boy," I said again. "Who's a good boy?"

He gave a short bark and rolled over so I could pet his belly. Okay, I thought, maybe dogs weren't so bad.

"Apollo," a smooth voice said from the front door. "Come."

Apollo's head lifted at his owner's voice. He licked my face and trotted to stand beside Nathaniel.

"I see you've made Apollo's acquaintance." Nathaniel was dressed casually today—a light gray sweater and darker gray pants. The man could wear a paper bag and look good. It really wasn't fair.

"Yes," I said, standing and brushing imaginary dirt off my pants. "He's a very sweet dog."

"He's not," Nathaniel corrected. "Normally, he doesn't take kindly to strange people. You're very fortunate he didn't bite you."

I didn't say anything. Nathaniel turned and walked into the house; he didn't even look back to make sure I followed. I did, of course.

"We'll have dinner tonight at the kitchen table," he said as he led me through the foyer. I tried to take in the decor—a subtle mixture of the antique and contemporary—but it was hard to take my eyes off Nathaniel as he strode along in front of me.

We walked down a long hallway past several closed doors, and all the while he talked. "You can consider the kitchen table your free space. You'll take the majority of your meals there, and when I join you, you may take it as an invitation to speak freely. Most of the time, you will serve me in the dining room, but I thought we should start the evening on a less formal basis. Is all this clear?"

"Yes, Master."

He turned, and there was ire in his eyes. "No. You have not yet earned the right to call me that. Until you do, you will address me as 'sir' or 'Mr. West.'"

"Yes, sir," I said. "Sorry, sir."

He resumed walking.

Forms of address were a gray area, and I hadn't known what to expect. At least he hadn't seemed too upset.

He pulled a chair out from a finely carved table and waited for me to sit down. Silently, he sat across from me.

Dinner was already on the table, and I waited for him to take a bite before I ate anything. It was delicious. Someone had baked chicken breasts and topped them with a delectable honey-almond sauce. There were also green beans and carrots, but I hardly noticed them, the chicken was so tasty.

It dawned on me, eventually, that there was no one else in the house, and dinner had been waiting. "Did you cook this?" I asked.

He inclined his head slightly. "I am a man of *many* talents, Abigail."

I shifted in my seat, and we resumed eating in silence. I was too nervous to say anything. We'd almost finished before he spoke again.

"I am pleased you do not find it necessary to fill the silence with endless chatter," he said. "There are a few things I need to explain. Keep in mind, you can speak freely at this table."

He stopped and waited for my response.

"Yes, sir."

"You know from my checklist I'm a fairly conservative dom. I do not believe in public humiliation, will not participate in extreme pain play, and I do not share. Ever." The corner of his mouth lifted. "Although as a dom, I suppose I could change that at any time."

"I understand, sir," I said, remembering his checklist and the time I'd spent completing mine. I really hoped this weekend hadn't been a mistake. My cell phone felt reassuring in my pocket; Felicia knew to call the police if I hadn't checked in within the next hour.

"The other thing you should know," he said, "is that I don't kiss on the lips."

"Like *Pretty Woman*?" I asked. "It's too personal?"

"*Pretty Woman*?"

"You know, the movie?"

"No," he said. "I've never seen it. I don't kiss on the lips because it's unnecessary."

Unnecessary? Well, there went the fantasy about pulling him to me with my hands buried in that glorious hair.

I took a last bite of chicken as I thought more about what he'd said.

Across from me, Nathaniel continued talking. "I recognize that you're a person with your own hopes, dreams, desires, wants, and opinions. You have put those things aside to submit to me this weekend. To put yourself in such a position demands respect, and I do respect you. Everything I do to or for you, I do with you in mind. My rules on sleeping, eating, and exercise are for your benefit. My chastisement is for your betterment." He ran a finger around the rim of his wineglass. "And any pleasure I give you"—the finger ran down the stem once and back up—

"well, I don't suppose you have any qualms concerning plea-sure."

I realized I was gaping at him when he smiled and pushed himself away from the table.

"Are you finished with dinner?" he asked.

"Yes, sir," I said, knowing I wouldn't be able to eat any more, my thoughts consumed by his remarks on pleasure.

"I need to take Apollo outside. My room is upstairs, first door on the left. I will be there in fifteen minutes. You will be waiting for me." His green eyes gazed steadily at me. "Page five, first paragraph."

I'm not sure how I made it up the stairs—every step felt like I wore iron shoes. But I had only fifteen minutes, and I needed to be ready when he returned. At the top of the stairs, I sent Felicia a text saying that all was okay and I was staying, adding our agreed-upon secret code so she'd know it was really me.

I pushed open the door to Nathaniel's room and gasped. Candles were everywhere. In the middle of the room was a large four-poster bed made of heavy wood.

However, according to page five, first paragraph, the bed wasn't my concern. I looked down. The pillow on the floor was.

Beside the pillow was a sheer nightgown. My hands shook as I changed. The gown barely skimmed my upper thighs, and the gauzy material would show every part of my body. I folded my clothes and put them in a neat pile beside the door. All the while I was chanting to myself:

This is what you wanted.

This is what you wanted.

After repeating that about twenty times, I finally calmed

down. I went to the pillow, knelt on it, and sat with my butt resting on my heels. I stared down at the floor and waited.

Nathaniel entered minutes later. I risked a peek and saw that he'd removed his sweater. His bare chest was muscular; he had the look of one who worked out frequently. His pants were still belted at the waist.

"Very nice, Abigail," he said when he'd closed the bedroom door. "You may stand."

I stood with my head down as he walked around me. Maybe in the candlelight he wouldn't be able to see how badly I trembled.

"Strip the gown off and place it on the floor."

Moving with as much grace as I could, I pulled it over my head and watched it flutter to the ground.

"Look at me," he commanded.

He waited until my gaze met his and then he slowly removed his belt. He gathered it in one hand and walked around me again. "What do you think, Abigail? Shall I chastise you for your 'Master' remark?" He snapped the belt, and the leather tip struck me. I jumped.

"Whatever you wish, sir," I managed to choke out, surprised by how turned on I felt.

"Whatever I wish?" He continued walking until he stood before me. He unbuttoned his pants and pushed them down. "On your knees."

I dropped to my knees and had my first glance at Nathaniel naked. He was magnificent. Long, thick, and hard. Very long. Very thick. Very hard. The reality was so much better than the fantasy.

"Service me with your mouth."

I leaned forward and took the tip of him past my lips. Slowly, I moved to take the rest of him in. He felt even larger in my mouth, and I couldn't help but think what it would feel like to take him inside my body in other ways.

"All of it," he said when he reached the back of my throat.

I raised my hands to feel how much more I had left to go.

"If you can't take it in the mouth, you can't have it anywhere else." He pushed forward, and I relaxed my throat to take him the rest of the way. "Yes. Like that."

I'd misjudged just how large he was. I made myself breathe through my nose. It wouldn't do to pass out on him.

"I like it hard and rough, and I'm not going to go easy on you just because you're new." He fisted his hands in my hair. "Hold on tight."

I had just enough time to wrap my arms around his thighs before he pulled out and rammed himself back in my mouth. He pumped in and out several times.

"Use your teeth," he said.

I pulled my lips back and scraped his length as he moved in and out. Once I got used to his size, I sucked a bit and wrapped my tongue around him.

"Yes," he moaned as he pounded into me harder.

I did this, I thought. I made him hard and had him moaning. It was *my* mouth. Me.

He started to twitch inside my mouth.

"Swallow it all," he said, pumping in and out. "Swallow everything I give you."

I nearly choked as he came, but I shut my eyes in order to focus. Salty spurts shot down my throat, but I managed to swallow.

He pulled out, gasping. "That, Abigail," he said with heavy breaths, "that is what I wish."

I sat back on my heels as he pulled his pants on.

"Your room is two doors down on the left," he said, calm

once more. "You sleep in my bed by invitation only. You are excused."

I pulled the gown back on and gathered my discarded clothing.

"I will take breakfast in the dining room at seven sharp," Nathaniel said as I left the room. Apollo slipped in past me through the open door and curled up at the foot of Nathaniel's bed.

Thirty minutes later, wide-awake and buried under the covers, I replayed the scene over and over in my mind. I thought of Nathaniel: his aloof manner, the calm way he issued commands, his absolute control. Not only had our encounter met my expectations, but it had exceeded them.

I couldn't wait for the rest of the weekend.

Chapter Four

I overslept the next morning, waking with a start and cursing under my breath when I saw the time. Six fifteen wouldn't give me enough time to shower if I was going to have breakfast on the table by seven. I hurried into the adjoining bathroom and brushed my teeth. Barely looking in the mirror, I pulled a brush through my hair and made a sloppy ponytail.

I grabbed a pair of jeans and a long-sleeved T-shirt out of the closet, surprised they fit until I remembered the papers I filled out had asked for my size. My gaze fell on the unmade bed as I stepped out the door. Leaving it crossed my mind briefly, but then I decided Nathaniel was probably a neat freak. I didn't want to make him angry my first weekend.

Your first weekend? my sensible side asked. *You think there will be more?*

I decided to ignore my sensible side.

The single bed wasn't big enough for two people, and I huffed in disappointment as I made it. Apparently, Nathaniel wouldn't be joining me in my bedroom. And from the sounds of it, nights spent in his would be few and far between.

I passed the indoor gym on my way to the kitchen and heard Nathaniel on a treadmill. I glanced at my watch and cringed.

6:35. No time to make my signature breakfast of French toast with bananas Foster sauce. Maybe another day.

Nathaniel walked into the dining room seconds after I set his scrambled eggs, toast, and cut fruit on the table. His hair was freshly washed and he smelled all outdoorsy and musky. Delicious. My heart raced just thinking about tasting him.

I stood by his right side as he ate. Not once did he look my way, but he gave a small sigh of satisfaction after the first bite.

When he finished eating, he looked up at me. "Make yourself a plate and eat in the kitchen. Come to my bedroom in an hour. Page five, paragraph two."

And with that, he left the dining room.

Why would he bother telling me to eat right before ordering me to his bedroom? Like I'd be able to eat anything, thinking about his words. But I scrambled an egg, cut up more fruit, and ate at the kitchen table like he'd told me to.

Sunlight streamed through the kitchen window, and I could see Nathaniel outside, walking with Apollo. The dog galloped through the large yard, scaring the birds on the lawn. Nathaniel was on the phone, but when Apollo came up to him, he reached down and ran a hand through his fur.

I sighed and looked around the kitchen. I wondered if the blonde ever ate at the kitchen table and if she was a good cook.

Regardless, she was gone. I was the one in his house, at least for the weekend.

I cleaned up the breakfast plates and made my way upstairs.

Page five, paragraph two was what I called the OB-GYN pose. Lying in the middle of Nathaniel's big bed, without a stitch of clothing on, I felt exactly like I was at the doctor's office. I actually missed that flimsy bit of paper they give you.

I closed my eyes and concentrated on breathing, telling myself I'd be up to anything Nathaniel had planned. Maybe he'd finally touch me.

"Keep your eyes closed."

I jerked. I hadn't even heard him enter the room.

"I like you spread out like this," he said. "Take your hands and pretend they're mine. Touch yourself."

He was driving me crazy. I'd tried to imagine how the weekend would go, and so far it was nothing like I'd thought. He hadn't touched me once. It was so unfair.

"Now, Abigail."

I lifted my hands to my breasts, and in my mind they became his hands. It was easy. I'd done this a hundred times.

Nathaniel's warm breath brushed across my ear as his hands caressed me. His touch started out soft and gentle but quickly grew rough as our breathing became choppy.

He was needy and I was what he needed.

He was hungry and I was the only thing he could consume.

With painful slowness, he rolled the tip of one nipple and then the other. I bit the inside of my cheek, awash in the sensations he created. He pinched, pulling hard, and then harder when I gasped.

I became the needy one. I needed him. Wanted him. Craved him. I trailed a hand down my stomach—aching and desperate to be filled. Wanting him to fill me.

He pushed my knees farther apart, and I was spread before him in offering. He would take me, finally. Take me and be done with it. He'd fill me like I'd never been filled before.

"You disappoint me, Abigail."

Dream Nathaniel disappeared. My eyelids fluttered.

"Keep your eyes closed."

He was inches from my face, and I smelled the maleness of him. My heart beat frantically while I waited for him to continue.

"You had me stuffed in your mouth last night, and now you use a single finger to represent my cock?"

I slipped another finger inside. Yes. Better.

"Another."

I added a third and started moving them in and out.

"Harder," he whispered. "I'd fuck you harder."

I wouldn't last long, not with that type of talk. I pushed deeper, imagining him stretching me. My legs tightened and a low groan escaped my lips.

"Now," Nathaniel said, and I exploded.

There was utter silence for several minutes as my breathing returned to normal. I opened my eyes and found him standing beside the bed, forehead glistening with sweat. His erection strained against the front of his pants.

"That was an easy orgasm, Abigail," he said, staring at me with those sultry green eyes. "Don't expect that to happen often."

But on the upside, I thought, at least it sounded like there *would* be more.

"I have a previous engagement this afternoon and won't be here for lunch. There are steaks in the refrigerator that you will serve me at six in the dining room." His eyes swept over my body, and I forced myself to remain still. "You need to shower since you didn't have time this morning."

Damn, the man didn't miss anything.

"And," he continued, "there are yoga DVDs in the gym. Make use of them. You may leave."

———————

I didn't see him again until six o'clock that night. If the steak dinner had been some sort of test and he wanted to see me fail, he would be sadly disappointed. I'd been known to bring grown men to their knees with my steak.

Okay, that was a lie. And I knew I had no hope of bringing Nathaniel West to his knees, but I could still cook up a pretty mean steak.

Of course, he didn't compliment my cooking. But he'd asked me to eat with him, so I sat in silence beside him.

I picked up a forkful of steak and put it in my mouth. I wanted to ask where he'd been all afternoon. If he lived in the city during the week. But we were at the dining room table and I couldn't.

After we finished, he told me to follow him. We walked through the house, past his bedroom to the room before mine. He opened the door, stepped to the side, and bade me enter first.

The room was dark. A single small lamp gave the only light. Two thick chains with shackles were suspended from the ceiling. I spun around to gape at him.

He didn't look surprised. "Do you trust me, Abigail?"

"I . . . I . . ." I stuttered.

He walked around me and unbuckled a shackle. "What did you think our arrangement would entail? I thought you were well aware of what you were getting yourself into."

Yes, I knew. But I'd thought chains and shackles would come later. Much, much later.

"If we are to progress, you must trust me." He unbuckled the other shackle. "Come here."

I hesitated.

"Or," he said, "you can leave and not come back."

I walked toward him.

"Very good," he said. "Take your clothes off."

It was worse than the night before. At least then I'd had some idea of what he wanted. Even earlier on his bed hadn't been too horrible. But this, this was madness.

The crazy part of me relished it.

When I was completely naked, he took my arms, stretched them above my head, and chained them. He stepped away and took off his shirt. Rummaging through a drawer in a nearby table, he took out a scarf and came back.

He lifted the black material. "Your other senses will be heightened when I blindfold you."

Then he tied the scarf around my eyes and the room went dark. I heard footsteps, and then there was nothing. No light. No sound. Nothing. Just the racing thump of my heart and my shaky breathing.

Light as air, something brushed my hair aside, and I jumped.

"What do you feel, Abigail?" he whispered. "Be honest."

"Fear," I answered in my own whisper. "I feel fear."

"Understandable, but completely unnecessary. I would never cause you harm."

Something delicate circled my breast. Excitement pulsed between my legs.

"What do you feel now?" he asked.

"Anticipation."

He chuckled, and the sound reverberated along my spine. I felt him draw another circle—teasingly, barely touching me. "And if I told you this was a riding crop, what would you feel?"

A riding crop? My breath caught. "Fear."

The crop swished through the air and landed sharply on my breast. I gasped at the sensation. It hurt briefly, but not too bad.

"See?" he asked. "Nothing to fear. I won't cause you harm." The crop hit my knees. "Spread your legs."

I felt even more exposed now. My heart doubled its tempo, but something inside me was lit with excitement.

He trailed the crop from my knees to the apex between my legs. Right where I was most needy. "I could whip you here," he said. "What do you think about that?"

"I . . . I don't know," I confessed.

The crop smacked three times in quick succession right near my clit. It stung, but the sting was replaced almost immediately by the need for more.

"And now?" he asked, the crop swishing gentle as a butterfly between my legs.

"More," I begged. "I need more."

The crop circled gently a few times before he snapped it against my aching center. Again and again it struck, each time bringing a pain laced with sweet pleasure. I cried out as it hit again.

"You look so good chained before me, pulling against my restraints, in my house, crying for my whip." The crop tickled my breast once more. "Your body is begging for release, isn't it?"

"Yes," I admitted, surprised at how much I needed release. I pulled against the chains, wanting to touch myself, to bring myself pleasure if he wouldn't.

"And you'll have it." The crop smacked against my core once more. "But not tonight."

I whimpered as I heard him walk away. Somewhere in the room, a drawer opened. I pulled on the chains again. What did he mean, not tonight?

"I'm going to unchain you now," he said. "You will go straight to bed. You will sleep naked and you will not touch yourself at all. There will be severe consequences if you disobey."

He undid the chains one at a time, gently rubbing a sweet-smelling lotion on each wrist. Then he removed the blindfold. "Do you understand?"

I looked in his deep green eyes and knew he meant what he said. "Yes, sir."

It would be a long night.

Chapter Five

The smell of bacon woke me the next morning.

I jumped out of bed and ran to my watch. Six thirty. Why was Nathaniel cooking? He hadn't said anything about what time to meet him for breakfast. Surely I couldn't be in trouble for not knowing he wanted breakfast earlier, right?

I rushed through another morning ritual of bed making, brushing my teeth, and dressing. I wasn't sure what time I'd be headed home. Maybe I'd have time later for a shower.

I made it downstairs right at seven. Nathaniel sat at the kitchen table and two places were out.

"Good morning, Abigail," he said. There was an excitement in his voice and eyes that hadn't been there before. "Did you sleep well?"

I'd slept horribly. It was bad enough I'd gone to bed all hot and needy, but sleeping naked had done nothing to help. Memories of what he'd done to me the previous night flooded my mind.

"No." I sat down. "Not really."

"Go ahead and eat."

He'd cooked for an army: bacon, eggs, and fresh blueberry muffins. I raised an eyebrow at him, and he smiled.

"Do you sleep?" I asked.

"On occasion."

I nodded as if that made perfect sense and dove into my food. I hadn't realized how hungry I was. I'd finished three slices of bacon and half my eggs before he spoke again.

"I've had a nice weekend, Abigail."

I tried to wrap my head around his calling the last two days a *nice weekend*. Must be some sort of crazy dom humor.

"I'd like to proceed with our relationship," he said.

I choked on a bite of muffin. "You would?"

"I'm very pleased with you. You have an interesting demeanor and a willingness to learn."

I was surprised he could tell anything from the little time we'd spent together, but answered, "Thank you, sir."

"You have an important decision to make today. We can discuss the details after breakfast and your shower. I'm sure you have a few questions for me."

It might be the only opening I had, and I took it. "Can I ask you something, sir?"

"Of course. This is your table."

I took a deep breath. "How did you know I didn't take a shower yesterday morning or this morning? Do you live here during the week, or do you have a place in the city? How did—"

"One question at a time, Abigail," he said, holding up a hand. "I am an extraordinarily observant man. Your hair didn't look like it'd been washed yesterday. I guessed you didn't take a shower this morning because you rushed in here like you had a demon chasing you. I live here on weekends and have a place in the city."

"You didn't ask if I followed your instructions last night."

"Did you?"

"Yes."

He took a sip of coffee. "I believe you."

"Why?"

"Because you can't lie—your face is an open book." He folded his napkin and placed it beside his plate. "Never play poker; you'll lose."

I wanted to be angry, but I couldn't. I'd tried to play poker once with Felicia and lost badly. "Can I ask another question?"

"I'm still at the table."

I smiled. Yes, he was. All that hard man-muscle, that gorgeous body, that smug grin—they were still at the table. With me. "Tell me about your family."

He raised an eyebrow, as if he couldn't believe that was what I wanted to know. "I was adopted by my aunt Linda when I was ten. She's chief of staff at Lenox. My uncle died a few years ago. Their only child, Jackson, plays for the Giants."

"I've seen his picture in the papers," I said. "My best friend, Felicia, asked if I knew whether or not he was single."

His eyes narrowed and his lips pressed together in a thin line. "How much did you tell your friend about me?" he asked. "I believe the papers from Godwin were very clear concerning my stance on confidentiality."

"It's not like that," I said. "Felicia's my safety call; I had to tell her. But she understands; she won't tell anyone anything. Trust me. I've known her since grade school."

"Your safety call? Is she in the lifestyle?"

I shook my head. "Quite the opposite, actually, but she knows I wanted this weekend, so she agreed to do it for me."

My answer seemed to satisfy him; he gave a slight nod. "Jackson doesn't know about my lifestyle and, yes, he's single." The corner of his mouth lifted. "I have a tendency to be a bit overprotective—he's had to deal with his share of gold diggers."

"Felicia's not a gold digger. Granted, it doesn't hurt that he's a good-looking professional athlete. But she's got the biggest heart of anyone I know and is loyal to a fault."

He didn't look convinced. "What does she do?"

"She's a kindergarten teacher. Petite, redheaded, and gorgeous."

"Why don't you give me her number? I'll pass it on to Jackson and he can decide if he wants to call her."

I smiled. Felicia would owe me big-time.

His expression grew serious. "Getting back to what I said earlier, I want you to wear my collar, Abigail. Please consider it while you shower. Meet me in my room in an hour and we'll discuss it further."

His collar? Already? I wasn't expecting to be collared so quickly. How come whenever I spoke with Nathaniel I always felt more flustered and confused at the end of the conversation than I did at the beginning?

From his spot on the floor, Apollo looked up at me and whined.

An hour later, Nathaniel waited for me in his room, holding a box. A cushioned bench was in the middle of the floor. He waved toward it. "Have a seat."

When I'd left my bathroom earlier, I'd found a silver satin bathrobe with matching panties and a bra waiting for me on the bed. I thought it was pretty high-handed of Nathaniel to set my clothes out, but I *had* agreed to his terms.

Which was why I gathered the robe around me and sat as daintily as possible on the soft bench. Nathaniel wore faded blue jeans and nothing else. Not even socks. I sighed. Even his feet were perfect.

He turned and set the box on the dresser by his bed. When he faced me again, he held a platinum choker made of two thick ropelike strands twisted together. Sunlight bounced from the facets of the numerous diamonds embedded in the platinum. "If you choose to wear this, you'll be marked as mine. Mine to do with as I wish. You will obey me and never question what I tell you to do. Your weekends are mine to fill as I wish. Your body is mine to use as I wish. I will never be cruel or cause permanent harm, but I am not an easy master, Abigail. I will have you do things you never thought possible, but I can also bring you a pleasure you never imagined."

My skin broke out in a cold sweat. He stepped even closer. "Do you understand?"

I nodded. "I understand, sir."

"Will you wear this?"

Again, I nodded.

He moved behind me, his hands brushing my neck as he fastened the collar. It was the first time he'd touched me all weekend, and I jumped at the contact.

"You look like a queen," he said, moving his hands across my shoulders and pushing the robe off. "And now you're mine." His hands moved under my bra and gently swept over my breasts. "These are mine." His hands ran down my sides. "Mine." He placed a kiss on my neck, then bit me gently.

His lips. His hands. His touch. I threw my head back and sighed at how wonderful they felt.

"Mine." His hands continued their descent. He reached the waistband of my panties and pushed it aside. "And this?" He slid a finger inside me. "All mine."

He moved his finger in and out, and I discovered I'd been right about his fingers—they could do wonderful things. They stroked hard and deep, but right when I was on the edge, he pulled them out. "Even your orgasms are mine."

I groaned in frustration. Damn it, would he ever let me climax?

"Soon," he whispered. "Very soon. I promise."

Soon, like sometime in the next hour? The choker felt heavy around my neck. I reached up to touch it.

"It looks very nice on you." He took a pillow from the bed behind him and put it on the floor. "Your safe word is *turpentine*. Say it and this ends immediately. You take the collar off, drive away, and never return. Otherwise, you will come here every Friday. Sometimes you will arrive at six and we'll have dinner in the kitchen. Other times, you'll come at eight and head straight to my room. My orders for sleep, food, and exercise remain. Do you understand?"

I nodded.

"Good." He continued. "I'm often invited to society functions. You will attend these with me. I have one such function next Saturday night—a benefit for one of my aunt's nonprofits. If you do not have a ball gown, I will provide you with one. Is all this clear? Ask me if you have any questions."

My brain was fuzzy. I couldn't think straight. "I have no questions."

He leaned forward and whispered in my ear, "*I have no questions . . .*"

He wanted something, wanted me to say something. What was it?

"Say it, Abigail. You've earned it."

The light dawned. "I have no questions, Master."

"Yes. Very nice." He pulled back, the excitement shining in his eyes once more. He went and stood behind the pillow and unbuttoned his jeans. "Now come and show me how happy you are to wear my collar."

Chapter Six

Felicia had raised an eyebrow when I returned home on Sunday, but hadn't said anything. I supposed as long as I made it home in one piece, she wouldn't comment. She'd told me I was stupid once, and in her mind that was enough warning. And she had other things to occupy her time—Jackson Clark called her that night to invite her to the black-tie benefit. She had accepted and they'd talked every day since.

That same Sunday evening, while Felicia had been talking to Jackson, I'd also been busy. I sat down at my computer and pulled up my browsing history. I had to see the picture of *her* again. Had to see if she had my collar on. I drummed my fingers on the desk as I waited. *My collar.* Could it really be mine if countless other women had worn it? The page loaded. There was Nathaniel, but my eyes weren't drawn to him, just to his date.

I breathed a sigh of relief when I saw she didn't have the diamond choker on. Instead, she wore a strand of pearls. I cocked my head to the side. Would Nathaniel have collared her with pearls? Frustrated, I shut off the computer.

Monday through Friday, I went to work as usual at one of New York's public libraries, surrounded by books and the people who love them. Books usually soothe me. "Usually" being the operative word. Two days a week, I tutored teenagers in English and literature. I enjoyed helping them, seeing the light in their eyes as they worked through an unusually hard problem or discovered a new skill—but on Wednesday one of my students had caught me fingering my collar. Just a simple "Nice necklace, Ms. King," had me all aflutter. Nathaniel had forbidden me to take it off. I tried not to think of what the boy's parents would say if they knew what I'd done last weekend. What I planned to do this weekend.

It's not anyone's business. My time is my time, I thought with a nod of my head. Then it hit me—my time on the weekends wasn't mine anymore. It was Nathaniel's.

By Friday it had been a long week. Technically, it hadn't even been a week since I'd seen him, just five days. But it felt like ten.

Nathaniel was waiting for me when I pulled up to his estate that night at six o'clock sharp. He'd set out plates of angel hair pasta with clam sauce.

"How was your week?" he asked when I'd swallowed my first bite.

"Long," I said. No need to lie about it. "How was yours?"

He shrugged. Of course he wouldn't admit to looking forward to the weekend. But even if he would, there was no way he had as many butterflies in his stomach as I did in mine.

What would we do tonight? Would he touch me? I remembered how his hands had run over my body on Sunday and I shuddered.

"Apollo killed a gopher."

I nodded. It was insane, both of us sitting and eating dinner like we were just a normal couple. Like it was a normal Friday night. Like he hadn't chained me up naked less than a week ago and whipped me with a riding crop. Like I hadn't *liked* it. I shifted in my seat.

"My friend Todd's wife, Elaina, brought a gown by earlier. They're looking forward to meeting you."

My head snapped up at that. "Your friends? Does everyone know about us?"

He twirled a strand of pasta around his fork and brought it to his mouth. That mouth. Those lips. I watched as he chewed and leisurely swallowed. Ugh. It was getting hot in the kitchen. I quickly ate a bite.

"They know you're my date," he said. "They don't know about our agreement."

Agreement. Yes, that was a nice way to put it. I concentrated on cutting my pasta. Across from me, Nathaniel ran a finger around the rim of his wineglass. He was taunting me, playing me like a violin. And doing a masterful job.

"So do you plan to touch me this weekend or not?" I blurted out.

His finger stopped and his eyes narrowed. "Ask me the question in a more respectful manner, Abigail. Just because this is your table doesn't mean you can talk to me any way you choose."

My face heated.

He waited.

I dropped my head. "Will you touch me this weekend, Master?"

"Look at me."

I did. His green eyes were blazing. "I plan to do more than touch you," he said slowly. "I plan to fuck you. Hard and repeatedly."

His words sent an electric shock from my head to the aching spot between my legs. There was a reason he was a master—he could do more with a few simple words than most men could do with their entire body.

He pushed back from the table. "Let's get started, shall we? I want you naked and on my bed in fifteen minutes."

Chapter Seven

I was starting to see how Nathaniel worked. How he could turn me on with just a look. Make me long for his touch with a simple word or phrase.

Like now, as I waited on his bed. Driving me mad and he wasn't even *in the room*. Dinner had been one long, drawn-out foreplay session. Watching him eat pasta, the way his fingers worked the wineglass, I was strung tight, ready, and nearly begging for him.

He hadn't even touched me.

He walked into the room with slow, purposeful steps. The candlelight illuminated his bare chest and made his eyes look darker. Silently, he went to the foot of the bed and lifted a shackle.

My rational self whispered that I should be afraid. I should be shouting "turpentine" at the top of my lungs. I should get out of the house and away from the man who had way too much control over my body and me.

Instead, I watched in suppressed excitement as he shackled me spread-eagle to the bed.

He spoke to me in that soft, seductive voice of his. "I wasn't going to do this tonight, but I can see you still don't understand completely. You are mine and you are to do and behave as I tell you. The next time you speak disrespectfully to me, I will spank you. Nod if you understand."

I nodded and tried not to show how much the idea turned me on.

"My last submissive could make me climax three times a night," he said, and I wondered briefly if he was talking about the blonde. "I want to try for four."

Four? Was that even possible?

From his pocket he drew out a black scarf. "And I want you totally at my mercy."

I took a deep breath. I could do this. I wanted this. I stared into his dark green eyes, and then he put the scarf in place and I couldn't see anything.

I heard the slow metallic sound of a zipper and I knew he was taking his pants off. He was as naked as I was now. My heart raced.

Two large hands started at my shoulders and ran gently down my sides. He moved past my breasts without touching them and circled my belly button. One finger dipped lower and skimmed my entrance. I groaned.

"How long has it been, Abigail?" he asked. "Answer me."

The last time I'd had sex? "Three years."

I hoped he wouldn't ask me any questions about why. We were both finally naked and on his bed—I didn't want to think about how none of my past boyfriends could satisfy me.

His finger dipped in again. I felt the bed shift as he leaned closer to me. "You're not ready yet. You need to be ready, or else I won't be able to ride you as hard as I want."

I felt him pull back and then his mouth was at my neck, slowly kissing his way lower until he was at my breast. He circled his tongue around my nipple, blowing gently. Then his mouth closed over it and he sucked, rolling his tongue around the tip. I gasped when he scraped me with his teeth.

He moved to the other side, starting gently, but gradually increasing his force until it became too much. I lifted my chest toward him without shame. If he kept up, I'd climax from his mouth alone. He continued his assault on my nipples while dipping a hand lower. Roughly, his fingers pressed against me, working their way down my body to where my legs were spread, open and waiting for him. His fingers rubbed harshly and I pushed against him, needing friction, needing something.

His fingers and mouth left, and I groaned as the cool air rushed in against my body. The bed shifted again and I felt him straddle me. His hard, thick length touched the valley between my breasts.

He thrust against me. "Do you think you're ready, Abigail? Because I'm tired of waiting. Are you ready?" He thrust again. "Answer me!"

"Yes, Master. Please. Yes."

He lifted his hips, and I felt his tip at my mouth. "Kiss my cock. Kiss it before it fucks you."

I pressed my closed lips against him and that's all I meant to do. Really. But I felt a drop of liquid at his tip and I couldn't help it—I stuck my tongue out and licked it off.

Nathaniel drew in a sharp breath through his teeth and lightly slapped my cheek. "I didn't tell you to do that."

Some part of me rejoiced that I'd made a slight crack in his carefully controlled demeanor, but then he moved down my body and lifted my hips with one hand and I didn't care about anything except what he was about to do. Every nerve ending I had tingled.

Slowly, he pressed into me and I groaned.

Yes!

He pushed more and I was stretched and filled. More than I'd ever been. He moved slowly, inching his way inside, until it got uncomfortable.

He wasn't going to fit.

"Damn," he said.

I sensed him move up. He took my hips in both hands and rocked back and forth, working his way in deeper.

"Move with me."

I lifted my hips and felt him slide in another inch. We both moaned. He gave a rough push and thrust in completely.

Beneath the blindfold, my eyes rolled to the back of my head.

He pulled out a bit and slid back in. Testing. Teasing. But I was finished with teasing. I needed more. I lifted my hips when he pushed in again.

"You think you're ready?" he asked. Before I could answer, he pulled almost all the way out, leaving me empty and wanting. He took a deep breath and slammed back into me, pulling out immediately.

I pulled against the restraints, frustrated, when he didn't return. And then he did. Again and again and again. Pushing me deeper into the bed with each thrust. I answered each one by lifting my hips to get more of him inside, wanting him even deeper. Wanting it even harder.

I felt my climax building with each slam of his body into mine. He moved above me, his hands holding my hips in an iron grasp.

"Come when you want," he panted, thrusting again, and I came apart in a million pieces.

He thrust deeper inside and held still, muscles shaking as he released into me. A few more quick thrusts and I came again.

Slowly, his breathing returned to normal.

Slowly, I came back to earth.

Hungry hands moved up my body. He pushed my hair aside and whispered in my ear.

"One."

He unbound my legs for our second time, though he left the blindfold on. He said he could go even deeper with my legs wrapped around him, and even though I knew he had lots more experience than I did, I wanted to tell him going deeper was physically impossible.

Good thing I kept that to myself, because when he entered me a second time and wrapped my legs around his waist, he did go deeper. He hit spots I didn't even know I had.

I was breathless when he moved off the bed. He rustled beside me. I still couldn't see anything, but I turned my head in his direction.

He unbound my arms and took off the scarf. "You'll sleep in my room tonight, Abigail. I'll take you again at some point during the night, and I don't want to be troubled with walking down the hall." He waved at the floor. "I made you a pallet."

Was he insane? He wanted me to sleep on the floor? I cocked an eyebrow at him.

"Do you have a problem with my order?"

I shook my head and, minutes later, fell asleep in between the cool sheets he'd laid out for me beside his bed.

"Wake up, Abigail."

It could have been hours or minutes later. I wasn't sure. It was still dark—only one candle lit the room.

"Hands and knees on the bed. Quickly."

I scurried on top of the bed, still half asleep, and positioned myself.

"Lean on your elbows."

I dropped to my elbows.

Two strong hands rubbed my backside and pushed my legs farther apart. "You were tight the other way, but you'll be even tighter like this."

Damn him and his sensual mouth. I was wide-awake within seconds.

His hands moved to my back, up to my shoulders and around my chest to roll my nipples. He gave each one a hard tug. His hands traveled back down to the spot where I pulsed for him, and he dipped a finger in lightly. The finger traveled to my backside and ran around my smaller hole.

I gasped.

He pushed against it. "Has anyone ever taken you here before?"

He knew the answer. It was on my checklist. I shook my head anyway, though, unable to speak. I wasn't sure I was ready for that.

"I will," he promised.

Every muscle I had tensed.

"Soon," he said, dropping his finger, and I let out a shaky breath. Soon, maybe, but not immediately.

He guided himself to where I was wet and ready. His hands made their way to my head, and he wrapped my hair around his wrists. His length pushed inside me as he pulled back on my hair. The delicious feel of him filling me was too much, paired with the sharp tug on my head. I let out a sigh of pleasure.

He pulled out and slammed back inside with a hard thrust of his hips and a quick jerk of my hair. Over and over, and he was right. I was tighter. I felt every inch of him. Every thrust forced him deeper inside and pushed my knees into the mattress. I grabbed on to the sheets and rocked my hips up and back to meet him. He groaned.

The familiar tingle of impending release built up, and my body screamed with the intensity of it. Or it might have been me. I couldn't tell. Didn't care.

Nathaniel gave one last thrust, and I yelled with the force of my climax. He quickly followed, releasing into me with a grunt.

I fell on top of the bed, panting. I might have dozed.

I came fully awake when he flipped me over and pushed his hips in my face. "Round four, Abigail."

He was already half hard. It shouldn't have been possible. Damn. What time was it? I turned my head to see if there was a clock beside the bed.

"Look at me." He turned my head back to his cock. "I'm your concern right now. Me and what I tell you. And right now I want you to serve me with your mouth."

I opened my mouth, showing my willingness. And later, when he'd released into me for the fourth time and lay on top of me gasping, I smiled.

I knew I'd served him well.

Chapter Eight

I woke to the feel of sunlight on my skin and blinked a few times in confusion. Where was I? I glanced to my right and saw the massive bed above me. Right. On the floor. By Nathaniel's bed.

I stretched my legs and groaned. I ached in places I didn't know I had and a few I'd long ago forgotten. I tentatively got to my feet and took a few steps. I'd give my right arm and part of my left for a bathtub, but it looked as though I'd have to make do with a hot shower.

After a long, thorough shower, I hobbled into the kitchen. Nathaniel sat at the table, *my* table, glued to his phone, texting or e-mailing, I supposed. He looked perfectly fine.

Biology totally screwed women.

Literally.

"Rough night?" he asked, not even bothering to look at me.

What the hell. He was at my table. I could speak honestly. "You could say that again."

"Rough night?" he asked again, a small smile lifting the corners of his mouth.

I poured my coffee and stared at him.

He was teasing me. I could barely walk, my back ached from sleeping on the damn floor, it was all his fault, and he was *teasing* me?

It was sweet in some sort of sick, twisted way.

I snatched a blueberry muffin from the counter and took a seat cautiously. I wasn't able to hide my wince.

"You need protein," he said.

"I'm fine," I answered, taking a bite of muffin.

"Abigail."

I stood up, hobbled over to the refrigerator, and took out a pack of bacon. Damn. Now I had to cook.

"I put two boiled eggs in the warming oven for you." His eyes followed me as I put the bacon away and retrieved my eggs. "The ibuprofen is on the first shelf, second cabinet beside the micro-wave."

I was pathetic. He was probably wishing he'd never collared me. "I'm sorry. It's just . . . been a long time."

"What a ridiculous thing to apologize for," he said. "I'm more upset over your attitude this morning. I didn't have to let you sleep in."

I sat back down and hung my head.

"Look at me," he commanded. "I have to leave. Meet me in the foyer dressed for the benefit and ready to leave at four thirty."

I nodded.

He stood up. "There's a large tub in the guest room across the hall from yours. Make use of it."

And just like that, he was gone.

I felt more human after a long soak and some ibuprofen. After drying off, I brewed a cup of tea, sat at the kitchen table, and called Felicia.

"Hey," I said when she answered.

"Abby," she replied. "I didn't know you were allowed phone calls."

"It's not like that."

"So you keep saying," she said in that I-don't-give-a-shit-what-you-say-I'm-not-going-to-believe-you voice. "Of course, since you're by yourself, it's not like you have anything better to do."

It wasn't often Felicia caught me off-guard. "How'd you know I was by myself?"

"Jackson said he was playing golf and having lunch with Nathaniel and some Todd guy before the benefit tonight. Of course, you're probably on a need-to-know basis with Nathaniel, so you wouldn't have known."

I could hear her smug smile through the phone, and I wondered why on earth I'd thought it was a good idea to call Felicia in the first place.

"We didn't have much time together this morning," I said offhandedly, like I couldn't care less why Nathaniel hadn't told me where he was going. It was a lie on my part—it hurt for some reason. "And remember, Jackson doesn't know about Nathaniel's—"

"Honestly, Abby, your kinky sex life isn't anyone's idea of appropriate first-date conversation."

The front door opened and closed.

"I have to go. Nathaniel's back," I said, thrilled to have a reason to hang up and thrilled Nathaniel was back.

"Are you sure?" she asked, interested for the first time. "It's far too soon—and Jackson said he'd call when they finished and I haven't heard from him."

"Got to go. Bye." I ended the call right as someone walked into the kitchen.

It wasn't Nathaniel.

A tall, willowy woman with short brown hair and red eyeglasses looked at me in shock. An expression that probably matched my own.

"Oops," she said. "I didn't know anyone was here."

"Who are you?" I asked, certain that if Nathaniel had expected someone to stop by he would have mentioned it.

"Elaina Welling," she said, holding a hand out. "My husband, Todd, and Nathaniel go way back."

I shook her hand. "Abby King. I'm sorry. Nathaniel didn't mention anyone stopping by."

She held up the black satin evening bag in her hand. "I forgot to bring this by when I dropped off the dress." Her eyes locked on my choker and, I swear, she gave a sly smile.

"Would you like some tea?" I asked.

"Yes," she said, sitting down. "I think I would."

I poured her a cup and we chatted pleasantly. After only fifteen minutes, I felt as if I'd known her forever. Elaina was the kindest, most down-to-earth person I'd talked to in a long time. She'd moved into the Clarks' neighborhood before high school and Linda had become a surrogate mom to her. Hearing that Elaina had lost her own mother as a child somehow made me feel even closer to her. When I spoke of my mom's passing four years ago, Elaina nodded, took my hand, and simply said, "You'll always miss her, but I promise it gets easier."

During our conversation, I noticed her eyes drift to my collar several times, but she never said anything about it. I wondered briefly if Nathaniel had lied when he said his family and friends didn't know about his lifestyle, but quickly decided he wasn't the type to lie.

Nearly half an hour had passed without our realizing it when Elaina looked at her phone and gave a little cry. "Oh no, look at the time! We need to get busy if we aren't going to be late." She kissed me on the cheek as she left and promised we'd talk more at the benefit.

I have an active imagination, and when I first tried to imagine the gown Nathaniel would have me wear, I'll admit my thoughts drifted toward leather and lace. But the gown waiting for me on my bed was gorgeous. A one-of-a-kind design I'd never have been able to afford with a two-year advance on my salary. Black satin, with a low gathered neck and delicate shoulder straps, formfitting without being vulgar or revealing. It was floor-length and flared just a bit at the bottom. I loved it.

I normally didn't wear makeup, but Felicia Kelly was my best friend and she never passed a cosmetics counter without stopping, so I knew a thing or two about proper application. With my hair swept up off my shoulders in the best up-style I could manage, I looked in the mirror. "Not too bad, Abby," I said to myself. "I think you might manage to make an appearance without embarrassing yourself or Nathaniel."

One quick stop in my bedroom to slip on the heels and I was off. Down the stairs to meet Nathaniel in the foyer, and, I'd admit, giddy as a teenager on her first date.

I stepped into the foyer and stopped.

Nathaniel waited with his back to me. He had a long, black wool overcoat on. A dark scarf was tucked around his neck and his hair brushed the collar. He turned around when he heard me.

I'd seen Nathaniel in jeans and I'd seen Nathaniel in a suit. But there wasn't a sight on this earth that compared to Nathaniel in a tuxedo.

"You look beautiful," he said.

"Thank you, Master," I managed to choke out.

He held out a black wrapper. "Shall we?"

I nodded, and when I walked to him, it was as if I walked on air. I wasn't sure how he did it, but he actually made me feel beautiful.

He draped the wrapper around me, hands lightly brushing my shoulders. Unbidden, images of last night flashed through my head. I remembered those hands. Remembered what they'd done to my body.

There was no other way to describe it, I decided as we walked outside—I was nervous. Nervous about being seen in public with Nathaniel. He'd said once he wasn't into public humiliation. I hoped that meant he wouldn't ask me to go down on him at the dinner table. And I was nervous about meeting his family. What would they think of me? He usually dated high-society types, not librarians.

January in New York was cold, and it had been one of the coldest on record. But leave it to Nathaniel—the car was running and toasty warm inside. He even opened the passenger side door, like a true gentleman, and closed it once I was inside.

We drove in silence for a long time. Eventually, he turned the radio on, and a soft piano concerto filled the interior.

"What kind of music do you like?" he asked.

The delicate melody playing had a soothing effect on me. "This is fine."

And that was all the conversation we had on the way to the benefit.

A valet took the car when we arrived and we walked into the building's entrance. Living in New York for as long as I had, I'd grown accustomed to the skyscrapers and crowds, but walking up the stairs that night, being part of the high-society crowd I typically just watched, made me feel overwhelmed. Thankfully, Nathaniel kept his hand on the small of my back, and it was oddly reassuring.

Taking a deep breath, I waited while Nathaniel gave my wrapper and his overcoat to the woman working the coat check.

Within minutes of our entrance, Elaina trotted toward us with a tall, good-looking man in tow. "Nathaniel! Abby! You're here!"

"Good evening, Elaina," Nathaniel answered with a slight inclination of his head. "I see you've met Abby already." He turned to me and lifted an eyebrow. I hadn't mentioned Elaina's visit to him—though I had no idea why, I felt he'd disapprove.

"Oh, lighten up." Elaina smacked his chest with her purse. "I had a cup of tea with Abby when I stopped by your house earlier today—so yes, Nathaniel, we've already met." She turned to me. "Abby, this is my husband, Todd. Todd, this is Abby."

We shook hands, and he seemed pleasant enough. Unlike his wife, his eyes showed no shock over my collar. I glanced around, wondering if Jackson and Felicia had arrived yet.

"Nathaniel," another voice said.

The woman in front of us stood with a grace and elegance that gave her a regal appearance. Even so, her eyes were kind and her smile welcoming.

I knew immediately she had to be Nathaniel's aunt.

"Linda," Nathaniel confirmed. "Allow me to introduce Abigail King."

Nathaniel could call me Abigail, but I'd be damned if everyone he knew would. "Abby," I said, holding out my hand. "Please call me Abby."

"Nathaniel said you work at the New York Public Library—at the Mid-Manhattan branch," Linda said after I shook her hand. "I go by there on my way to the hospital. Maybe we could meet for lunch sometime."

Was that even allowed? Could I have lunch with Nathaniel's aunt? It seemed way too personal. But I couldn't turn her down; I didn't want to turn her down. "I'd like that."

She asked me about the release date for several new books by her favorite authors. We chatted a few minutes about our likes and dislikes—we both enjoyed thrillers and read very little science fiction—before Nathaniel interrupted.

"I'll get us some wine," he said to me. "Red or white?"

I froze. Was this a test? Did he care what type of wine I wanted? What was the correct answer? I'd been so comfortable talking with his aunt, I'd forgotten I wasn't the average dinner date.

Nathaniel leaned close, so that only I heard him. "I don't have a hidden agenda. I simply want to know."

"Red," I whispered.

He nodded and went off to get our drinks. I watched him move away—it was such a joy simply watching him walk. A young teenager interrupted him, though, halfway to the server. The two embraced.

I turned to Elaina. "Who's that?" I couldn't imagine anyone having the nerve to walk up and hug Nathaniel like that.

"Kyle," she said. "Nathaniel's recipient."

I felt totally clueless. "Recipient?"

"Nathaniel's bone marrow, of course." She waved to the banner at the front of the room, and I read for the first time that this was the New York Bone Marrow Association Benefit.

"Nathaniel donated bone marrow?"

"It was a few years ago. Kyle was eight, I think, and Nathaniel saved his life. They had to drill into Nathaniel in four different places, and he was awake the entire time. He said it was worth it, though, to save a life."

I think my eyes were still bugged out when Nathaniel returned. Fortunately, we were called to dinner shortly and I could turn my attention to other matters.

Jackson and Felicia were already at our table. They sat turned to each other, engrossed in conversation. Nathaniel held my chair out for me while I sat down. Felicia smiled briefly, but quickly went back to Jackson.

"Looks as if they both owe us one," Nathaniel said after he sat down.

"Abby," Jackson finally said, standing up and shaking my hand across the table. "I feel as though I already know you."

I shot Felicia an angry look.

It wasn't me, her expression said. *I don't know what he's talking about.*

"Hey, Nathaniel," Jackson said. "How cool is it you and I are dating besties? The only thing better would have been if they were sisters."

"Shut up, Jackson," Todd said. "Act like you have some manners."

"Boys, please," Linda chimed in. "Felicia and Abby will be afraid to join us again if you keep this up."

The *boys*, as Linda called them, managed not to make too much of a ruckus again. I could see that they must have made for a boisterous childhood growing up. They all played off one another. Even Nathaniel joined in on occasion, but he was the most reserved.

Our appetizers were served first. The waiter put a plate of three large scallops in front of me.

"Hell, Mom," Jackson said. "Three scallops? I've got play-offs starting soon." But he dug in and ate anyway, mumbling the entire time about "pansy" food.

"Jackson was raised by bears," Nathaniel whispered to me. "Linda let him in the house only every so often. It's why he fits in so well on the team. They're all animals."

"I heard that," Jackson said across the table.

Felicia giggled.

Salads and entrées soon followed, and I didn't know about Jackson, but I was getting quite full. Through it all, everyone kept a steady conversation going. I learned Elaina was a fashion designer, and after she entertained everyone with runway mishaps, Jackson chimed in with football stories.

I turned to Nathaniel when we'd finished our entrées. "I need to find the restroom." I stood, and all three men at the table did the same.

I almost sat back down. I'd read about it, seen it in a movie even, but I'd never had an entire table full of men stand up simply because I had. Even Felicia looked shocked.

Fortunately, Elaina covered for me. "I think I'll go with you, Abby." She walked over and took my hand. "Come on."

We weaved through the tables to the restrooms, Elaina leading the way. "I guess it can be a bit overwhelming, seeing all of us together," she said. "You'll get used to it."

I didn't have the heart to tell her I didn't think I'd be invited to many family functions. We made it into the restrooms. A large sitting room, bigger than my kitchen, met us. When I finished in the back part of the bathroom, Elaina was waiting for me at a large lighted dresser.

"Do you ever know something, Abby?" she asked. She swept powder over her nose, although I wasn't sure why—she looked perfect. "You know, *really* know something? Deep in your heart?"

I shrugged, took Elaina's example, and reapplied my makeup.

"I do," she continued. "And I want you to know—you're good for Nathaniel." She glanced at me. "I hope you don't mind me saying that. It's just I feel as though we've known each other forever."

"I feel the same," I said. "Like you and I have known each other forever, I mean." Not that I was good for Nathaniel. I didn't mean that at all.

"I know he can be a prick and I know he's hard to get to know, but I've never seen him smile more than I have tonight." She turned to face me. "It has to be you."

My hands shook as I redid my lipstick. I'd think about the

conversation later, when I was alone in the dark that night. Or maybe sometime during the week when Nathaniel wasn't so close. Sometime when I wouldn't have to look in his eyes and wonder what I was seeing reflected.

I dropped the lipstick back in my bag. Elaina hugged me. "Don't let the hard exterior get to you," she said. "He's a great guy."

"Thanks, Elaina," I whispered.

Dessert and coffee were waiting for us when we returned. All the men stood up again and Nathaniel held my chair out. Across the table, Elaina winked. I looked down at my chocolate cheesecake. Was she right?

After dessert, a small band started playing. Couples from around the room got up and began to dance.

The first two songs were fast and I sat back in my chair, happy just to watch. When the third song started, it was slower. A simple piano melody.

Nathaniel stood and held out a hand. "Will you dance with me, Abigail?"

I don't dance—I've been known to clear a dance floor faster than a bad rendition of the "Macarena"—but my mind was still reeling after what Elaina had told me, and across the table, Linda's hand fluttered to her lips, as if to hide a smile.

I looked up at Nathaniel; his green eyes were dark and I knew this wasn't an order. I could turn him down. Politely decline and nothing would be said. But at that moment, I wanted nothing more than to be in his arms, to feel him in mine.

I took his hand. "Yes."

We'd been together in the most intimate way there was, but I'd never felt closer to Nathaniel as he put his arm around my waist and pulled me close, our joined hands tucked against his chest.

I was certain he could feel me tremble in his arms. I wondered if this was his plan all along——to have me trembling and aching in public. I wouldn't have put it past him.

"Are you having a nice time?" he asked, his breath hot in my ear.

"I am," I said. "Very nice."

"Everyone is quite taken with you." He pulled me closer, and we spun slowly across the dance floor as the song continued.

I tried to wrap my head around everything I'd learned about Nathaniel that night. How he'd donated bone marrow to a total stranger, the way he played with his family and friends. And I thought about Elaina most of all, about what she'd said in the bathroom. Thought about it all and tried to reconcile it with the man who'd had me tied to his bed the night before. The one who claimed he wasn't easy to serve. I couldn't do it.

And as we danced, I knew one thing——I was dangerously close to falling more than just a little bit in love with Nathaniel West.

We made it back to Nathaniel's house right before midnight. It'd been a quiet ride back. Fine with me. I wasn't in the mood to carry on a conversation. Not with anyone. Especially Nathaniel.

Apollo ran up to us when Nathaniel opened the door. I stood back, afraid he would soil my gown.

"Keep the gown on and wait in my room," Nathaniel said. "The way you did in my office."

I walked up the stairs slowly. Had I done something wrong? I thought back over the evening and pondered the many, many mistakes I might have made. I hadn't told Nathaniel that Elaina had come by. I insisted everyone call me Abby. I told Linda we'd have lunch. What if it was a test when he'd asked what kind of wine I wanted? What if I should have said white? What if I should have said, *Whatever you wish, Mr. West?*

My mind came up with three thousand things I'd done wrong, each one more ridiculous than the last. I wished he'd given me some instruction before we'd left.

He was still dressed when he entered. At least I think he was. My head was down; all I saw were his shoes and pants as he walked in front of me.

He moved behind me, each step slower than the one before. His hands came up and softly traced the top of the gown. "You were spectacular tonight." He started taking the pins from my hair. Soft curls fell around my shoulders. "And my family will talk about nothing but you now."

Did that mean he wasn't mad? I hadn't done anything wrong? I couldn't *think* with him so close.

"You pleased me tonight, Abigail." His voice was smooth, his lips dancing along my back, close but not quite touching. "Now it's my turn to please you."

He drew the zipper of my gown down and slowly pushed the straps from my shoulders. His lips were on me then. Trailing my spine as the gown made its way down and fell to a puddle at my feet.

He swept me into his arms and carried me to his bed. "Lay down," he said, and I could do nothing but obey.

I hadn't worn any hose, and he knelt between my legs and slipped my heels off. Dropped them to the floor. He looked up, met my eyes, and then bent down to place a kiss on the inside of my ankle. I gasped.

But he didn't stop. His lips kissed gently all the way up my leg as his hand softly brushed the other. He reached my panties, and a long finger hooked at the waistband.

I knew exactly what he was doing, what he was going to do. "Don't," I said, putting a hand on his head.

"Don't tell me what to do, Abigail," he whispered. He slipped the panties down, and I was naked and spread before him once more.

No one had ever done this to me before. Kissed me *there*. And I was sure that was what he was getting ready to do. I ached for it, needed it, and I closed my eyes in anticipation.

He kissed me gently, right on my clit, and I grabbed the sheets, all coherent thought leaving me. I didn't care what he did anymore. I just needed him. Needed him badly. In whatever way he wished.

He blew on me and went back to kissing. Taking his time, moving slowly, letting me grow used to him. Placing kisses sporadically, soft as whispers.

He licked me and I bucked off the bed. Shit. Forget his fingers. His fingers had nothing on his tongue. And he was soft and slow, licking me, nipping me. I struggled to close my legs, to keep the sensation inside, but he slipped his hands to my knees and pushed them apart.

"Don't make me tie you up," he warned, and his voice vibrated against me, causing shudders to work their way up and down my body.

His tongue was back, licking where I needed it, and his teeth nibbled gently. All the while, the familiar tingling of my climax built up, starting where his mouth was and spreading down my legs, up my torso to my breasts, circling my nipples.

But no, that wasn't me, those were Nathaniel's hands. And he was working me with his mouth, while his fingers stroked my nipples. Tugged. Pulled.

And licked and nibbled down below.

I twisted the sheets, wrapping them around my wrists, pulling hard as I pressed against him. His tongue swirled around my clit, and I gave a small cry when pleasure overtook my body, starting where Nathaniel stroked softly and spiraling outward.

"I think it's time for you to go to your room," Nathaniel whispered when my breathing had returned to normal.

He was still completely dressed.

I sat up. "What about you? Shouldn't we . . ." I didn't know how to say it. But he hadn't climaxed. It didn't seem fair.

"I'm fine."

"But it's my place to serve you," I argued.

"No," he said. "It's your place to do as I say, and I say it's time for you to go to your room."

I slipped off the bed, warm and weightless. I was surprised my legs kept me up.

Between the emotions of the day and the relaxing release I'd just experienced, it wasn't long before I fell asleep.

That was the first night I heard the music—a piano somewhere, playing soft and sweet. Delicate and haunting. I searched for the sound in my dream, tried to find out who was playing, where the music was coming from. But I kept getting lost and each endless hallway looked the same. I knew somehow that the music was home, but I couldn't get there and, in my dream, I fell to my knees and sobbed.

Chapter Nine

I slept restlessly that night, twisting and turning, and at one point I woke up in a daze. An unexpected sadness filled me, but I couldn't remember what made me sad. Just something about music and not finding it, and in my confusion, I rolled over and went back to sleep.

I woke up at five thirty and realized why Nathaniel wanted me to get eight hours of sleep during the week—sleep on weekends was prime. I rolled out of bed with a groan.

I was showered and dressed by six fifteen, leaving plenty of time to finally make my signature French toast. A light shone from under the door of the gym. Nathaniel must already be up and working out. I wondered if I'd ever wake up before he did.

I yawned while dicing the bananas and beating the eggs. I loved to cook. Loved creating a meal that would give sustenance and taste good. If I didn't love books so much, I'd have been a chef.

I was sautéing the bread when Apollo plodded in. "Hey, Apollo," I called. "What's happening?"

He gave a soft woof, yawned, and rolled to his side.

"You too?" I asked, yawning again.

I thought over the previous night while the banana sauce cooked. It still seemed surreal. But it'd been a lot of fun.

Everyone had been so nice. And Nathaniel . . . I especially thought about Nathaniel, dancing with him and then up in his bedroom . . .

I almost burned the sauce.

At seven o'clock I served him breakfast, placing the toast on a plate and pouring the sauce over everything.

"Make yourself a plate and have a seat," he said. There was no trace of the gentleman of the previous night, but I knew he was there somewhere.

I sat down with my own food and had just taken a bite when he spoke again.

"I have plans for you today, Abigail," he said. "Plans to prepare you for my pleasure."

Plans to prepare me for his pleasure? What the hell? I'd been doing the yoga. I'd been running. I'd been following the diet plan—what else did he expect?

But we weren't at my table.

"Yes, Master," I said, looking down at my plate. My heart pounded. I wasn't hungry anymore. I swirled some sauce around my plate with a piece of bread.

"Eat, Abigail," he said. "You can't serve me on an empty stomach."

I wasn't too sure I'd be able to serve anything if my nerves caused me to throw up all over him, but I kept that thought to myself. I ate a bite of toast. I might as well have been eating cardboard.

After I'd finished enough of my breakfast to please Nathaniel, I cleared the table and went back to the dining room to stand beside him.

"You have far too many clothes on," he said. "Go to my room and take them all off."

My mind wrestled with itself on the way to his room. What else could we do that we hadn't done? I thought, trying to calm myself down. We'd had sex three times, he'd gone down on me the night before, and I'd served him orally at least three times. I could handle whatever was coming.

I'd done a halfway successful job of calming down. But then I entered his room and stopped short.

There was some sort of bench in the middle of the room—at least I thought it was a bench. It was waist high. And had a step.

The nervous excitement returned. I took off my clothes and put them in a messy pile beside the door. Then I stood and stared at the wooden contraption.

"It's a whipping bench," Nathaniel said, strolling into the room. "I use it for chastisement, but it serves other purposes as well."

Say it, rational brain side begged. *Turpentine. Say it.*

No, crazy side countered. *I want this.*

My inner struggle was lost on Nathaniel.

Or else he ignored it.

"Step up," he said. "And lie on your stomach."

Three little syllables and you can be on your way home, rational brain tried again.

Three little syllables and you'll never see him. He won't hurt you. Crazy side wanted to stay. Crazy side wanted Nathaniel.

He said he wouldn't cause you permanent harm. He never said it wouldn't hurt. Rational side had a point.

"Abigail." Nathaniel took a deep breath. "This is getting tiresome. Either do it or say your safe word. I won't ask again."

I considered my options for five seconds. Crazy side won. Rational side threatened to take a long vacation.

I took a deep breath and stepped on the bench. The wood was smooth and had a scooped area for my body.

Okay, this isn't too bad.

Nathaniel was doing something behind me. I heard him opening and closing drawers. Something was placed beside my hips.

"Do you remember what I told you Friday night?" he asked. It was a rhetorical question. I wasn't supposed to be talking unless he told me to specifically. He was messing with my mind.

I thought back to Friday night. Lots of sex, no sleep, lots of sex, aches and pains, sex, clam sauce, more sex . . . Total blank—I had no idea what he was talking about.

He placed two warm hands on my waist, stroked my backside, and I remembered him asking about anal sex.

Turpentine! rational brain side screamed. *Turpentine!*

I clenched my teeth to keep the word inside my head where it belonged. I clenched other parts of my body. Hell, I clenched my *entire* body.

"Relax." He stroked down my back. Any other time, it would have felt good. Any other time, I'd have purred with the pleasure of his hands on me. But not if he was going to want anal sex.

True, I hadn't marked it as a hard limit. I just thought it would come later.

There was rustling; he was taking his clothes off. I sucked in a deep breath and kept my body rigid.

Nathaniel sighed. "Move to the bed, Abigail."

I jumped down so quickly, I almost tripped. Nathaniel followed me to the bed—he was naked and magnificent, but I barely noticed.

"You have to relax." He took me in his arms. "This won't work if you don't." His mouth was on my neck, and I threw my arms around him. Yes, this I knew. This I could handle.

That wonderful mouth was doing unbelievable things to my skin. My body started to loosen as his mouth made its way down. His lips brushed my nipples, and I threw my head back as his tongue swirled around and around.

He placed kisses up and down my torso, his hands always stroking, always moving, igniting me with their touch.

"What I do, I do for your pleasure as much as mine." He nibbled my ear. "Trust me, Abigail."

And I wanted to. I wanted to trust him. The gentleman of last night I trusted. The dom with a whipping bench? Well, he was a bit harder to trust.

They're the same man, I told myself.

I was so confused, I didn't know what to think. I was trying so hard to work out what was happening. What would be the right thing to do. Who he was.

And the entire time, Nathaniel kept up his soothing murmurings.

"I can bring you pleasure, Abigail," he whispered. "Pleasure like you've never imagined."

He was knocking down my resistance. Erasing all my excuses. And I let him. I had no choice, really. He'd already claimed me.

He pulled back and looked in my eyes as he entered me. I moaned and tightened my arms around him.

It was then I realized that for the first time I had my arms free during sex. I ran a tentative hand down his back.

"Let it go, Abigail." He pushed farther into me. "Fear has no place in my bed."

He pulled out and started a fast tempo, all the while soothing me with his voice. All the while reassuring.

After a while, I couldn't remember what I was afraid of. Couldn't remember anything. Just Nathaniel and his bed and the feel of him pounding into me over and over and his voice whispering of promised pleasure.

My release began to tighten in my belly. Nathaniel pulled back from me, lifted my hips, and thrust in deeper. I was close, so close. I wrapped my legs around him, pulling him toward me. And just as he thrust in for the last time, something warm and slick pushed inside my backside, and I screamed as my climax overtook my body.

He said it was a plug. That it would help stretch me and I should wear it a few hours every day. Anal sex was totally outside of my experience. I had no idea what to expect, just nerves and anticipation. But he said he would give me pleasure, and until he did differently, I decided to believe him. He had never lied to me.

I left after lunch on Sunday. My last words from Nathaniel were that I was to return Friday night at six.

Felicia was all giggles that night when I got home.

"I've been waiting all day for you to get home," she said as I let her in. "Have I got a surprise for you."

Felicia's surprises typically involved new lipstick. But I sat down on the couch, tucked my legs under me, and told her to lay it on me.

"First off," she said, "you are the best friend, ever, for giving Nathaniel my number to give Jackson. Jackson is the best. I thought he'd be all into himself because he's a pro ball player, but he's not; he's so down-to-earth. And his mom? Can you believe her? She's so nice! And the way all the guys stood up when you had to pee? And Elaina stood up and went with you? And then——"

"Felicia," I interrupted. "At what point do we get to my surprise? Because I can do a replay of the entire evening all by myself." And I planned on doing just that. As soon as I was alone.

"Right," she said. "Sorry."

"No problem. Just get on with it."

She leaned close. "On the way home, I asked Jackson about his childhood. How long they've known Todd. How long Todd has been married to Elaina. If Nathaniel dated a lot of women—"

"Felicia Kelly!"

"I'm your best friend, Abby. It's my job to look out for you. Now, Todd grew up next door to the Clarks. He's known them all his life." She looked at me with an evil grin. "Nathaniel's dated three women seriously. Paige first, then Beth, and Melanie was the last one. Jackson called Melanie the 'Pearl Girl' because she always had on this strand of pearls." She looked at my choker. "Hate to know what he'll call you. Can't Nathaniel give you a ring like a regular guy?"

She kept on talking, but my mind was still processing what she'd just said. Three women. Three submissives. Three that the family knew of.

Felicia was still talking, "Nathaniel and Melanie broke up five months ago. Jackson said she was a real bitch and he was glad to see her go." She gave me another evil grin. "He also said you weren't Nathaniel's normal type, but that you seemed to be good for him."

That was the second person close to Nathaniel in two days who'd said I was good for him. They couldn't both be wrong, could they?

A new burst of energy shot through me, and I wasn't as sleepy as I'd been minutes before.

"That new movie we wanted to see comes on tonight," she said. "Want to watch it?"

It'd been too long since Felicia and I had bonding time—we were seriously overdue. "How long does it stay on?" I asked.

"Until eleven."

The movie finished at eleven. I had to be up at six. That was still seven hours of sleep—longer than I'd had the last two nights.

"Sure, let's watch it."

Chapter Ten

Apprehension gnawed at me as I was driven to Nathaniel's house on Friday night. His admin had called me at the library on Wednesday and said, "Mr. West will see you at eight on Friday—his car will pick you up, as usual." That was all. No details. No explanations. No nothing.

I was a bit disappointed—I rather liked our Friday night dinners. Eating with him before heading to his room eased me into the weekend nice and gently. And maybe it was just me, but I had the feeling he liked them as well. If for no other reason than to tease me. To work me up to what he had planned. Of course, I had a pretty good idea of what he had planned for the weekend. I had used the plug as directed and felt ready.

But still. I had the strangest feeling I was missing something.

It was dark when the car pulled into his driveway. No Apollo to meet me. No Nathaniel opening the door before I knocked.

I rang the doorbell.

The door opened slowly, and Nathaniel waved me inside.

"Abigail."

I nodded. Why were we standing in the foyer? Why was he looking at me like that?

"Did you have a good week?" he asked. "You may answer."

"It was fine."

"*Fine?*" he asked, both eyebrows going up. "I'm not entirely sure *fine* is the appropriate response."

I thought back over the week. Trying to see where this was going.

Nothing out of the ordinary sprang to mind. Work was the same. Felicia was the same. I did all the jogging. All the ridiculous yoga. I got eight——

Oh, no.

Oh, no. Oh, no. Oh, noooooo . . .

"Abigail," he said calmly. "Is there something you wish to tell me?"

"I got only seven hours of sleep on Sunday night," I whispered, looking at the floor.

How the hell did he know?

"Look at me when you speak."

I looked up at him. His eyes were blazing.

"I got only seven hours of sleep on Sunday night," I said again.

"Seven hours?" He took a step closer. "Do you think I put together a plan for your well-being because I'm bored and have nothing better to do? Answer me."

My face was hot. I was certain I'd pass out at any moment. Passing out would be good. Passing out would be preferable. "No, Master."

"I had plans for this evening, Abigail," he said. "Things I wanted to show you. Instead we'll have to spend the evening in my room, working on your punishment."

He looked as if he wanted me to say something. I wasn't sure I could speak. "I'm sorry to disappoint you, Master."

"You'll be sorrier still when I finish with you." He jerked his head toward the stairs. "My room. Now."

I've always wondered what it felt like for a condemned criminal to walk to their execution. How did they get their feet to move? Did they look over the streets or cells they passed and remember better times? Could they feel the eyes of the observers watching them as they passed?

I'm not saying it's the same. I know it's not.

You can only die once. You don't feel anything after you're dead.

I would feel what was coming my way.

But I made up my mind on the way to Nathaniel's room that I would take my punishment without complaint. He'd made the rules and I'd agreed to them. I'd broken one. There would be consequences. I could accept that.

I wasn't surprised to see the whipping bench back out. I took a deep breath and stripped my clothes off. I trembled a bit when I stepped up to the bench and leaned over it.

But where did my hands go? Crossed under my chest? That didn't seem right. I hung them down. That was uncomfortable. Above my head? No, that probably looked stupid.

I heard Nathaniel enter the room and, all of a sudden, my hands didn't matter anymore.

Part of me wished I could see his face, but another part of me was glad I couldn't. I was acutely aware that I was naked and exposed to him.

A warm hand touched my bottom and I jumped.

"I use three different types of spankings," he said, stroking me. "The first is an erotic spanking. It's used to heighten your pleasure, to excite you." His hand swept down my bottom and landed between my legs. "The riding crop, for example."

His stroking got progressively rougher and he pinched me. "The second spanking is for chastisement. You won't feel any pleasure. The purpose is to remind you of the consequences of disobedience. I make rules for your well-being, Abigail. How many hours of sleep are you supposed to get Sunday through Thursday? Answer me."

"Eight," I choked out. Could he not get on with it?

"Yes, eight. Not seven. You obviously forgot, so perhaps a sore backside will help you remember in the future."

He was silent. The only sound I heard was the beating of my heart thumping in my head.

"The third spanking is a warm-up spanking. It's used before a chastisement spanking. Do you know why I have to use a warm-up spanking?"

No, I'd never heard of a warm-up spanking. Damned if I'd say anything, though.

He placed a leather strap by my head. Right where I could easily see it.

"Because your ass can't handle the chastisement spanking first."

My hands groped madly for something to hold me to the bench.

"Twenty strokes with the leather strap, Abigail." He stopped. Waited. "Unless you have something you'd like to say."

He was goading me into saying my safe word! The nerve of him to think I'd give up so easily. I forced myself to remain completely still.

"Very well."

He started with his hand, smacking me lightly at first, and it wasn't too bad. It was almost pleasurable, actually. Nothing worse than the riding crop. But he kept on. And kept on. And kept on. It started to get uncomfortable and my body strained with the effort to hold still.

After a while, perhaps about five minutes, I started tensing before his hand landed and dreading when he'd strike me again. Because, damn it, it hurt and he hadn't even really started.

Tears sprang to my eyes. How long was this going to last?

Again and again his hand came down. Over and over. And, damn, this was only the warm-up.

He stopped, ran his hand over my backside as if he were gauging something on my skin. Then he took the strap from beside my head. "Count, Abigail."

Without warning, the strap whistled through the air and landed on my sore butt.

"Ow!"

"What?" he asked.

"One. I meant one."

Again it came down.

"Shit! I mean, two."

"Watch the language." Harder this time.

"Th . . . three."

Four hurt so badly, I reached out to cover myself. He stopped for a second and leaned over to whisper in my ear, "Cover yourself again and I'll tie you up and add an additional ten."

I crossed my arms and put them under my chest.

I was sobbing by eleven. Had a hard time catching my breath by fifteen. By eighteen, I'd decided I'd get ten hours of sleep. Every night. Just, please, stop.

"Quit begging."

I'd been talking out loud. Begging. I didn't care. The strap landed again. I blurted out something that might have been nineteen.

One more and it'd be over.

"How many hours of sleep are you to get, Abigail? Answer me."

I took a deep breath. Choked on snot. "Ei . . . ei . . . eight."

One more and it would be over.

"Twen . . . ty."

The only sound in the room came from me. Sobs and snorts. My body shook. I wasn't sure I could move off the bench.

"Clean your face and go to your bedroom," Nathaniel said. He wasn't even breathing heavily. "You have sleep to catch up on."

Chapter Eleven

The face looking back at me from the mirror was red and splotchy.

Well, Abby, I told my reflection, *no more bonding time with Felicia, huh?* Or if there were, it would end well before my ten o'clock bedtime.

I hobbled to the bedroom and lay on my stomach. I certainly hoped Nathaniel wouldn't want to do any . . . experimenting . . . this weekend. Plug or not, I was too sore even to think about it.

And what if he did? Would I say my safe word? The spanking, okay, I could handle that. I'd messed up. He'd let me know tonight, in no uncertain terms, that rules were rules were rules. But what if he wanted to try anal sex?

I just didn't think I could do it—not tonight. Not this weekend. I'd have to use my safe word.

I decided then and there, that was my limit. You needed to have limits. Had to tell yourself how far you'd go. And that was mine. No anal sex this weekend.

I thought about leaving Nathaniel.

And I got sad. Whether it was disappointing Nathaniel, the spanking, the thought of never seeing him again, or all three, I started crying. I pushed my face into the pillow—I didn't want *him* to hear. What if he came in?

As I cried, I heard footsteps echoing in the hallway. I stopped and held myself still. Had he heard? The steps stopped. I saw his feet underneath the door.

He continued walking.

I let out a shaky breath and forced myself to go to sleep.

The dream came back that night. The one with the music. It started out faster this time. Angry. Fierce. Then gradually grew into the same sweet longing of the song I'd heard the previous weekend. Sweetness laced with a hint of sorrow. In my dream, I ran from room to room. Desperate. I would find it this time. I would find out where the music was coming from. I pushed open door after door after door. But, like before, each one opened to another hallway and each hallway ended with a new door.

The music stopped. I reached another door and shoved it open. Only to see that it led to nothing . . .

Another Saturday morning. Another early-alarm-clock wake up. As I got ready, I thought about facing Nathaniel. What would he say? How would he act? What did he have planned for the weekend? Would the day see me saying my safe word and leaving?

I walked gingerly to the kitchen, my body achy all over. No sounds from behind the door of the gym. The kitchen was empty. My eyes swept over the room. There. On the table. A folded note.

On the outside, in neat script, was my name.

I opened it.

I'll be back at noon for lunch in the dining room.

I took a deep breath. He wasn't telling me to pack up and leave. Some part of me had feared he would.

I fixed a quick breakfast of oatmeal, stirring in a few nuts and diced bananas. I ate standing up, staring at the cabinets that lined two walls of the kitchen. I decided to dig through them after I'd finished eating. It would give me something to do, since I didn't feel like jogging and yoga moves were out of the question.

I took some ibuprofen and then explored for an hour. Nathaniel had a wonderful selection of cookware, gadgets, and dishes. And his pantry was well stocked. Four deep shelves contained a chef's dream world of supplies. The top shelf, I couldn't reach. I'd investigate it later.

I decided to make bread. Kneading dough would be the perfect way to work through my feelings. And it had the extra bonus of being work I could do standing.

As I pounded the dough, I went over and over my feelings for Nathaniel. I had been stupid last week to think—to hope—that he was falling for me. I was his submissive. For now, that would be enough. I wouldn't think about the future. Just the here and now. Besides, after I saw him again, maybe I would discover my feelings toward him had cooled.

I took a cold cooked chicken from the refrigerator and cut it up. Chicken salad would go nicely with the fresh bread. I'd serve it with grapes and carrots.

The morning passed quickly. I heard Nathaniel return at some point. Apollo ran into the kitchen. He spotted me, let out a "woof" and jumped up to give me a sloppy kiss.

At noon, I carried a plate into the dining room, where Nathaniel sat waiting. My heart pounded. I hoped he didn't see the way my hand shook when I set his plate down.

"Eat with me," he said simply.

I didn't feel liking sitting down, but there wasn't a snowball's chance in hell I was going to disobey him. I made a plate, carried it into the dining room, sat it on the table, and pulled out the chair across from him.

It had a pillow on it.

I hesitated for just a minute. Was he trying to be *funny*? Because there wasn't a damn thing funny about anything. I shifted my eyes over to him. He was staring straight ahead, chewing.

No. He wasn't trying to be funny. The dining room chairs were hard. He was being considerate.

I sat down cautiously. Okay. It hurt a bit. Not too bad. Nothing I couldn't handle.

We ate in silence. Again.

I didn't mind silence normally. Silence was good. Silence gave you time to think. But I'd had nothing but silence this morning, and I was tired of thinking. I was ready for noise.

"Look at me, Abigail."

I jumped. Nathaniel was looking at me with those strangely intense green eyes. I couldn't breathe.

"I didn't like chastising you. But I have rules, and when you break them I *will* chastise you. Swiftly and soundly."

Of that, there was no doubt.

"And I don't give gratuitous compliments," he continued. "But you did well last night. Far better than I thought you would."

Something inside me I thought dead flickered back to life. Not a lot. Not even a spark. Just a flicker. But to hear him say I'd done well . . . it was the highest praise I could hope to get from him.

He pushed back from the table. "Finish eating and meet me in the foyer in half an hour in your robe."

I quickly tidied the kitchen and went to my room, hoping to lie down and rest, even if it was just for a few minutes. I was tired and, despite the ibuprofen, still feeling very sore. Instead, I put on my robe and went to meet Nathaniel, who was waiting for me in the foyer in his own robe—not quite what I'd expected. I had no idea what he was planning.

"Follow me," he said, turning and walking through a door I'd never used.

We made our way through a masculine living room. There was a large television above a massive fireplace. Leather couches provided ample sitting room and a tall, wide window overlooked an expansive patio.

He opened the French doors leading to the patio and waited for me to go outside.

Outside? In this weather? In a *bathrobe*?

But again. Snowball's chance and all. I stepped outside and waited.

He led me to a bubbling hot tub that sat low in the ground, surrounded by steam and fluffy white towels. It looked like heaven.

He untied my robe and slipped it off. "Turn around."

I turned, just a little embarrassed to have him look at my backside, although why, I wasn't sure. He'd seen plenty of it the previous night.

"Good." His hand skimmed over me lightly. "It won't bruise."

It wasn't a question, so I didn't say anything. But I was happy. And surprised. It certainly felt like it would bruise.

When he took my hand, I noticed he'd taken off his robe. He led me to the side of the tub and stepped in, still holding my hand.

"It'll sting a bit," he said. "But that should disappear soon."

I gasped as I entered the hot water. It felt so good after the icy coldness of the winter air. And it did sting, but as I grew accustomed to the water, I felt the pain slip away.

"No pain today," Nathaniel said, taking me in his arms and drawing me down to sit on him. "Just pleasure."

The steam was heavier when I sat down on his lap. I couldn't see him clearly. He was all fuzzy and buried in the fog. Like he was a dream. Like this was a dream.

His lips nibbled on my neck and his hands ran down my arms. "Touch me," he whispered in my ear.

My hands ran down his chest. I hadn't touched him like that before. It was new. His chest was rock-hard and perfect, like the rest of him. My hands went lower, stroked his stomach. He sucked in a breath when my hands went even lower. Then I brushed his cock and he was hard. I took him in one hand.

"Two hands," he whispered. I took the length of him with both hands and, because I knew he'd like it, squeezed him hard.

"You learn fast." He slipped his arms to my waist and spun me to straddle him. Gentle, though, careful not to touch where he'd struck me last night.

The entire experience was a lesson in opposites. The frigid temperature of the air and the heat of the water. The pleasure Nathaniel brought to my body and the soreness that reminded me of the pain he'd inflicted last night. But mostly it was Nathaniel himself—the man who could be hard as nails and still touch me as light as a feather.

I breathed in the warm, enveloping steam as he worked me with his magical hands. I'd thought that maybe my feelings for him had cooled. Especially after the previous night. But being in his arms, being so close and feeling what he could do to my body, the flicker grew to a spark, and I knew I was dangerously close to igniting completely.

Chapter Twelve

I looked over my shoulder to make sure no one was watching. No one. I went back to the computer in front of me.

Do it, Bad Abby encouraged.

But it's wrong, Good Abby countered.

No one will know. Bad Abby was so bad.

You'll know. Good Abby was a stick-in-the-mud.

My fingers were poised over the keyboard. Poised and ready. *Nathaniel West.* It'd take me seconds to type his name.

Nathaniel. The man was starting to fill my weekdays as well as my weekends. I couldn't stop thinking about him. Even after the horrible spanking. I should have wanted nothing to do with him. I should have taken the collar off and mailed it back to him.

Instead I was counting down the hours until Friday night. *At six.* Six o'clock this weekend. There had been no impersonal phone calls this week. No need for one.

I looked at my watch. *Thirty and a half hours left.* I was such a dork. I bet none of his other submissives had counted down. Then again, we were talking about Nathaniel West. On second thought, I bet *all* his submissives had counted down.

But back to the business at hand. I took a deep breath, closed my eyes, and typed his name as fast as I could.

Oh, yeah. Sure, Good Abby snorted. *It doesn't count if you don't look.*

The computer whirred as it pulled up the information I asked for. My heart pounded. I looked over my shoulder again. Then back to the screen.

And there it was. Jackpot.

Nathaniel West was a public library patron. Or at least he could be. He had a card. He just never used it. Interesting. When had he been issued a card? I counted backward. Six and a half years ago. Hmmm . . . I'd been working at the library six and a half years ago.

Wonder who issued him a card. I glanced around. So many people had come and gone in six and a half years. It could have been anyone. The only thing I knew was that it wasn't me. If I clicked on the next link—

"Abby?"

"Ahhh!" I jumped ten feet in the air.

Elaina Welling was staring at me strangely when I came back down from the ceiling.

"Elaina!" I said, putting a hand over my pounding heart. "You scared the crap out of me." She had a sly grin on her face, and I wondered if she'd seen the screen. "Ready for the big game?" I asked.

Jackson and the Giants were in the play-offs the upcoming weekend in Philadelphia. He'd given Felicia tickets to the game. She had been beside herself all week. Hard to live with, truth be told. All Nathaniel had given me was a spanking.

Stop it. Here and now, remember?

I was sure Nathaniel would be going to the game, which meant we had only tomorrow night. Just one night . . .

"Getting ready, but I was hoping I could take you to lunch today," Elaina said, dragging me away from thoughts of the next night.

"Oh." I looked at my watch. "I don't take lunch until noon."

"That's okay. I have a few things to take care of. How about Delphina's at ten past?"

We agreed, and half an hour later I walked into the bistro Elaina had picked out.

She was waiting for me in a secluded corner booth. We both ordered iced tea, and when the waitress left, Elaina leaned across the table.

"I'm going to tell you a secret," she said. "I know what you are. I know about Nathaniel."

My jaw hit the table. Elaina knew. If Elaina knew, then Todd knew, and if Todd knew—

"You're in shock. I should have said it differently. It's j-just," she stammered, "I thought it'd be better to lay it all out. And I don't care. You're great. And I love Nathaniel. I'd love him no matter what."

"Wait a minute," I said, holding up a hand. "Does Nathaniel know? Does he know you know and does he know you're taking me to lunch?" Because, damn it, she wouldn't be the one with the sore ass.

She nodded. "He knows I'm taking you to lunch. He doesn't know I know."

I really didn't want to keep secrets from Nathaniel. I sighed. Why did this have to be so complicated?

"Todd knows?" I asked instead.

"Yes. Linda doesn't, though, but I'm not sure about Jackson." She took a sip of tea. "Todd and I wouldn't have known if Melanie hadn't shown up at our house four months ago, crying her eyes out."

Pearl Girl had cried her eyes out to Elaina and Todd? Okay, this was too juicy not to hear.

"Melanie, his last submissive?" I asked.

She leaned across the table again. "Melanie was never his submissive."

The waitress interrupted us. It took me three tries to get my order out. Melanie wasn't his submissive? What the hell was she?

"I don't guess you could call her a submissive," Elaina continued once the waitress left. "I don't know the proper terms for all this stuff. He never gave her a collar. Pissed her off something horrible."

That didn't make sense. "But Jackson called her Pearl Girl because she always wore pearls."

"That was just Melanie. Maybe she was pretending to have a collar. I don't know." Elaina shook her head. "Not long after Nathaniel broke it off with her, she came to our apartment. She's known Todd since grade school."

I took a long sip of tea. This was too much information to process.

"Melanie grew up with them," Elaina said. "She's always had a crush on Nathaniel. He tried his best to ignore her, but she was persistent. She finally got him, but for only six months or so."

I sat back and tried to decide if it was good or bad that he'd never collared her. What did that say about me?

"Did Nathaniel kiss her?" I asked.

"Kiss her? Yeah, sure he did."

Damn. It was just me, then. He didn't want to kiss me.

"I thought back, after she left," Elaina said, oblivious to my disappointment. "To the other girls. I remember Paige and Beth. They both wore collars, plain ones, though." She waved at mine. "Nothing like yours. I'm sure there have been others. He just never introduced us."

"Why are you telling me all this?"

"Because you deserve to know what you've done for him and he won't tell you."

I was totally confused.

"He gives you this great collar, almost immediately after you meet," Elaina said. "He talks about you. He has a spring in his step I haven't seen in forever and . . . I don't know. He's just changed." She raised an eyebrow. "I hear you make mean French toast."

He talked about me? Mentioned my cooking?

The waitress set our salads down.

"Abby," Elaina said. "Listen to me. You have to handle Nathaniel carefully. His parents died in a car accident when he was ten."

I nodded. I'd heard this before.

"He was in the car with them," she said. "It was mangled up so badly, it took hours to cut them out." Her voice dropped to a whisper. "I don't think they died immediately. I don't know. He won't talk about it. Never has. But he changed after the accident. He was always so happy before they died and so withdrawn and sad afterward." She looked at me with hopeful eyes. "And now you're changing him back. You're bringing Nathaniel back."

After that little bombshell, we talked about other things—Elaina's work, my tutoring, Felicia and Jackson. The time passed quickly, and all too soon I had to leave to go back to work.

I climbed into a cab, thinking about what Elaina had said, that I was changing Nathaniel, bringing him back.

I wanted to believe her, but I couldn't.

So he'd collared me quickly. That didn't mean anything. And so what if he took me to his aunt's nonprofit benefit? None of it mattered. He was who he was and our relationship was what it was. Nothing had changed.

I turned around. Elaina stood on the sidewalk behind me, looking in my direction and talking on the phone to someone. Her expression changed. She was screaming.

Why was she screaming?

Metal collided with metal. Horns blared. The earth spun in a crazy twirl. My head struck something hard.

And then nothing.

Chapter Thirteen

I was in pain.

For the longest time, that was all I could concentrate on. Pain.

Then the lights came. And the noise. And I wanted to tell everyone to be quiet and turn the lights off because the light and the noise hurt. And if it could just be dark and quiet, I'd be fine. But even though I could hear, I couldn't talk.

Then I was aware of moving, and that was worse, because moving hurt. And numerous hands were pulling at me. They didn't stop when I told them to leave me alone.

The noise got louder.

"Abby! Abby!"

"BP steady at one twenty over sixty-nine."

"Pupils equal and reactive."

"Call CT; she's . . . too long."

"Possible intracranial hemorrhage . . ."

And mercifully, the darkness came back.

I woke again to the sounds of arguing.

Felicia. She was arguing.

"Heart of a fucking animal . . . don't even know . . ."

"Don't know anything . . ."

"Why don't you . . ."

"I refuse . . ."

"Have to ask you both . . . disturbing the patients . . ."

And again the darkness fell.

The next time I woke, I was able to open my eyes. It was dark. And there was no sound but a steady *beep, beep, beep.*

"Abby?"

I turned my eyes to the noise. Linda.

I licked my lips. Why were they so dry? "Dr. Clark?"

"You're in the hospital, Abby. How are you feeling?"

Like hell. Like utter and complete hell. "I must be badly off to have the chief of staff in my room."

"Or else you're very important." She stepped to the side. Nathaniel stood behind her.

Nathaniel!

"Hey," I said.

He came forward, took my hand, and lightly ran his thumb over my knuckles. "You scared me."

"Sorry." I wrinkled my forehead, trying to remember. "What happened?"

"Your cab was hit by a dump truck," Nathaniel said. "Damn driver ran a stop sign."

"You have a moderate concussion, Abby." Linda typed something on her laptop. "I'm keeping you overnight. You were more deeply unconscious than we'd usually expect in concussion cases. But there's no internal bleeding. Nothing broken. You'll be sore for the next few days."

I tried to nod, but it hurt too much. "Did I hear Felicia?"

Linda smiled. "New hospital regulation. Nathaniel and Felicia aren't allowed within twenty feet of each other."

"We had a slight misunderstanding," Nathaniel said. "She's with Elaina. They've been talking to your dad."

"Can I—?"

"You need to rest," Linda said. "I'll go let the others know you're awake. Nathaniel?"

Nathaniel nodded.

When she left, I looked up at him and waved him close. He leaned over for me to whisper in his ear.

"I missed yoga class this afternoon."

He brushed the hair back from my forehead. "I think I can overlook it this one time."

"And I'll probably miss my jog tomorrow morning."

He smiled. "Probably."

"But on the upside," I said, feeling slightly dozy again, "I seem to be getting lots of sleep."

"Shh." Long fingers skimmed along my forehead right before my eyes closed.

They were whispering about me. I kept my eyes closed so they wouldn't know I was awake.

"Abby?"

I opened my eyes. Felicia.

"Don't you think I know you well enough to know when you're faking?"

Yeah, she did. "Hey, Felicia."

She squeezed my hand. "Scare me like that again and I rip you from limb to limb."

"She'll have to stand in line," Elaina said from behind her.

"Hey, Elaina."

"Thank God you're okay. Honestly, when I saw that truck run the stop sign . . . I lost it . . . I kept thinking . . ." Her eyes misted. "And Nathaniel was yelling and I thought you were dead." Tears ran down her face. Even Felicia wiped her eyes. "You wouldn't wake up, Abby. Why wouldn't you wake up?"

"Sorry." I tried to sit up, but gave up. Sitting up hurt. "I'm awake now."

And hungry. I was hungry.

Felicia pushed me back down. "I don't think you're supposed to be up yet."

Nathaniel. Nathaniel had been here earlier, hadn't he? Had it been a dream?

Linda walked up behind Elaina. "Nathaniel went to get you something to eat. He said he wouldn't feed Apollo what passed as food around here."

Yes, that sounded like Nathaniel. Make a meal plan and stick with it.

"I ripped your boyfriend a new one earlier," Felicia said. "He took it like a man. You have my blessing."

"Blessing for what?" I asked.

"To continue seeing him." She rolled her eyes.

"Thanks," I said. "But I wasn't aware it was up to you."

She shrugged her shoulders.

I rearranged my blankets. Wait a minute—

"Where are my clothes?" My hand went to my throat. "Where's my . . ."

"They had to cut your clothes off," Elaina said. "It was wild. They used these huge scissors." She winked at me. "I have your necklace in my purse."

"Thanks, Elaina." It felt odd not to have my collar on; my neck felt so light.

"Did Sleeping Beauty wake up?" Nathaniel walked into the room, carrying a tray, still wearing his suit and tie. He set the tray on the rolling table by my bed, pushed it to me, and lifted the lid off a bowl. "You should see what they call food in this place. They serve chicken broth out of a *can*."

I pointed to the broth. It smelled delicious. "Did you make this?"

"No." He crossed his arms. "They wouldn't let me. But I dictated."

I just bet he did.

He glanced around the room. "Did you tell her?"

Linda shook her head. "No. She just woke up. Come on, Elaina. Let's get something to eat." She looked back. "Felicia, would you like to come?"

Felicia waved them on. "I'll be down in a minute."

Once Linda and Elaina left, Nathaniel unwrapped a spoon and put it beside the bowl. He adjusted the bed to lift me into a sitting position. "Eat."

"Damn, Nathaniel," Felicia said. "She's not a dog."

He glared at her. "I know that."

"Do you?"

"Felicia," I warned.

Felicia scowled at Nathaniel and stomped out the door.

"I'm sorry about that. Felicia is . . ." I sighed. "Felicia."

"Don't apologize." Nathaniel sat at the end of my bed. "She cares for you and is looking out for your best interests. There's not a thing wrong with that." He pointed to the bowl. "You do need to eat."

I took a sip. "This is good."

He grinned. "Thank you."

I ate half the bowl before talking again. "Elaina has my collar."

He rubbed my leg over the blanket. "I know. She told me. We'll get it later."

I took another sip. *We'll get it later.* I liked the sound of that. Another sip. I'd pretend we were sitting at the kitchen table. After all, we'd never talked about proper hospital etiquette. "What did you mean earlier—had they told me? Told me what?"

He was still rubbing my leg. "About the weekend. Tomorrow, Felicia and everyone will head on to Philly as planned. But since you shouldn't be alone this weekend, you'll stay with me."

But I stayed with him every weekend.

And then I remembered. Jackson's game.

"I'm sorry. You'll miss Jackson's game because of me."

"Do you know how many times I've watched Jackson play football?" he asked.

"But this is the play-offs."

"And I've seen him in the play-offs too many times to count. I don't mind missing this one. We can watch it on TV." He grinned again. "But I am disappointed you'll miss it."

"Me?" But I wasn't going.

"You and I were going to take my jet to Philly tomorrow evening. Spend the weekend in the city. Watch the game on Sunday." He patted the blanket. "Now we'll have to make do with the couch and takeout."

He was going to take me to Philly on his private jet?

"Don't worry," he said. "If they pull this off, there's always the Super Bowl."

Chapter Fourteen

I pushed the tray away. "Is there a mirror around here?" I'd never been a horribly vain person, but I wanted to see if I looked as bad as I felt.

"I don't know . . . I don't think," Nathaniel stammered, and I looked at him in shock. He'd never seemed unsure about anything before. Everything was always so black-and-white. Yes and no. Do this and do that. I wasn't sure I'd ever heard him say *I don't know* before.

I lifted a hand to my face. "Is it bad? Do I look that awful?"

Nathaniel found a hand mirror by the sink and brought it to me. I lifted it slowly.

One part at a time, Abby, I told myself. *Focus on one part of your face at a time.*

I started with my eyes. "Ugh. I'm going to have a black eye. I'll look like I've been beaten."

Total silence from Nathaniel. I moved the mirror. There was a bandage covering the left side of my forehead. "What was this? What happened?" I asked, touching the bandage. Ouch.

"Head wound," Nathaniel said. "There was blood everywhere. It wouldn't stop and they weren't trying. They were too concerned with whether you had a broken neck or internal bleeding." His eyes took on a distant look. "Head wounds bleed a lot. I remember."

And in that second, Nathaniel wasn't a thirty-four-year-old man anymore. He was a ten-year-old boy, stuck in a car.

"But it stopped," I said softly.

"What?" he asked, snapping back to the present.

"My bleeding. It stopped."

"Yes," he said. "Once they decided you hadn't broken your neck, they bandaged your head." He stood up and took my dinner tray. "Let me put this outside."

Nathaniel and Felicia got into another argument over who would stay overnight.

"I already brought an overnight bag with a change of clothes and a toothbrush," Felicia said.

"Linda's bringing me a set of scrubs," Nathaniel countered.

"I think that's improper use of hospital equipment." Felicia pointed at his chest. "Maybe I'll report it to the board."

Nathaniel took a step closer to her. "Linda's *on* the board."

A nurse entered my room and sidestepped them. She gave me a look: *Should I kick them out?*

I shook my head.

"We'll both stay," Nathaniel said.

The nurse took the IV from my hand and placed a bandage on the wound. "Sorry, Mr. West. Only one visitor in the room overnight. It's a rule."

I felt my face heat at the word *rule*. Probably turned eighteen shades of red.

Nathaniel straightened. "I see. Felicia, you can stay." He walked over to me. "I better leave before they call security. I'll see you first thing in the morning." He leaned over and whispered in my ear, "Sleep well."

Things got quiet after he left. Felicia settled into the recliner in the corner of my room, and soon I drifted off.

It's impossible to sleep in a hospital. They're forever running into the room to check on you or take your blood pressure or something. I dozed off and on all night, but probably slept better than Felicia did. The recliner didn't look very comfortable.

Felicia looked bad when I woke up the next morning. Her normally perfect hair was tousled and she had bags under her eyes.

"I should have taken Nathaniel's advice and gone home," she said.

"You'd have slept a lot better, that's for sure," I said, experimentally moving various body parts.

"I mean, it's not even like it mattered." She got up and stretched. "He stayed in the waiting room all night anyway."

I stopped all movement. "Nathaniel? He stayed here? All night?"

"All night." She walked over to my bed. "He was standing in the hallway every time a nurse came in. I totally misjudged him. I think he really cares for you."

I was still working that out in my mind when the man in question came in. He glanced warily at Felicia, but she was ignoring him, straightening up the room. A hospital worker entered after him, carrying a tray.

"Breakfast time," Nathaniel said, pushing the table back into place for me to eat. "Ham and cheese omelet this morning."

"I've got to run, Abby," Felicia said, coming over and kissing my cheek. "I still have to pack. You take it easy. I'll call you when I can." She turned to Nathaniel. "Hurt her and I cut off your dick and feed it to you for *your* breakfast."

"Felicia Kelly!" I gasped in astonishment.

"Sorry. It just came out." She pointed at him. "But I mean it."

"I don't know what's gotten into her," I told Nathaniel after she left.

He sat down on the edge of the bed. "She was pretty upset yesterday. She just doesn't want you to get hurt."

"Are you going to tell me what you two argued about?"

"No."

I really didn't expect him to anyway. I took a bite of the omelet. It was, not surprisingly, very good. "Are other hospital patients eating ham and cheese omelets for breakfast?"

"I find myself rather unconcerned with what other hospital patients are eating for breakfast."

Linda came in, followed by a nurse. The nurse took my blood pressure *again*.

"Good morning, Abby," Linda said. "I'm going to have another CT ordered and, if all's clear, you're free to go. You'll be staying with Nathaniel?"

I nodded.

"Good," she said. "And to be honest, the sooner I get you out of here, the better. My kitchen staff is threatening to quit if Nathaniel shows up down there again. Let's get you discharged before lunch."

The CT was clear and I was discharged before noon, saving Linda the task of replacing her kitchen staff. Elaina dropped off a blue cashmere sweater and soft khaki pants, so I didn't have to leave the hospital in a backless gown.

It wasn't until I was settled into Nathaniel's car that I remembered the accident.

"What happened to the cabdriver?" I asked as Nathaniel navigated traffic.

"Minor scratches. He was released yesterday. I don't like cabs. I'm buying you a car."

"What? No."

He looked sharply at me and, for once, I didn't care. This wasn't some dom weekend thing. This was . . . well, I didn't know. This was different.

His grip on the steering wheel tightened. "What's wrong with me getting you a car?"

I shook my head. "It feels wrong." I didn't want to explain it to him. He should understand. I blinked back hot tears.

"Are you crying?"

"No." I sniffled.

"You're crying. Why?"

"I don't want you to get me a car." Could he not just say *okay* and drop it? I closed my eyes. No, he wouldn't. "It'd make me feel . . ."

"Make you feel what?"

I sighed. "Make me feel dirty, like a whore."

His knuckles turned white. "Is that what you think you are?"

"No." I wiped away a tear. "But I'm a librarian. You're . . . you're one of the wealthiest men in New York. How would it look?"

"Abigail," he said calmly. "You should have thought about how things would look long before now. You wear my collar every day."

Yes, I did, and I'd gotten quite a few stares. "That's different."

"It's the same. My responsibility is to take care of you."

"By buying me a car?"

"By making sure your needs are met."

He drove in silence for several miles. I looked out the side window at the passing landscape. After a time, I closed my eyes and pretended to sleep. Why was he so dead set on getting me a car? I lived in the city. I didn't need a car.

When we finally pulled up to his estate, he walked over and opened the door for me. "The car conversation is not finished, but you need to get inside and rest. We'll talk later."

He set me up in the living room, on one of the leather couches. Apollo jumped up and curled around my feet. Nathaniel came in minutes later with a sandwich and fruit.

There was a desk in the living room, and while I rested on the couch, mindlessly flipping through TV channels, Nathaniel worked. I was certain he had a lot to catch up on from the day before.

I dozed off and on. Sometime around three thirty, I woke up. I looked around; Nathaniel glanced up from his computer.

"Feeling better?" he asked.

I wasn't sure if he was talking about the car situation or my various aches and pains.

"A little," I said, answering both questions at once, and then popped the pain pills sitting on the table beside me. I stood up and stretched. Ahh. That felt good.

Nathaniel turned off the computer.

"Come with me." He held out his hand. "I want you to see the southern part of the house."

The southern part of the house? I took his hand. It was warm and reassuring in its strength.

We walked through the main hallway, through the foyer, and into a section of the house I'd never been in. At the end of the hall was a set of double doors.

Nathaniel dropped my hand, smiled at me, and pushed the doors open.

I gasped.

No wonder he never used his library card—he could open the doors to this room and service the people of New York himself. I knew people had libraries in their houses, but I'd never seen anything like this before. Never knew such rooms existed.

The room was large, and the late-afternoon sun slanted through windows that ran floor to ceiling along one wall. But the other walls . . . they held shelf after shelf of books. Nothing but books. There was even a movable ladder attached to one wall, so you could reach the upper shelves.

Two overstuffed couches sat near the center of everything. But in the very middle of the room, in the place of honor, was an exquisite grand piano.

"I want this to be your room," Nathaniel said. "When you're in this room, you are free to be you. Your thoughts. Your desires. It's all yours. Except for the piano. The piano is mine."

I walked in awe around the room, dragging my hand along book spines. It was an unparalleled collection—first editions, antique volumes—I couldn't take it all in. The rich wood, the leather-bound books, it was too much.

"Abigail?"

I turned to look at him.

"You're crying," he whispered. "Again."

"It's so beautiful."

He smiled. "You like it?"

I walked back to him and put my arms around him. "Thank you."

Chapter Fifteen

It had been a long two days.

Not that I was bored or anything. Exploring the library was my new favorite pastime, and I spent hours discovering new books and reacquainting myself with old friends.

Nathaniel was considerate. Polite. Perhaps a bit distant. He kept me well fed and rested. He even joined me in the library on occasion, but didn't stay very long. I rather missed his domineering side. Not enough to purposely antagonize him or anything. I didn't miss it *that* much.

The car conversation never came back up. I thought back to what he'd said, how it was his responsibility to care for me. To ensure my needs were met. He was doing exactly that over the weekend. And as much as I wanted to pretend his gestures at the hospital and giving me the library as free space were romantic, I knew better. He was doing what he said in the car—making sure my needs were met. It was a means to an end. He needed a healthy submissive, and he'd do anything within his power to make me healthy. That's all there was to it. Bottom line.

But I was the littlest bit peeved he hadn't touched me. I'd rested all weekend. I felt perfectly fine.

And I had needs that *weren't* being met.

I put the glass I'd been using in the dishwasher and left the kitchen. I glanced at my watch—one o'clock. The football game didn't start until three. Plenty of time.

I walked past the gym. Empty. No Nathaniel in the living room. I wondered if he was outside or in his bedroom. No, he was working in the library. Sitting at a small desk in the corner.

He glanced up when I walked in. "Everything all right? Do you need something?"

"Yes. You." I slipped the shirt over my head.

He put down the papers he'd been reading. "You need to rest."

That didn't sound like a direct order, so I didn't say anything. I unbuttoned my pants and slipped them down. Stepped out of them. And it was *my* library.

He sat looking at me with a blank expression. What was he thinking? He wasn't going to tell me to leave, was he? I reached behind my back and unhooked my bra. I didn't think I could handle it if he turned me down.

What if he turns me down?

I pushed my panties down and they fell to the floor. It was my library, but he had free will as well. He could turn me down.

I'd never felt more exposed in my life.

Nothing from Nathaniel.

He was going to turn me down.

Slowly, ever so slowly, he pushed his chair back. Opened the desk drawer and took something out. Seven steps and he stood before me. He ran his hands down my shoulders, along my arms, and took my hands. He placed them on the front of his button-down shirt, slipping something into my hand.

"Okay," he said.

I looked inside my fist. A condom.

Because antibiotics invalidated birth control pills.

Victory surged through me. Excitement shot from my head straight to the center of my being and down to the aching spot between my legs.

I dropped the condom on the floor. My fingers fumbled with his buttons, but I worked my way through them. Pushed the shirt from his shoulders, yanked it from his pants. I ran my hands down his chest, remembering the feel of him, tracing the planes of his stomach. I walked around him. I loved the sight of a man's back.

His back was perfect, of course. I circled his shoulder blades and reached up on tiptoe to place a kiss at the juncture between them. He sucked in a breath, but didn't touch me, allowing me to explore on my terms. I licked down the line of his spine, savoring his taste.

I walked back around to face him and dropped to my knees. He was erect and straining the front of his pants.

Well, well, well.

I brushed him with my fingertips, eliciting a hiss. Very slowly, I unbuckled his belt and unbuttoned his pants, making sure I stroked him every so often through the material. I went even slower with his zipper, roughly dragging my fingers the entire way.

He grew even harder.

I pulled his pants and boxers down at the same time, freeing him at last. His cock bobbed in front of my face. I leaned forward and took him forcefully into my mouth, wrapping my arms around his backside and pulling him toward me at the same time. He steadied himself briefly by resting his hands on my head. Gently.

I sucked him hard, relishing the feel of having him in my

mouth again. I ripped open the foil package at my knees, rolled the condom down his length, and got to my feet. The couch was behind him; I pushed on his chest and he moved backward. We landed on it together, my legs straddling him.

He leaned forward and drew a nipple into his mouth, swirling his tongue around it until I groaned in pleasure. But this was my show, so I pushed him back down and positioned myself right above his cock.

I lowered myself on him, inch by delicious inch, delighting in how he filled me.

"Abigail," he groaned, trying to thrust up against me.

I held him down and pushed until he was completely inside. Then *I* groaned. I stopped for a few seconds to concentrate on how it felt. How it felt to have him under me and in me. *Heaven*. I leaned forward onto his chest, and he sucked my nipple into his mouth again. *Ohh. Even better*.

I started a slow, grinding rhythm, pressing down and lifting up as my hips moved around and around. Nathaniel helped, thrusting up to meet me. We began a sultry, erotic dance. Up and down and around. Over and over.

His hands weren't still. They circled my waist, ran up my back, cupped my breasts. His breathing got choppy. Then he grabbed my waist and worked me up and down, thrusting into me harder, even as I pushed down. I couldn't get enough of him. Couldn't get him deep enough.

"Damn it, Abigail." He groaned and thrust upward again, hitting a new spot.

I was close, so I moved quicker. He realized what I was doing and joined me, driving into me, helping me reach it.

Release flooded my shaking body, and he followed seconds later, thrusting one last time, grunting as he came.

We lay on the couch, letting our breathing return to normal.

Waiting for our limbs to work again. Or maybe that was just me. The accident had taken more out of me than I'd thought.

Nathaniel rolled us so we were on our sides and I was between him and the couch. "Are you okay?"

"I am now," I said with a smirk. The library was my new favorite room, for sure. He could remove all the books and it would still be my favorite. I ran a hand down his chest. *Mine.* In this room I could pretend he was mine.

He took my hand and held it to his chest. "I want you to take it easy the rest of the day."

"Okay." I could do that, since I'd gotten what I wanted.

He rolled off the couch, threw the condom away, and gathered his clothes. "What type of pizza do you like?" he asked, buttoning his shirt.

Mr. Eat-this-and-not-that wanted pizza? For real?

He sensed my hesitation. "The Clark family has to eat pizza and hot wings during every play-off game. If we didn't and the Giants lost, Jackson would disown us."

"I've heard of crazier superstitions," I said, getting off the couch. "Just don't tell me if he wears the same unwashed underwear."

"My lips are sealed."

In more ways than one, I thought, wondering if he'd ever kiss me.

"Mushroom," I said, deciding not to dwell on his lips. "I like mushroom pizza. And bacon."

"Mushroom and bacon it is." He pulled his boxers back on. "Picnic on the floor sound good?"

Nathaniel on the floor surrounded by pillows and pizza? My mind wandered . . .

"Abigail?"

"Yes. Picnic on the floor would be great."

But I hadn't fooled him one bit.

"You will take it easy the rest of the day."

He brought my collar out during halftime.

Up to that point, we'd been doing our part for Jackson, eating hot wings and pizza. And it was working—the Giants were up by a touchdown.

He turned the TV off and stood by me, holding out the collar. "Elaina gave it to me at the hospital."

I couldn't lie to him, even if it was a lie by omission. "Elaina knows," I said, then hastened to add, "But it wasn't me. I didn't tell her."

He nodded. "I thought as much. Thank you for being honest." He hesitated for a minute. "I want to make sure you still want this. I wasn't sure . . ." His eyes met mine. "You know more now. Maybe you don't . . . want it."

"I want it."

Surprise lit his eyes for just a second. *He thought I would say no.* I rose to my knees and dropped my head, ready for him to put the collar back on.

"Look at me, Abigail."

I looked at him. He faced me, dropping to his knees and reaching around my neck to fasten it, then ran his fingers through my hair. His eyes darkened, dipped to my lips, and back to my eyes. He moved the tiniest bit forward.

He's going to kiss me.

I was frozen. I couldn't move, couldn't breathe.

He closed his eyes and sighed.

Then his eyes opened and he got to his feet to turn the game back on.

Disappointment swept over me. *Stupid. Stupid. Stupid.* I

brought my hand to my neck. But I still had his collar. Still had that part of him. He still wanted *me*.

New York won by a point.

"You know what this means?" Nathaniel asked as they showed a close-up of Jackson pumping his fist in the air.

"We're going to the Super Bowl?"

"Yes," he said, fingering the collar. "And I have plans for the Super Bowl."

Chapter Sixteen

Felicia came over Monday night all abuzz. Philly was great. The game was great. The Wellings were great. But mostly Jackson. Jackson was great. She was one hundred percent, totally, head over heels in love. After what? Two weeks? It was crazy.

I was thrilled for her.

Once she calmed down, I asked her about her argument with Nathaniel.

She tucked a strand of hair behind her ear. "It was nothing, really."

"Felicia," I said. "My subconscious heard you. It wasn't nothing."

She bit her lip. "I was just shocked that Nathaniel was already there. I'm your best friend. I should have been there first. It's stupid. Like I said, nothing."

I tried to think back. It was hard. The memories were fuzzy. "When did you get to the hospital?"

"When they brought you to your room. Right after your CT scan."

That made sense. "When did Nathaniel get to the hospital?"

She sighed and plopped down on the sofa. "He was in the trauma room with you. The nurses had to kick him out." She raised an eyebrow. "Why don't you ask him?"

I ignored her. "Why did you call him a fucking animal?"

"Because I thought he was one. You're his, like, sex slave or something. You fill one need for him and he comes running to the hospital when you're injured as if his world were falling apart. It ticked me off."

"But you like him now?"

"I wouldn't use the word *like*, but yeah, I'll put up with him." She walked to the door. Conversation over. "You going to the Super Bowl with him?"

"Yes. He mentioned something about it."

On Wednesday afternoon at around one thirty, I was working the front checkout desk. I had my back to the front door while cataloging new releases.

"I need to see something in the Rare Books Collection."

Heaven save me from dimwits who don't know library regulations. "I'm sorry," I said, not even bothering to look around. "The Rare Books Collection is open by appointment only, and we're a little short-staffed at the moment. I really don't have time this afternoon."

"That's rather disappointing, Abigail."

You know how what you expect to happen clouds what you see and hear? Well, it never occurred to me that Nathaniel would wander into my branch of the New York Public Library at one thirty on a random Wednesday afternoon. Which was why I didn't grasp who he was until he said my name.

I spun around.

He stood in front of me, bundled in a woolen overcoat with only a hint of tie seen above the collar of his coat. Smug grin firmly in place.

Nathaniel West was in my library. On a Wednesday.

I tilted my head.

To see the Rare Books Collection?

"Is this really such a bad time?" he asked.

"No," I croaked out. "But I'm sure you have the exact same books at your house."

"Probably."

"And," I continued, still not understanding what he was doing, "someone will have to escort you the entire time."

"I certainly hope so. It'd be rather boring in the Rare Books Collection all by myself." He slowly pulled his gloves off, one finger at a time. "I know it's not a weekend. Please feel free to tell me no. There will be no repercussions. Will you escort me to the Rare Books Collection?"

Oh. My. Word.

"Ye-ye-yes," I stammered, watching as he stripped off the other glove.

"Excellent."

I stood frozen.

"Abigail," he said, pulling me from my stupor. "Perhaps that lady right there"—he pointed over my shoulder—"can work the front desk while you are . . . otherwise occupied?"

Gah.

"Abigail?"

"Martha?" I called, moving away from my post. "Watch the desk for me, will you? Mr. West has an appointment to see the Rare Books Collection."

Martha waved.

"Just for my education," Nathaniel said as we walked, "does the Rare Books Collection room happen to have a table?"

A table? "Yes."

"Is it sturdy?"

"I suppose so."

"Good." He followed me up the stairs. "Because I plan to have more than books spread out for me."

My heart doubled its tempo.

I scuffled with the keys, trying to find the one that fit the lock to the Rare Books Collection room. I finally found it, unlocked the door, and pushed it open.

"Oh, no," Nathaniel said, holding the door. "After you."

I walked into the Rare Books room, eyes scanning the space. It was empty and, unless something unexpected came up, would remain that way for the foreseeable future.

Nathaniel closed the door behind me and locked it. He took off his coat and slung it over the back of a chair, then walked around the room, inspecting the various shelves and tables.

"This one," he said, pointing to a waist-high table in the middle of the room, "is exactly what I had in mind."

I was going to have sex in the Rare Books Collection.

With Nathaniel.

"Strip from the waist down, Abigail," he said. "And hop onto the table."

Shutting out the part of my brain that warned I shouldn't do so, I slipped out of my shoes and undid my pants. Slid them and my panties past my hips and onto the floor. Nathaniel watched as I scrambled onto the table.

"Very nice." He unbuckled his belt. "Put your heels and ass on the edge of the table and spread those pretty knees for me."

The temperature in the Rare Books Collection was kept lower than in other parts of the library. I was usually cold when I went in there, but now I was hot. Burning hot. And getting hotter watching him unzip his pants and boxers and step out of them. He rolled a condom onto his already erect cock.

"Beautiful." He walked to the table, spread my knees farther apart, and then looked down, moving me ever so slightly, lining me up with his cock. Teasing me. Making me savor the anticipation.

"Tell me, Abigail," he said. "Have you ever been fucked in the Rare Books Collection before?"

"No."

His head shot up. "No, what?"

"No, sir."

He pressed his cock into me the slightest bit. "Much better."

He waited a minute and thrust in all the way. My hips moved back. He reached out to grab my backside and pull me closer.

"Lean back on your elbows, Abigail. I'm going to fuck you so hard, you'll still be feeling it Friday night."

He didn't have to tell me twice. I leaned back and scooted my hips forward, moving farther onto him as I did.

Nathaniel thrust forward, pounding into me over and over, and I held on as tightly as I could. I pushed up on the balls of my feet so I could meet his thrusts.

"You're mine," he said, ramming forward again.

My head dropped back. I was so exposed in this position, everything felt so much more intense. *Yes*, I wanted to say. *Yours and yours only*.

"Mine." He held my hips steady as his cock battered me. "Say it, Abigail."

"Yours." I repeated it as he thrust again and again. "Yours. Yours. Yours."

I started moaning as my climax built. It just felt *so good*. But I was at work; I bit my lips together as my climax grew and grew, until it spiraled out of control and I let out a little squeak. Nathaniel sucked in a breath and then held still as he came powerfully into the condom.

He leaned over me, breathing heavily, and trailed kisses

down my belly. "Thank you for escorting me on my tour of the Rare Books Collection."

"Anytime," I said, running my fingers through his hair.

He placed one last kiss on my belly before we straightened our clothes.

I slipped my shoes back on, and it hit me what we'd just done. What if someone heard us? What if there were people standing outside? Nathaniel had locked the door, but several employees had keys.

He cocked his head. "Are you okay?"

"Yes," I said, wanting to leave the room as quickly as possible. I took the condom from Nathaniel and headed out into the corridor. "I'll take care of this."

He nodded. "I'll see you Friday at six."

"Yes, sir."

We went our separate ways, him to leave and me to the bathroom. I felt wobbly and tingly inside——I'd probably be wearing a stupid grin for the rest of the day.

When I made it back to the front desk, there was a rose waiting for me on top of the books I'd been cataloging. A cream-colored rose, tinted at the tips with a blush of pink.

I picked it up and inhaled its fragrance.

Fifty-two hours and counting.

Chapter Seventeen

I sat at the front desk, twirling the rose.

"Someone's got it bad," Martha sang out, sitting at the desk and placing her chin in her hands.

"Who, me?" I twirled the rose again.

"Obviously," she said. "But so does that delicious slice of man cake who left the rose for you." She blinked her eyes dramatically several times.

"Nathaniel West?" I asked, delighting in the sound of his name on my lips. "He's just someone I've been seeing." Okay, that was a lie. I'd been doing a hell of a lot more than *seeing* Nathaniel. And the rose was nothing but a thank-you for not turning him down.

Martha stood up. "A cream-colored rose with a touch of pink is serious business."

"Really?" I stopped twirling. "Why?"

"John Boyle O'Reilly?" she asked. "The Irish poet?"

I shook my head. Never heard of him.

Martha clapped her hands. "This is so romantic. It's from his poem 'A White Rose—'"

"It's not white."

Martha shot me an evil look. "I know that. I'm just telling you the title."

"Sorry." I waved, interested in seeing where she was going. "Go on."

She cleared her throat:

> " 'The red rose whispers of passion,
> And the white rose breathes of love;
> O the red rose is a falcon,
> And the white rose is a dove.
> But I send you a cream-white rosebud
> With a flush on its petal tips;
> For the love that is purest and sweetest
> Has a kiss of desire on the lips.' "

I dropped the rose.

It doesn't mean anything. Doesn't mean A THING. He liked the way the rose looked, is all. It's all a coincidence.

But when did Nathaniel ever do anything coincidental?

Never.

"Abby?" Martha asked.

A kiss of desire on the lips.

Nothing. It means nothing, Rational Abby whispered. Or maybe it was Crazy Abby. Who knew at this point?

Sure. Keep telling yourself that. Tell yourself it's just a thing he does every weekend. Whatever. It really doesn't matter anymore, does it? It means more to you, Crazy Abby said. Or perhaps it was Rational Abby who said that.

"Abby?"

"Sorry, Martha." I picked the rose up and set it on the desk. Stared at it. "It's a beautiful poem. Very romantic."

A kiss of desire on the lips.

I looked up at Martha. "I think I'm going to visit the poetry section, check out some more O'Reilly."

I'd had a crazy fantasy about being Nathaniel West's submissive. Submitting to his control, being under his will. I'd come to terms with the fact that I'd fallen for him, but what about how he felt about me?

Was it possible he had fallen, too?

I thought Friday night would never come. The minutes dragged by and the hours trudged on forever. Yoga. Work. Walking instead of jogging.

But Friday did come. I arrived at Nathaniel's house at ten to six and heard Apollo barking inside the house when I got out of the car.

Nathaniel opened the front door. Damn, he looked good in his long-sleeved button-down shirt and black dress pants. My legs felt wobbly just looking at him. His eyes followed me up the stairs.

"Happy Friday, Abigail," he said, his voice so smooth I nearly swooned.

It is now.

"Come inside." He stepped back and let me pass. "Dinner's ready."

And what a dinner it was. Coq au vin served at the kitchen table. Delicate chicken breasts in a savory wine sauce. Every bite was scrumptious. While we ate, it hit me that Nathaniel and I shared a passion for cooking. What would it be like to work in the kitchen with him?

Chopping and dicing. The steamy heat of a simmering pot. Tiny sips to test the spiciness. Subtle touches here and there. Brushing against him as I moved around the counter. Reaching over his head to grab something.

A replay of the library table, but this time on the kitchen countertop.

Yours. Yours. Yours.

"How are you feeling today?" Nathaniel asked, bringing me back to reality as we finished eating.

I remembered his words from Wednesday: *You'll still be feeling it Friday night.*

I smiled. "Sore in all the right places."

"Abigail," he chided. "Have you been a naughty girl this week?"

I blanked.

He, very precisely and intentionally, set his fork by his plate. "You do know what happens to naughty girls, don't you?"

I shook my head.

"They get spanked."

Ah, hell no!

"But I did the yoga and I got my sleep and did the walking instead of jogging, just like you said." This couldn't be happening. I broke the rules last time. I got that. But this week—this week—I'd done nothing wrong. Damned if I'd be splayed out on that whipping bench again. I'd have to use my safe word.

Damn it.

"Abigail." Nathaniel was calm and collected. He didn't look angry or disappointed. Not at all like last time. "How many types of spankings are there?"

What? Who cared how many there were? They all hurt.

"Three," he said, answering his own question. "What was the first one?"

I was missing something. What was it? My brain frantically ran back to that night. What had he said? Warm-up, chastisement, and erotic.

Erotic.

Oh.

He raised an eyebrow. "Get your ass upstairs."

I pushed back from the table and ran up the stairs. To be honest, I actually expected the whipping bench to be out. I let out a sigh of relief that it wasn't—there was just a stack of pillows in the middle of Nathaniel's bed.

Nathaniel's bed.

Fear has no place in my bed. I believed him. Tonight would be about pleasure. He would see to it. Excitement ignited in my belly.

I stripped off my clothes and waited. Nathaniel came into the room seconds later. He nodded toward the bed and started unbuttoning his shirt. "On your stomach over the pillows."

I crawled on top of the bed and positioned myself over the pillows so my butt was high in the air. Nathaniel walked to the head of the bed and pulled out a tie-down.

"We can't have you trying to cover yourself, can we?" he asked, tying my hands together and pulling them so I rested on my elbows.

The bed shifted as he moved behind me. I felt his hands run over me. "Have you been using your plug, Abigail?"

I nodded.

"Good." He pushed my legs apart. "I want you open for me." His finger skimmed my throbbing entrance. "Look at this, Abigail. So slick already. Does the thought of me turning your backside red excite you?"

I bit the inside of my cheek.

He rubbed me and then gave me three smacks in quick succession. They stung, but it was the tingly yes-sir-may-I-please-have-another type of sting.

"The good people of New York pay your salary so you will work in the library, not sneak off into the Rare Books Collection." He smacked me again and again, his hand landing on a different area each time.

But instead of pain, I felt a growing pleasure. Instead of hurt,

I felt a warmth that spread from his hand and throbbed through my lower body. I needed him. Needed him to touch me. Needed him inside me.

"You're so wet." He dipped a finger into me briefly and then spanked me right where I was slick and aching.

I moaned.

"Do you like that, Abigail?" He struck me again.

There. Yes, please. There.

Smack.

I shifted my hips back toward him. He started smacking my backside again.

"Your ass is a beautiful shade of pink." I felt his cock press up against me and I held my breath. "Soon I'll do more than spank it. Soon I'll fuck it."

A wrapper ripped open, and he shifted to slide right into where I was wet and ready.

I couldn't help groaning.

He pulled out. "No noise tonight or you can't have my cock." He smacked me again. "Do you understand? Nod if you do."

I nodded.

"Good." He plunged inside me forcefully, and I pushed back to meet him. "Greedy tonight, aren't you? Well, that makes two of us."

He started thrusting long and hard and deep, and I squeezed my inner muscles around him each time he entered. Over and over, he pushed. And I answered each thrust by pushing back onto him, drawing him deeper.

Deeper.

Deeper.

He reached to where we were joined and rubbed my clit. And he'd never done that before. My body exploded with pleasure, and he jerked against me, joining me in my release.

Afterward, I rolled off the pillows, and Nathaniel lay beside me, catching his breath.

His hand skirted up my side and over my breast to cup my shoulder, still pulled above my head. ·

"I don't believe I saw everything I wanted to on Wednesday," he said. "Perhaps you would be so kind as to set up an appointment for me to visit the Rare Books Collection again this coming Wednesday?"

Yes and *sir*.

Late that night, I crept out of my bedroom and walked down the hall to the steps. The half-moon's golden light illuminated my path, giving everything a surreal glow. The door to Nathaniel's room was closed as I sneaked past. He'd never told me I couldn't explore in the middle of the night, but I didn't want to be caught.

Down the steps I went, quiet as a mouse. Into the library. My library.

I walked over to the shelves that held Nathaniel's poetry collection. My fingers danced across spine after spine.

It has to be here. It has to be. Please be here.

My fingers stopped.

The Collected Works of John Boyle O'Reilly.

With nervous hands, I pulled the book from the shelf and walked to stand closer to the window. The book fell open naturally at a spot three-quarters in, right at the page containing "A White Rose."

Something fluttered to the floor. I bent to pick it up—a cream-colored rose petal, with just a hint of pink on the tip.

Chapter Eighteen

I slipped the rose petal into the book and shoved them both back on the shelf right as footsteps echoed in the hallway. It sounded like someone was headed straight to the library.

I was caught.

Nathaniel strolled into the room. He was shirtless and wore only a pair of tan drawstring pants. If he was surprised to see me, it didn't show. He turned a small lamp on.

"Abigail," he said, like it was the most natural thing in the world that I'd be in the library at two o'clock in the morning.

"I couldn't sleep."

"Decided poetry would knock you right out?" he asked, noting where I was standing. "Let's play a game, shall we?

> " *'She walks in beauty, like the night*
> *Of cloudless climes and starry skies;*
> *And all that's best of dark and bright*
> *Meet in her aspect and her eyes . . .'* "

Nathaniel smiled at me. "Name the poet."

"Lord Byron." I crossed my arms. "Your turn.

> " *'I sleep with thee, and wake with thee,*
> *And yet thou are not there;*

> *I fill my arms with thoughts of thee,*
> *And press the common air.'* "

Amusement lit his eyes. "I should have known better than to suggest such a contest with a librarian and English major. I don't know that one."

"John Clare. One point for me."

A wicked grin lit his face. "Try this one," he said.

> " *'Let not thy divining heart*
> *Forethink me any ill;*
> *Destiny may take thy part,*
> *And may thy fears fulfill.'* "

Well, that was cryptic. I narrowed my eyes. "John Donne."

He nodded. "Your turn."

I took a deep breath and thought of the poem I'd read Wednesday night, the one that would give me away. Would he recognize it?

> " *'You gave me the key of your heart, my love;*
> *Then why do you make me knock?'* "

I know, I told him with my eyes. *I know. I want this. I want you.*

No surprise from Nathaniel, just the grin that warmed my heart. "John Boyle O'Reilly," he said. "I give myself a point for knowing the next line:

> " *'O, that was yesterday, Saints above!*
> *And last night—I changed the lock!'* "

This is new for me, his expression warned. *Let me do it my way.*

I could do that.

"A tie, then." I walked away from the shelf, trailing a finger along the leather couch. "So, why are you visiting my library this time of the morning?"

He nodded toward the piano. "I came to play."

"May I listen?"

"Of course." He sat down at the bench and started playing.

My breath caught.

It was the song from my dream. It was real.

It was Nathaniel.

I listened in shock to the song I'd tried so hard to find in my dreams. I'm not sure how much time passed as I sat and listened. Maybe time ceased.

And Nathaniel . . .

I could have sat forever and watched Nathaniel. It was as if he were making love. His face became a portrait of utter concentration; his fingers were soft and gentle, caressing the keys. I think I forgot to breathe at times. The melody echoed in the night, adding a touch of melancholy to the moonlight. Finally, the song came to a haunting crescendo and softly faded to nothing.

For a long while, we sat in silence. Nathaniel broke it first.

"Come to me," he whispered.

I crossed the floor. "It's my library."

"It's my piano."

I approached the bench. Not sure if I should sit or stand. Nathaniel took charge by putting his arms around my waist and pulling me into his lap to straddle him. I faced his chest, with the piano at my back.

He ran his hands through my hair, across my shoulders, and down my back to my waist. His head fell forward between my breasts, and he sighed. I lifted my hands to his head, burying my fingers in his thick hair.

Please, please, please kiss me, I wanted to beg. Wanted to pull his head to mine and kiss him myself. It was my library, after all. But I wanted him to kiss me.

Otherwise, it wouldn't be the same.

Otherwise, it wouldn't mean as much.

He kissed my right breast through the flimsy material of my gown. Pulled my nipple into his mouth and sucked it.

Okay, I decided, maybe I wouldn't think. I'd just feel.

"I want you," he said, looking deeply into my eyes. "I want you here. On my piano. In the middle of your library."

And again, he was giving me an option. It was my library—I could turn him down.

I would sooner stop breathing.

"Yes," I whispered.

We both stood. He ran his hands down to my waist and pulled my gown up and over my head.

"My pocket," he whispered as I worked his pants down.

Oh, yes. The condom.

"Pretty sure of yourself, aren't you?" I asked, ripping the package open.

He didn't answer. He didn't have to.

He was already erect, and I worked the condom on, teasing him with a rough squeeze as I did so. He sat down on the piano bench and I wrapped my legs around his waist, facing him once more.

"Play for me," I whispered, putting my arms around him, running my fingers down his back.

He couldn't reach many of the keys with me sitting in his lap, but he tried, and the song he played was one I'd never heard before. It started slowly and sensuously. Delicate. Taunting.

I lifted my hips and lowered myself onto him. He skipped a note or two—even I could tell.

"Keep going," I whispered, lifting up and pushing myself back down on him. He kept playing.

I held my hips still, leaned down and nibbled his ear. "I love the way you feel inside me." He missed more notes. "During the week, I fantasize about your cock—how it tastes." I squeezed my inner muscles. "How it feels." His arms shook. "I count the hours until I see you." I rode him slowly. "Until I can be with you like this." His hands fell from the keyboard to grip my ass, trying to push me harder, but I held still. "Keep playing."

The song got faster, more intense, and I worked myself up and down while he played.

"I've never felt this way before," I said. "Only you. Only you can do this to me."

His playing was chaotic now; it didn't even sound like a song at all, just disjointed notes. Sweat formed on his body, and I knew he was fighting. Fighting to retain the control he valued so much. Fighting to keep the music going.

Fighting and losing.

The music stopped, and with one swift move, he grabbed my waist and thrust up into me with all he had.

"You think it's different for me?" he ground out in a husky voice. He hooked his arms around my shoulders, forcing himself deeper. "What makes you think it's different for me?"

We moved faster, each trying to hold out for the other, as if climaxing first would be giving in. I bit my lip in concentration, willing him to let go first. He dropped a hand between us and rubbed circles around my clit.

Damn it.

I grabbed handfuls of his hair and pulled. He moaned against my shoulder and rubbed harder.

Finally, it became too much. He was the master, after all. He could do what he wanted with my body. I had no weapons to use against him. I gave up and allowed my climax to overwhelm me. He followed seconds later.

As our hearts and breathing slowed, I felt him putting the wall back up. Brick by brick. Closing himself off. Becoming distant once more.

"Breakfast at eight in the dining room, Abigail." He lifted me from his lap and placed me on the floor. The control was back.

"French toast?" I asked, slipping my gown on, wanting to see if any of the Nathaniel I'd just glimpsed remained.

"Whatever you prefer."

No. He was gone.

Chapter Nineteen

It took longer than usual to make breakfast the next morning. I prolonged each step, dreading what I would find waiting for me in the dining room. How far removed would Nathaniel be this morning from the fevered lover of the night before?

I set a plate for myself on the counter after I made Nathaniel's plate. I wasn't sure where I'd be eating this morning. I wasn't sure where I wanted to eat. No. That wasn't true. I knew where I wanted to eat——at the kitchen table with Nathaniel.

What was it Elaina told me at lunch right before the accident? *You have to handle Nathaniel carefully.*

I could be careful. I would handle him with kid gloves, draw him out so slowly, he wouldn't know what hit him. Handle him carefully, indeed.

And bring the wall down, brick by brick.

I placed the French toast in front of him. Was it my imagination, or did the corner of his lip lift ever so slightly?

Do you think it's different for me? What makes you think it's different for me?

He might as well have said it out loud again. The words rang through my head, and I knew it didn't matter he was eating in the dining room. I'd made a small crack in his exterior last night. I just needed time to make it bigger.

"Make a plate and join me," he said, picking up his fork and spearing a piece of toast.

I joined him minutes later.

"Last night doesn't change anything," he said as I sat down. "I am your dom and you are my sub."

Keep telling yourself that, Nathaniel. Maybe you'll convince yourself eventually. Last night changed everything.

"I do care for you," he continued. "It is not unheard of. It's to be expected, actually."

I started eating.

"But sex is not the same thing as love." He put a banana slice in his mouth, chewed, and swallowed. "Although I suppose many people confuse the two."

He didn't look at me while he ate, almost as if he felt it easier to speak that way. I felt certain I'd seen glimpses of his true feelings the night before. But his actions at the table made it seem as if he were preparing for a mighty big battle. I wondered if it was with himself or me. Himself, I decided. Definitely his own self.

I hear you, Elaina. I hear you loud and clear.

After breakfast, he instructed me to wait in his room.

The curtains were mostly closed, letting in just a small amount of light. I glanced around—there were no pillows on the bed. No ties. No whipping bench. Just the bed.

Then I saw the pillow on the floor, which could mean only one thing, and I dropped to my knees, fully clothed.

Nathaniel walked in, still wearing the tan drawstring pants from last night.

"Very nice, Abigail," he said, coming toward me. "It pleases me that you anticipate my needs."

He took his pants off and I saw that he was only partly erect.

I leaned forward and took him in my mouth, putting my arms around his hips. His fingers dug into my hair.

I swirled my tongue around his cock, running it up and down his length as he moved slowly in and out of my mouth. He could pretend this was nothing but sex, but I knew better and I poured my heart out in the only way he'd allow. The only way I could.

I couldn't tell him how I felt, but I could show him. Show him by being what he needed. Taking from him what I needed in return.

His breathing grew choppy and his thrusts harder. I relaxed my throat to take him all the way, to allow him the release he needed. The fingers in my hair pulled harder. I reached up to gently cup his sac. Stroked it.

I risked a peek at him and his face almost stopped me in my tracks. His teeth were clenched and his expression . . . his expression was a picture of pain. As if he were on the whipping bench.

In that second, I knew what he was doing. Trying to prove to himself that we were only about sex. And that made me angry, because last night had been beautiful. We could be beautiful. He just wouldn't admit it. He could be my dom, I could be his sub, and it could be beautiful.

He twitched inside me, and I knew he was close. I sucked him harder, and when he came in my mouth, I swallowed frantically.

I felt him relax, and the hands on my head loosened. He must have felt better about himself, because he looked more peaceful when he lowered a hand to help me up.

His nimble fingers made quick work of my shirt and pants.

Honestly, I'm not even sure why I bothered getting dressed. It was a complete waste of time. The clothes never stayed on.

My eyes traveled to the bed, and I saw a tube of lubricant off to the side—I'd missed seeing it before. My body tensed.

"Look at me, Abigail." Nathaniel took both my hands. "I want you to answer my questions," he said, drawing me to the bed. "Where are we?"

"Your room." I climbed onto the bed and scooted to the middle, focusing my attention on him.

He crawled to me, still looking in my eyes. "Where in my room?"

"Your bed."

He ran a hand up and down my side. "What happens in my bed?"

My stomach grew all tingly. "Pleasure."

"Yes," he said, bending down to kiss my throat, lowering me to the bed.

I closed my eyes as the sensations rippled through me. His lips, his tongue, his teeth. He nibbled, licked, and sucked.

"Just feel, Abigail," he whispered. His hands dipped and brushed through my curls, stroked lower still to where I ached for him. But instead of moving on top of me, he moved again. His mouth nibbled the slope of my stomach; his tongue dipped into my belly button.

His finger entered me slowly, swirling around my entrance, dancing in and out. I rocked my hips.

"Yes," he soothed. "Just feel."

He moved between my thighs, bent my knees, and pushed them apart. I lifted my hips, begging for friction.

"Wait," he said against my wetness, and the vibration of his voice felt so good, I moaned. "Wait."

His tongue replaced his fingers, right where I needed him.

Then, in one swift move, he hitched my legs over his shoulders and his tongue slipped in and out of me. Slowly. Too slowly. I pushed against him, needing him, wanting more. One of his fingers drew lazy circles around my clit.

I was so close. I teetered on the edge.

His hands left, and some part of me knew what he was doing, but the bigger part of me didn't care because his tongue had replaced his finger, going around and around, but never giving me exactly what I needed.

Slick fingers came back, circling my lower opening, matching the rhythm his tongue continued. He pushed a fingertip inside at the same time as he licked my clit.

I gasped.

"Pleasure, Abigail," he said, slowly moving his fingertip in and out, while his voice did that wondrous vibration thing. "Just pleasure."

His finger slowly went deeper and deeper while he continued licking and nibbling at my growing ache. He slipped his tongue inside me, in and out, in and out. His finger moved slower.

My body once more teetered on the edge and, damn it, I never expected what he was doing to feel good, but it did. So much better than the plug. So much better than I thought possible.

"Relax," he whispered, but it must have been in jest, because I couldn't have been more relaxed. He added a second finger and I felt a stretching pain, but his tongue was back. Swirling. Licking. Teasing me. Keeping me from my release. And his fingers moved in and out.

He moved his mouth so that his tongue was thrusting in and out while his teeth grazed my clit. And his fingers kept up their rhythm.

I lifted my hips to get some of him, any of him, farther inside.

"That's it, Abigail," he said. "Let it go. Let me make it good."

I believed him. He could make it good. He would make it good. I had no more doubts.

His teeth grazed across my clit roughly, right as his fingers thrust deeply inside.

My climax washed over me, throwing me off the edge completely.

When I came back to my senses, Nathaniel was looking down at me, a touch of smugness on his face.

"Are you okay?" he asked.

"Mmmmm," I mumbled.

He lay down beside me and took me in his arms. "Can I take that as a yes?"

I nodded and pushed my head onto his chest. And there, for just a second, I had him back.

Chapter Twenty

Nathaniel surprised me when he visited the Rare Books Collection that Wednesday. Surprised me in a good way.

"I've been giving some thought to what you said about the car issue," he said, zipping his pants up.

"You have?" I slipped my socks on quickly, wanting to be dressed completely if we were going to fight. There was no way, no how I'd ever agree to him buying me a car.

He straightened his tie. "I've decided not to press the issue."

"What?"

"The idea made you extremely uncomfortable, and though part of me still thinks it'd be safer for you to drive, your mental well-being is just as important to me." He walked over and stood in front of me. "I won't have you ever thinking you're a whore."

I was a little surprised he'd drop the subject without further discussion, but pleased that he wasn't going to push his will on me. "Thank you."

"Give and take, Abigail, that's what relationships are." He took his coat on his way to the door. "I appreciate you being honest with me about your feelings. I have difficulties with that myself."

No shit, Sherlock.

I slipped down from the table and slid my shoes on. "Maybe we can work on that together."

He held the door open for me. "Maybe."

I met him at the private airport terminal at four o'clock Friday afternoon. He stood waiting by a beautiful private jet. At least, I assumed it was beautiful—it's not like I'd ever seen a private jet up close before, so I had nothing to compare it to.

"Good afternoon, Abigail," he said. "Thank you for making arrangements to leave work early."

I nodded and took the outstretched hand he offered to help me up the stairway into the plane. The interior was spacious and sleek. It looked like a fancy apartment: it had a bar, leather couches, even an open doorway leading to a bedroom and, of course, leather chairs.

The pilot waved when he saw us enter the main cabin. "We'll be ready for takeoff shortly, Mr. West," he said.

Nathaniel motioned toward the chairs. "We should be seated."

I sat beside him, butterflies in my stomach, while the handful of staff prepared for flight. I was nervous for several different reasons—seeing Nathaniel's family again, concern over the expectations Nathaniel had of me, wondering just how the game would go, and, okay, I won't lie, I was driving myself crazy over what Nathaniel's *plans* involved.

In no time at all we were airborne. I took a deep breath and closed my eyes.

"I want to discuss the weekend with you," Nathaniel said. "Your collar will remain on. You are still my submissive. But my aunt and Jackson have no need to know of our private life. Also, you will not address me as Master, sir, or Mr. West. If you try, you can avoid using my name at all." He met my eyes. "You will not call me by my given name unless it is unavoidable."

I nodded.

"Now, today," he said, "you're going to learn about control."

An older lady walked into the cabin. "Can I get you or Ms. King anything, Mr. West?"

"No," Nathaniel said. "We'll page you if we need anything."

"Very good, sir."

"She'll spend the remainder of the flight with the pilot unless we need her," Nathaniel said, unbuckling his seat belt. "Which we won't." He held out his hand. "Come with me."

We walked to the bedroom and Nathaniel closed the door. "Remove your clothing and get on the bed."

I did as he said, watching him move around the small room. I estimated we had about two hours. Thinking of the things he could do to me in two hours made me giddy.

I got on the bed, staring up at the ceiling. Anticipation bubbled in my belly as I wondered what he meant by "control."

I didn't have to wait long. Nathaniel, fully dressed, walked around the bed, and stretched out my arms so they were perpendicular to my body. My legs he left alone. "Stay like this and I won't tie you up."

He sat on the bed, holding what looked like a bowl in his hand. "This is a battery-operated hot plate," he said. "Normally, I'd use a candle for this, but the pilot won't allow it." He gave a small smile. "And rules are rules."

A candle? Was there wax somewhere?

He took a blindfold from his pocket. "This works better blindfolded."

Soon, I was wrapped in darkness. Once again naked and waiting.

Nathaniel spoke in that smooth, seductive voice. "Most people find the sensation of the heat very pleasurable."

I hissed as a drop of wax landed on my upper arm, surprised at how good it felt.

He rubbed it in. "This is special candle wax. It turns to body oil once heated."

Another drop landed on my other arm, followed again by the gentle feel of Nathaniel's hand. The uncertainty of where the wax would land next had me tense and waiting. Then it would come—dribbled down my belly, across my upper thigh, down between my breasts. The initial heat gradually subsided into a warmth that left me weak and jellylike. After every drop, Nathaniel would rub the oil into my body with long, sensuous strokes.

The heat landed on my nipple and I gasped.

Ohhhhh. Damn, that felt good.

Again he followed with his hand, rubbing the oil in.

"Do you like the heat, Abigail?" he asked, his breath hot in my ear as another drop landed on the opposite nipple.

I could only moan.

He dribbled a stream of wax over both breasts. The bed moved and I felt Nathaniel straddle me, both hands rubbing up my torso, cupping my breasts and running the length of my arms.

"Control," he said. "To whom do you belong? Answer me."

"You," I whispered.

"That's right," he said. "And by the end of tonight, you'll be begging for my cock." His thumbs rubbed over my nipples, pinching, pulling. "If you're good, I might just let you have it."

The bed moved again and he left. I felt weak with anticipation. Still naked, still at his mercy and, suddenly, very much alone.

Our hotel was a five-star resort in Tampa. I'd wondered over the week what the arrangements would be. Would I share Nathaniel's bed at last? Would he make me sleep on the floor? Would we have two separate rooms?

I stood with him as he checked in, acutely aware of his body next to mine. I could almost feel the electricity coming from him. I wondered how the hotel clerk kept from fanning herself. Of course, he hadn't massaged her less than an hour ago with hot body wax.

"Here you go, Mr. West," she said. "The presidential suite is ready for you."

She glanced at me.

Yes, I wanted to say. *I'm with him. Deal.*

"How many keys will you need?" she asked.

"Two, please."

She handed the keys to him, and he stuck both of them in his pocket. "Your luggage will be up shortly," she said.

He thanked her, and we made our way to our room.

"I booked us a suite so you could have your own room and bathroom without the hassle of being down the hall or in a separate room from me." He handed me a key. "You might need this."

The suite was spacious and airy. Nathaniel pointed out my room and told me we had an hour before we met everyone for dinner. Our bags were delivered shortly after we arrived, and I settled on a dress that Elaina must have given him for me to wear. Tasteful, sexy, and sophisticated all in one.

I met Nathaniel in the suite's living room right before we needed to leave.

"Very nice," he said, looking me over. "But go back and remove the hose."

Remove the hose? The dress hit right above the knee and it was cold outside.

"I want you totally bare beneath that dress," he said. "I want you to go out knowing I can lift your skirt and take you anytime I want."

My brain worked hard to comprehend that. Worked hard and failed. I went back to my bedroom and took off my hose and panties. Slipped my shoes back on.

Nathaniel was waiting for me when I returned. "Lift the skirt."

My face heated as I pulled the skirt up.

He held out his arm. "Now we're ready."

We met everyone at a steakhouse downtown. New York fans and photographers lined the windows and blocked the doorway. It took me a few seconds to realize they were waiting for Jackson.

"All these people," Nathaniel murmured as a passerby bumped us into each other. "No one even notices us. I can do anything I want and no one will notice."

My knees threatened to give out from under me.

"Nathaniel!" Elaina called from inside the restaurant, pushing her way through the crowd. "Abby! Over here."

Fortunately, the restaurant staff were doing an excellent job of keeping the crowd out. Even so, our table received numerous stares, and nearly every eye was on us as we took our seats with the Clarks and the Wellings.

"Can you believe this weather?" Elaina asked as Nathaniel pulled my chair out for me. "We must have brought it with us from New York."

I laughed and sat down. "I think it was warmer at home."

"Which would certainly explain why you would choose not to wear hose," she said, nodding at my bare legs.

I looked over to Nathaniel, but he simply shrugged.

"Hate the damn things," I said. "Always seem to find a way to poke a hole in them."

"How are you feeling, Abby?" Linda asked, sparing me any more questions about my lack of hosiery. "After the accident?"

"I'm feeling great, Dr. Clark," I said. "Thank you."

"Hey, Abby," Felicia said. "How was the flight?"

I blushed. I'm sure she noticed. "Fine, Felicia. It was just fine."

"Fine?" Nathaniel whispered in my ear. "I poured hot wax over your naked body and it was *fine*? I'm rather insulted."

I *think* he was teasing.

The waiter came by and poured Nathaniel and me a glass of wine while we looked over the menus. I felt a bit unsure of myself. This was not the type of restaurant I normally frequented. It was too high-class. Too intimidating.

"The lobster bisque is excellent," Nathaniel said. "So is the house Caesar. I would also recommend either the filet or the strip steak."

"Lobster bisque and the filet, then." I closed my menu. "So, Jackson. Ready for the game?"

He pulled his eyes away from Felicia. "You know it!"

He laughed and then launched into football talk. I had trouble following what he was saying, and it was an effort to feign polite interest, but I noticed Felicia was hooked on his every word. At one point, Jackson reached over and took her hand. I was so happy for her. She deserved a nice guy and, from what I could tell, Jackson treated her like a queen.

Elaina gave me a wink and pointedly asked me a question, drawing me away from all the football talk. She and Todd were very kind, asking me about my family and what school I'd been to, trying to set me at ease. As it turned out, Todd had attended medical school at Columbia, which was where I'd gone for my undergraduate degree. We spoke for a while about our college days and discovered we had favored several of the same hangouts. Nathaniel had attended Dartmouth, but that didn't stop him from joining in our conversation and adding in his favorite college memories. We all laughed when he described working the coin-operated washer and dryers for the first time.

There was a slight lull in the conversation as our appetizers were delivered. I placed my napkin in my lap, noticing for the first time just how close I was sitting to Nathaniel. I could feel his body heat if I tried hard enough.

I'd just taken a sip of soup when his hand started drawing circles on my knee.

Control.

Heaven help me.

Chapter Twenty-one

"Abby," Linda said across the table, totally clueless that her nephew was making love to my kneecap. "I keep meaning to call you for lunch. This coming week isn't good. How would the next Wednesday work for you?"

The hand on my knee continued stroking.

"Wednesdays aren't good for me," I said. "There's a patron who comes in every Wednesday to see the Rare Books Collection—and we don't let researchers in unaccompanied, so I have to be there with him."

Nathaniel chuckled under his breath.

"That must be a bit tiresome," Linda said. "But I suppose that's what customer service is all about."

"I don't mind," I said. "It's refreshing to find someone so thorough."

The hand stroked down my knee, brushed the underside.

"How would that Tuesday work?" she asked. "He doesn't come on Tuesdays, does he?"

Not yet.

"Tuesday will be fine," I said.

"It's a date, then," she said, smiling at me.

Conversation flowed freely. At some point, Nathaniel and

Todd started a debate over politics. Elaina looked at me and rolled her eyes. Perfectly normal dinner conversation. Nothing out of the ordinary.

Above the table, that is.

I'll give him this much—Nathaniel was a sneaky thing. He'd play with my knee for a few minutes and then pass the bread to Felicia or cut his salad, something requiring two hands. Later, without warning, his hand would be back. Stroking, squeezing, gently working higher. Retreating.

I was a complete mess of nerves.

I took a sip of bisque. Nathaniel had been right. It was incredible. Creamy. Rich. Just the right amount of chunky lobster. I crossed my legs out of habit. When Nathaniel's hand came back, he pushed my left leg off my right and continued stroking. Going higher this time.

Lobsters, I told myself. *Think about lobsters.*

Lobsters. Lobsters were sea creatures. They had huge pincers and had to have their claws rubber-banded. They turned a red color when you boiled them.

Does the thought of me turning your backside red excite you?

I choked on a mouthful of bisque.

Fortunately, Nathaniel's hands were both in plain view, above the table, at the time. He pounded me on the back. "Are you okay?"

"Fine. Sorry."

The waiter came to take our bowls and plates away. Everyone at the table was chatting or laughing, caught up in conversation.

Nathaniel poured me more wine and started caressing my thigh through the dress. "What do you read besides poetry?"

He wanted to discuss my reading habits? "Just about anything," I said, curious as to where this was going. "Classics are my favorite."

" 'A classic,' " he said, " 'is a book which people praise and don't read.' Mark Twain."

I knew then I was in real trouble. To tease me with provocative caresses was one thing; to engage me in verbal sparring was quite another. Especially where literature was concerned. My body he had already mastered. Was my mind next on his agenda? But I thought back to the library and knew I could give as well as he did.

" 'I cannot think well of a man who sports with any woman's feelings,' " I said. "Jane Austen."

He smirked. " 'But when a young lady is to be a heroine, the perverseness of forty surrounding families cannot prevent her.' " His hand went up my skirt. "Jane Austen."

" 'Truth is more of a stranger than fiction,' " I said. "Mark Twain."

He laughed and moved his hand. "I give up," he said. "You win." His eyes grew serious. "But only this round."

I wondered how many rounds there might be.

Our entrées were delivered, and once more Nathaniel didn't disappoint—the filet was so tender, I could cut it with a fork.

"Hey, you two," Elaina said to Felicia and me. "Linda and I are hitting the spa tomorrow for massages and facials and to get our nails done. We made you both appointments as well. Our treat. Will you come?"

Felicia looked over to Jackson. He picked up her hand and kissed it. "I'll be busy tomorrow anyway. You go and have a good time."

"How very thoughtful," Nathaniel said, caressing my knee once more. "I suppose Todd and I can amuse ourselves with golf. Would you like to go with the girls, Abigail?"

"Sure," I said. "I'd love to."

Elaina beamed at me.

A spa day sounded delightful. But what about my collar? Wouldn't it be odd to wear it to a spa? Nathaniel's hand inched farther up my skirt, and rational thought was beyond me for several long minutes.

It wasn't as easy for Nathaniel to keep up his under-the-table moves while we ate, but I was tense all the same. On the edge of my seat waiting for what he'd do next.

Which was probably exactly where he wanted me.

When the entrées were cleared away, we all sat back and waited for dessert. Two young teenagers came by our table for pictures and autographs from Jackson. He chatted with them for a bit, told them he'd see them Sunday. Like I said, a totally normal dinner.

Right. Who was I kidding? There was nothing normal about this dinner.

Nathaniel refilled my wineglass, and I tried to remember how much I'd had to drink. Three glasses? Four? Surely not four.

His hand came back, but instead of reaching for my leg, he took my hand and, ever so subtly, placed it on his crotch. He was erect and straining against his pants. He thrust up into my palm. Barely moving. No one at the table suspected anything.

I could control myself, but feeling the evidence of his need just about did me in. I chewed my lip. How long until dinner was over? I glanced at my watch. Eight thirty. Still early. It wouldn't take much for me to beg for his cock tonight. I was almost there as it was.

Soufflés were delivered to the table. Nathaniel's hand went straight up my skirt, brushed right where I was wet and aching and then reappeared above the table. I bit the inside of my cheek.

Control.

I wasn't tipsy, I told myself. I was just really relaxed. And happy. Couldn't forget happy. And warm. Warm and tingly inside. Weightless.

Nathaniel continued his teasing in the car. It was easy. We were alone and there was no one to see. He flipped my skirt up with one hand.

"You're going to mess up the interior of the rental," he scolded, dipping a finger inside. "Wet as you are."

I wanted to tell him to spank me. But we weren't in the kitchen or my library. We were in a rental car, headed back to the hotel. Where there was a bed.

Nathaniel and a bed . . .

I'd even beg.

Now.

Please.

We made it back to the hotel and got into the elevator for the long ride up to our suite. Nathaniel squeezed my backside and I groaned.

"Not yet," he said.

Someone had been busy while we were out. The lights were muted, and Nathaniel's bed had been turned down. He led me to the bed and fumbled with a duffel bag on the floor. He placed a tube of lube and a vibrator on the bed.

"I've been patient, Abigail," he said. "And I'll be as gentle as I can, but tonight's the night. You're ready."

Pure adrenaline shot right through me. I surely never thought I'd be looking forward to this.

You'll be begging for my cock.

I had no reason to think he was wrong.

"Undress me," he said.

Trembling, I slid the jacket from his shoulders, feeling his firm muscles, powerful and hard under his shirt. I had to see them. I unbuttoned his shirt and yanked it from his pants. Unbuckled his belt. Pushed his pants and boxers down his hips and feasted on the sight of his erection.

"All for you," he said. "Because you did so well at dinner tonight, I'll let you have a little taste."

I dropped to my knees and took him into my mouth. We both moaned. He wrapped my hair around his hands and thrust in and out of my mouth.

Mmmm. His taste.

Much too soon, he pulled back and helped me to my feet. I was a little unsteady.

"Undress for me," he said. "Slowly."

I stepped out of my shoes, reached behind my back, and undid the zipper. Pushed the dress slowly down my arms. His eyes were hungry, like he wanted to devour me. The dress fell to a puddle at the floor. I undid my bra and added it to the pile.

"Touch yourself," he commanded, sitting on the edge of the bed.

I brought my hands to my breasts and rubbed them, circling them slowly, dragging my fingers across my nipples. Pinched them. Rolled them between my fingertips. Squeezed harder because it hurt so good. I ran one hand down my side, across my hips, circled my belly button, and stroked lower. Rocked into my palm.

"Enough," he said. "Come here."

I walked to the bed, feeling the wetness drip onto my thighs. He grabbed me by the waist and flipped me so I was under him. His hands and teeth explored everywhere. Biting and scraping me. Pinching and taunting. I was overwhelmed by pure sensation.

I moaned with my need for him, glad he wasn't telling me to be quiet, because I knew I couldn't.

His hands grew less frantic and his nibbles softer. I strained against him, wanting him back. Needing him back. Something. Please.

He turned me so I was on my side, my back to his chest, and

took the tube of lubricant at my elbow. When he touched me again, his fingers were warm and slick.

How did he get it warm?

Like during the previous weekend, one finger circled my clit while the other one slipped in the lower hole. He took his time, moving slowly, stretching me, eventually adding a second finger.

Why does it feel so good?

The finger at my clit rubbed softly and I thrust against it, wanting it harder. Rougher. His other hand lifted my leg and he slipped in behind me—his warm, slick cock pressing against my opening.

He moved forward, pressing the head into me. I gasped as I stretched. Surely he wouldn't fit. There was no way. But he held still, working my clit again. Relaxing me. Moved forward a little, stretching me. It hurt, but I trusted Nathaniel. I knew he wanted my pleasure as well.

He slowly worked his way inside, pushing against the natural resistance and then held totally still after he popped the head of his cock in. Allowing me time to adjust. He stopped circling my clit and took my hand. "Are you okay?" he asked.

Ow, ow, ow.

I waited until I could be honest. "Yes."

He squeezed my hand and kissed the back of my neck. "You're doing great."

And just that simply, I was his.

I heard something turn on. *The vibrator.* One hand held me close to him, and with the other, he ran the vibrator gently down my body until it came to rest at my wet entrance. He slowly pushed it in while working his cock deeper.

I was stretching in ways I never knew possible. Being filled two ways. I didn't know I could feel so full. But he was still moving, still pushing forward. Inch by inch. All the way.

Oww.

"Still okay?" he asked, and his voice was strained.

"Yes," I answered, my voice matching his.

Again he was still. Making sure I was fine, giving me the time I needed to adjust.

Slowly, I focused on the buzzing inside me that felt so good. He started to move, both his cock and the vibrator, working them opposite each other. I held still, awash once again in sensation. Allowing it to sweep over me.

I sucked in my breath through my teeth. The pain mixed with the pleasure. It was too much, too much. I gasped as he moved a little faster. The buzzing overtook me, vibrated throughout my whole body.

I wasn't going to last long. Nathaniel's breathing grew heavy, uneven, and my belly tightened. Something was building, building deep inside and threatening to shatter me.

I whimpered as the feeling grew. I'd never felt anything so intense. So utterly and completely intense. I couldn't bear it. In and out, he moved. His cock. The vibrator. He kept on and kept on and the vibrator was hitting a new place now.

Oh, please. Oh, please. Oh, please.

Almost. Almost. Almost.

"Yes!" I screamed as the world shattered all around me in bright flashes of light.

He thrust one more time and released into me. I shuddered as a second orgasm hit.

I was vaguely aware of water running.

I tried to roll over, but my body wouldn't work. I felt that weak.

Two arms lifted me and carried me into the bathroom. The

light was dimmed, barely enough for me to see as he placed me carefully in the warm water.

He took his time bathing me. Washed me tenderly, taking care to be gentle. He was still naked and he must have been cold, but all his attention was focused on me. When he was finished, he took me from the tub, sat me on the edge, and dried me completely with soft towels.

"You were wonderful," he whispered, brushing my hair. "I knew you would be."

Then he lifted me in his arms, carried me to my bed, and tucked me in.

Chapter Twenty-two

The sound of hushed voices from the living room woke me the next morning. I rolled over and squinted at the clock beside my bed. Seven thirty.

Seven thirty!

I sprang from the bed and threw my robe on before I realized I wasn't at Nathaniel's house. I was in the hotel. In Tampa. There was no kitchen. No need for me to fix breakfast.

Relieved, I sat back down on the bed and noticed the bottle of water and two ibuprofen on the bedside table. This reminder of his care for me made me all tingly inside.

I swallowed the pills with the cold water and went into the bathroom. Elaina and Linda hadn't said what time to meet them at the spa, so I took my time showering and getting ready. To be honest, I spent most of my time thinking about the previous night.

I'd thought the night in the library had changed everything for Nathaniel and me, but looking back, I knew I'd been mistaken. The night before changed everything.

Last night I had been worried about wearing my collar to the spa. This morning I'd walk across broken glass for Nathaniel. Or hot coals. Broken glass with hot coals sprinkled around. Anything, absolutely anything he wanted me to do, I'd do. And I'd wear the collar to the spa with pride.

I walked out into the main living room. Nathaniel sat at the dining table adjoining the living area. I dropped my head when I saw him.

"Come sit down and have breakfast, Abigail," he said.

I walked to the table. It must have been room service knocking that woke me up. My food was still warm. Bacon, eggs, fruit, and toast. Fresh orange juice and coffee. My stomach gave a loud gurgle.

"Linda and Elaina want you and Felicia up in the spa at nine thirty," he said. "I'm not sure what they have planned, but apparently you won't finish until sometime this afternoon."

Suddenly, I was a bit sad I wouldn't spend the day with him. Our one whole weekend day and I'd be at a spa and he'd be golfing. Ridiculous that I'd be sad, but I was.

I ate in silence, thinking about how I could get out of spending the day away from Nathaniel—perhaps I could complain of a stomachache, a sudden case of the flu, maybe the ever-popular PMS. But it was a spa day and I would be with Elaina and Felicia and Linda.

And there was always the coming night . . .

When I finished eating, Nathaniel told me to stand.

He walked behind me. "Elaina and Felicia know of our lifestyle. I'd like to think my aunt doesn't, but even if she does"—he unlatched the collar—"there's no reason to flaunt it." He walked around to face me. "You'll get your collar back this afternoon."

I dropped my head.

He lifted my chin with his finger, and his eyes sparkled as they looked into mine. "You're still mine. Even with this off."

That made me all tingly again.

I met Felicia outside the spa. "Felicia," I said, jogging up to her. "Hey!"

She turned to me, all smiles. "Hey, how was your night?"

I was certain my smile rivaled hers. "Earth-shattering," I said, wiggling both eyebrows.

She took my arm. "I so do not want to hear this. Ask me how my evening was."

Which was just as well—I really didn't feel like sharing my evening with her. "How was your evening?"

"Oh, Abby," she said, blissful. "It was perfect. After dinner we went down to the waterfront. It was so funny, Jackson trying to be inconspicuous and failing, because you have seen him, right? There's nothing inconspicuous about him. People kept walking up to him, wanting shirts signed and all. And he was so nice to everyone, even though you could tell he just wanted us to be alone. But we finally found this quiet little spot and we just talked and talked, and guess what?"

She didn't stop long enough for me to guess. Rhetorical question, obviously.

"He doesn't want to play pro football much longer," she said. "He wants to retire soon and coach high school. And, Abby, he wants four kids."

To anyone else, this would have been a statement of fact, but for Felicia . . . it was so much more. She'd wanted a large family from the first day I met her.

"After he dropped that little bit on me," she continued, "I told him how I wanted to open a school, and he didn't think it was funny or strange at all." She stopped walking and grabbed both my hands. "I'm probably being stupid, but, Abby, I think he's *the one*."

I hugged her. "I don't think you're being stupid at all. And I'm so very, very happy for you."

"Thanks. Hey, where's your"—she waved at my throat—"thingie."

"It's a collar." I rolled my eyes. "Nathaniel didn't want to flaunt our lifestyle in front of Linda. She doesn't know."

Elaina and Linda arrived soon after we did, and we were all escorted around the spa. We ended up in a plush locker room, where we were given schedules for the day and bathrobes. We all had separate services scheduled for the first part of the morning, but we'd meet up again for lunch.

Felicia and I went off to change.

"Damn, Abby," Felicia said. She pointed to my back.

"What?" I said, twisting around.

"You've got a scratch mark or a bite on your shoulder. What were you doing last night?"

I sighed, remembering.

"On second thought," she said, "never mind. I don't want to know."

We were called then and went our separate ways—Felicia to a massage and me to a facial.

The facial was completely relaxing. I actually fell asleep halfway through. Not that it would have been difficult. The bench was warm and covered with fluffy towels. Soft music played in the background, and the room smelled like spicy lavender.

The technician shook me gently to wake me up and then led me to a room down the hall for my massage.

It started with a salt scrub. Again, lavender, this time combined with the gentle exfoliation of salts. I washed the salt off in a large shower with multiple showerheads.

But thinking about showers got me thinking about Nathaniel and the bath he had given me the night before. His hands. The way he washed me—almost reverently. And then he'd taken his time to brush out my hair and dry every part of me . . .

A knock on the shower door interrupted me. "Ms. King," the massage therapist called, "are you ready?"

Once again, I found myself under warm blankets. I promised myself I'd stay awake this time so I'd remember the massage. Up to that point, I'd only had the one Nathaniel gave me on the plane. Hot wax and Nathaniel. Yum. I wondered what he had planned for the flight home.

"Any sore areas you need me to work on?" the therapist asked.

I wondered briefly what she'd do if I mentioned the particular soreness I had as a result of the previous night's activities . . .

"No," I said. "Not really."

Before too long, I was in the spa's ivory-colored dining area, waiting for Felicia, Elaina, and Linda. Soft music played in the background and candles flickered on the tables. I lay back in a thickly padded lounger and closed my eyes as I waited.

"Abby?" Linda said.

I sat up. "Linda, hey. I was just relaxing a bit."

She sat down beside me. "Did you have a good morning?"

"Oh, yes, the best. It was so nice of you and Elaina to arrange this for us."

She reached for a glass of water. "It was Elaina's idea. I'd planned to spend the day shopping. This was a much better idea."

Felicia and Elaina came in together as Linda was talking. They were laughing at something Elaina had said. They sat down right as four grilled chicken salads were delivered. They looked delicious—fresh greens, feta cheese, almonds, and cranberries. I smiled. Nathaniel would approve.

"Did everyone have a good night last night?" Linda asked, spearing a chunk of chicken.

Elaina smiled at her. "You and I have discussed the benefits of hotel sex many times in the past, Linda."

Just a hint of color spread across Linda's cheeks. "Yes, Elaina, but I was actually asking to make sure Jackson and Nathaniel were being good hosts and acting like the gentlemen I raised them to be."

"I'm not sure *gentleman* is the right word for Todd," Elaina said, putting a napkin in her lap, "but he was good all right."

Felicia snorted on her water.

Elaina and Linda obviously had a closer relationship than I'd thought. Regardless, I loved the way they could tease each other. The way they talked about sex and men like sisters would.

"Abby," Linda said, changing the subject, "I remember last night you said you went to Columbia."

"Yes," I said. "Same as Todd, right?"

Elaina chimed in. "He did his graduate work there."

"And Nathaniel went to Dartmouth." I took a bite of cranberry with feta. You could never have too much feta. Feta went with everything.

"Yes," Linda confirmed. "For the longest time he wanted to go to the Naval Academy. We had even arranged an appointment for him. But he changed his mind and went to Dartmouth instead." She got a faraway look. "He was always a withdrawn child. I guess you can understand why. My sister's death was very hard on him."

I looked down at my plate, remembering the haunted look he'd had while I was at the hospital.

"Now, Jackson," Linda said, taking Felicia's hand, "Jackson was always my wild child. It's a good thing we steered him toward sports—there's no telling what kind of trouble he'd have gotten himself into otherwise."

"He still gets in plenty of trouble," Elaina said in between bites. "Remember the skydiving incident?"

Linda laughed. "The coach made him sit out the next game as a result of that little incident. I don't think he's ever tried skydiving again."

After we ate lunch, we changed into swimsuits and hung out in the hot tub. I pulled my hair to the left side to cover up the mark Felicia had noticed. I thought back to the previous night, trying to remember when Nathaniel might have marked me, but I couldn't. I remembered pain in other parts of my body, but not my shoulder. Mostly I remembered the pleasure.

I think I spaced out in the hot tub for several long minutes just thinking back to the night before. I glanced up at the clock they had in one corner of the pool room. How long until I saw Nathaniel again?

"Abby," Elaina said. "Did Nathaniel tell you?"

"Tell me what?" I asked.

She walked through the tub to sit next to me. "Linda's turning in early and Jackson and Felicia are hanging out with some of his teammates, so you, me, Todd, and Nathaniel are having dinner together."

Normally, I'd have loved to have dinner with Todd and Elaina, but after spending the entire day apart from Nathaniel, my thoughts had been drifting toward an intimate dinner in the suite. Dinner in the suite naked.

"Don't look so disappointed," she said, bumping my shoulder gently. "Nathaniel sees you all the time—I only get you for today." She leaned in close. "And we'll have you back plenty early. Tomorrow's the big day, you know. Better get plenty of sleep."

Sleep, right. Who needed sleep?

Chapter Twenty-three

After the hot tub, we went to another room to have our nails done. The four of us were lined up with different techs doing our manicures and pedicures. We all decided to go for the same deep red polish, called After Sex. Elaina had a good laugh over the name, and we all joined in like a group of crazy sorority sisters.

We hugged each other goodbye afterward and headed to our rooms. There was a brunch the next day we'd all be attending. Elaina blew me a kiss and told me she'd see me soon.

I was so ready to see Nathaniel.

He was waiting in the suite, reading a newspaper. When I came in, he looked up. His eyes smoldered.

"Did you enjoy your day?" he asked, being the gentleman. Like his eyes weren't telling me in six different ways he wanted me. Wanted me badly.

"Yes, Master."

He stood up, the collar in his hand. "Miss something?"

I nodded.

"Do you want it back?" he asked, walking to me.

I nodded again.

"Say it," he said. His voice dropped. "Say you want it."

"I want it," I whispered as he moved behind me. "I want your collar."

He drew my shirt over my head, swept my hair to the right. Kissing the mark on my shoulder, he murmured against my skin, "I marked you last night. Marked you as mine and I'll do it again." His teeth grazed my shoulder. "There are so many ways I can mark you."

It took all my self-control not to beg him, because, damn it, I wanted him to mark me. My legs felt all wobbly just thinking about it.

"Unfortunately," he said, fastening the collar, "we have to have dinner with Todd and Elaina. Go change. I have your clothes out on the bed."

A long-sleeved cotton dress waited for me, with a pair of flats on the floor. No hose. I took the hint and left my panties off.

Nathaniel stood by the couch when I reappeared. "Bend over the arm of the couch, Abigail."

I did as he asked, wondering where he was going with this. We had to leave soon. He stood behind me and lifted my skirt, ran his hand over my bare skin. He chuckled.

"How well you read my mind. Too bad. I was looking forward to giving you a spanking before dinner."

I made a mental note to wear panties next time.

We drove to a waterfront bistro, probably not far from where Jackson and Felicia had talked last night.

"There will be several fish dishes on the menu," Nathaniel said in the car. "You will order one of them."

Fortunately, I loved fish. I wondered what would happen when he asked me to do something I didn't want to do.

We arrived before Todd and Elaina and went inside to sit down at a booth. Nathaniel motioned for me to enter first.

I was looking over the menu, trying to decide between salmon and grouper, when Todd and Elaina arrived.

"Abby," Todd said in a tight voice.

I was surprised. Had I done something to make him angry? I looked up, but he was glaring at Nathaniel—he wasn't mad at me after all.

I glanced over to Elaina. She shrugged her shoulders. Either she didn't want me to know what was wrong or she didn't know herself.

The waiter came to take our drink order. When he left, Todd slapped his menu on the table. Nathaniel scowled at him.

"So, Nathaniel," Elaina said, eyes bouncing from Nathaniel to her husband. "Where's Apollo this weekend?"

"At a kennel," Nathaniel said, still looking at Todd.

"He's better, then?" she asked. "You can leave him there?"

I wanted to ask why he wouldn't be able to leave Apollo at the kennel, but I couldn't get past Todd's expression. What had happened between him and Nathaniel?

"He's made marginal improvements."

Todd mumbled something under his breath.

The waiter came back with our drinks. "Everyone have a chance to look over the menu?" he asked. His gaze traveled to Elaina's hand. Her large engagement ring and wedding band sparkled in the light. He wrote their order down and looked to our side of the table. "Ma'am?" he asked me.

"I'll have the salmon," I said, handing the menu to Nathaniel.

"Wonderful choice," he said. "The salmon's one of our bestsellers." He winked at me.

Nathaniel cleared his throat.

"Yes, sir," the waiter said, shifting his gaze to him. "What would you like?"

"The salmon," Nathaniel said and handed him our menus.

The waiter wrote the order down and rocked back on his heels. "You guys in town for the game?" he asked, looking at me.

I scooted closer to Nathaniel. *Sorry,* I tried to tell the waiter. *Taken.*

His lips lifted at the corner.

"Of course," Elaina piped up when no one else did. "Giants all the way."

"You know," Nathaniel said to the waiter, "if you put in our order, we'll get our food faster and get out of here quicker."

The waiter shot me one more glance and left.

We all sat in silence for several long minutes. I glanced out the window to the water, still trying to figure out what was wrong between Todd and Nathaniel. I wondered if it had something to do with me.

"I need to hit the restroom," Elaina said. "Abby?"

"Sure," I said.

Nathaniel stood to let me out.

"What in the world is going on?" I asked once we were in the bathroom.

"I have no idea," she said. "I think something happened after the golf game, but I'm not sure. I hope they're over it by tomorrow. It'll make for a long day if they're not."

"Do you think it's something to do with me?"

She shook her head. "I really don't think so. He knows about you and Nathaniel." She turned to the mirror and played with her hair. "It's strange Todd won't tell me."

As we left the bathroom, I saw Nathaniel and Todd arguing. Todd looked up, saw us approaching, and they stopped.

Dinner was tense. Elaina kept trying to start a conversation, but it never went anywhere. Even the waiter picked up on it, dropping our dinners off and coming back only to refill our drinks.

Nathaniel and I were both out of sorts by the time we made it back to the hotel room. He slammed the door behind us and I jumped. In one swift move, he had me against the door.

"Damn it, damn it, damn it," he said against my skin as his hands drew my dress up and over my head. He tore my bra off, throwing it to the floor.

His wild, uncontained actions excited me, and a surge of pure lust pulsed through my body. I wanted him. Wanted him as badly as he wanted me. He stepped back and jerked his pants down. Kicked them off.

He picked me up and pushed me against the door. "Next weekend you're not wearing a bit of clothing from the time you arrive until the second you leave my house."

Yes. Yes.

His hands dipped down and he slipped two fingers inside me. I was already wet. "I'll take you whenever and wherever I want." His fingers twisted. "I'll fuck you five times Friday night alone."

Please.

"I want you waxed bare next weekend, Abigail," he said. "Not a bit of hair left."

Uh, what?

"Spread your legs and bend them," he said. "I'm not waiting any longer."

I did as he asked and he bent low, thrusting into me and lifting me up in one movement. I gave a short squeak, marveling at how deep he went with that one thrust. Then he pulled back and thrust again, pounding me into the door. I wrapped my legs around him.

He slammed me into the door again and again. My arms went around his back and my nails scratched him.

"Yes," he shouted with another thrust that sent him deeper into me than he'd ever been. So deep, I sucked in a breath, trying to grow accustomed to him, and held him tighter. "Damn it. Yes."

Bang.

Bang.

Bang.

I hoped no one was walking by our room. Each slam sent vibrations through my arms, down my spine, and right to where we were connected.

The familiar feeling of impending release built up inside. I groaned as it threatened to overtake me.

"Not yet, Abigail," he said with another thrust. My back slammed into the door. "I'm not finished."

I groaned again. Squeezed my internal muscles around him.

"You better not come before I tell you," he said, pulling back and then slamming us into the door again. "I brought the leather strap."

I clawed at his back, his muscles tense under my hands. Again we hit the door. I couldn't last much longer. Again. He angled his legs, and when he thrust, my butt hit the door, pushing him deep. *Damn, he is good.* Again.

I bit the inside of my cheek. Slam. Bad move. I tasted blood. Slam. I couldn't last. I was going to explode. Slam. I whimpered.

He dropped his head. "Now."

I threw my head back and let my climax overtake me. His release shot into me, and he bit my shoulder, sending another wave of pleasure through my body.

He was breathing heavily as he lowered me to the floor minutes later. My legs were quivering, and I could barely stand. He left for the bathroom and came back with a washcloth, then cleaned me gently, the way he had the night before.

"I'm sorry," he said, and for a moment I thought he was apologizing for the rough sex. "I have to go out. I'll be back later."

I didn't hear him come back at all that night, although I'm sure he did at some point. I eventually went to bed and fell into a restless sleep.

Chapter Twenty-four

Brunch wasn't until eleven, so I slept late again and took my time getting dressed. Nathaniel hadn't said anything about what to wear, so I decided on black pants and a gray cashmere sweater. I also wore panties.

Because he hadn't told me not to.

Because I wanted to see what he'd do when he found them.

Of course it was a calm, cool, nothing-but-collected Nathaniel who met me. No trace of the wild man who had taken me against the wall, biting my neck as he came . . .

Damn it, yes.

But I had to spend the morning with his aunt, his friends, and several strangers. It wouldn't do to get all flustered just because I'd had amazing sex the night before.

Amazing fuck-me-now-against-the-door sex.

Stop it, Good Abby said.

Show Nathaniel you have panties on, Bad Abby said.

I decided Bad Abby was the stuff. Nathaniel watched as I walked over to the coffeepot and poured a cup. I turned so my butt was in plain sight. Gave a little wiggle.

"Abigail," he chided. "Do I see panty lines?"

I held still, coffee cup in hand. *Hell, yes, you see panty lines. What are you going to do about it?*

"Come here," he said, setting his coffee cup down.

I walked over, heart thumping in my throat.

He stood up and moved behind me. "You're wearing panties. Take them off. Now."

I undid my pants and pushed them down over my hips. I stepped out of my panties.

"Over the arm of the couch, Abigail."

I leaned over the couch arm, butt facing him.

He smacked my backside. "No more panties the rest of the weekend." Another smack. "When I finish, you will go to your room and bring them all out to me." Smack. "You'll get them back when I say." Smack. "Which won't be next weekend either." Smack. "I told you last night what will happen next weekend."

He gave me another smack. The warmth was spreading, reaching between my legs. Everything he did felt so good. Damn. Absolutely everything. I pushed back toward him, wanting more.

"Not this morning." Another smack landed on my backside. "Put your pants on and bring me what I asked for."

Damn it. No release.

We took the elevator downstairs to a private ballroom where the brunch would be held. I recognized only Linda and Felicia, although I knew several of Nathaniel's business associates would be in attendance.

Felicia and Linda stood talking in a far corner. Elaina and Todd arrived shortly after we did.

"We're a bit early," Nathaniel said, placing a hand on my lower back. "I need to go speak with a few people. Should I take you over to Felicia and Linda, or are you okay here?"

If I stayed where I was, maybe Elaina would come talk to me. "I'll be fine here."

He brushed the top of my arm. "I won't be long."

I watched as he moved into a crowd of people. Elaina slid to my side minutes later.

"Come here," she said, pulling me behind a tall vase.

I glanced toward Nathaniel. He was deep in conversation with a handsome older couple.

"Nathaniel came to our room last night," she said. "Todd left with him shortly after he showed up." She looked to where her husband stood. "He won't tell me what's going on, but I think you're right. I think it's about you."

Was that what the door sex was about? Proving a point to Todd? Or was he proving a point to himself?

Proving a point to me?

"I'm trying to take your advice," I told her. "I'm being real careful with him. Sometimes"—I thought back to the library—"sometimes I think I'm breaking through and sometimes"—I thought back to the night before last—"sometimes I don't even care."

"Todd was in a better mood when he came back," she said. "I think whatever Nathaniel said calmed him down."

I chewed on my lip, trying to figure that one out.

"My advice is, whatever you're doing, keep doing it." She squeezed my hand. "It's working."

"How long was Todd gone last night?" I asked. I couldn't remember what time I went to sleep, but it was pretty late.

"A few hours," she said. "Todd did say that Nathaniel stayed downstairs looking for a piano."

A piano made sense. He always seemed to feel better once he played. I thought about the time I rode him while he played—I knew I certainly felt better after. I looked back to the crowd. Nathaniel was still in conversation with the older couple.

"Who are they? Business associates?" I asked, not wanting to think about the library and the piano with Elaina so close. After spending the day with her in the spa, I was certain she had a sixth sense about sex.

"No," she said, her voice dropping to a whisper. "Those are Melanie's parents."

My jaw dropped. *Melanie's parents.*

"What are they doing here?" I asked.

"Friends of the family."

"Where's Melanie?" I glanced around. Was she here?

"Not invited," Elaina said with a little grin on her face.

Todd walked up to us. "Ladies."

Elaina took his hand. "Time to eat?"

There was a buffet for brunch. I selected my normal breakfast items, throwing a few finger sandwiches on my plate as well. Todd and Elaina sat at our table along with Felicia.

"How long have you worked at the library, Abby?" Todd asked at one point when the conversation drifted away from the upcoming game.

"At the public library for seven years," I said. "But I worked at one of the campus libraries before then."

"You did?" he asked. "I wonder if I ever saw you. I spent a lot of time in the campus libraries."

I squinted my eyes at him. He was handsome enough, although not as striking as Nathaniel. "I don't know," I said, thinking back. "I'd probably remember you."

"One would think," he said, almost under his breath.

Elaina looked from Todd to Nathaniel and then back to me. What was going on? What was I missing? I glanced at Nathaniel. Nothing.

"You like the public library better than the campus one?" Todd asked.

"The people are a lot more diverse," I said. "Plus college students can be a bit obnoxious." I smiled, trying to lighten what had turned from a simple question into a tense conversation. "Did I ever have to tell you to tone it down or to stop ripping pages from the reference books?"

Todd laughed. "No, I definitely would have remembered that."

The conversation went back to the upcoming game, and maybe it was just me, but I was almost certain I felt Nathaniel give a sigh of relief when it did.

We had a box booked at the stadium. The weather was still cold, and I was thankful we'd be inside as opposed to watching the game outside in the frigid temperatures.

New York was up by three right before the half. Nathaniel took my hand and led me to the door of the box, telling everyone we'd be back later. He picked up a duffel bag on the way out.

"My plan?" he whispered in my ear. "Starts now."

Funny, I thought he'd already completed that plan—that night in his suite, when he had taken full possession of me, the night that everything had changed. My heart raced . . . What in the world could he have planned for the stadium?

He gave me the bag. "Go change. I have an extra ticket in the bag. Meet me there before the half starts."

I took the bag into the bathroom. Inside was a short skirt. *In this weather?* There were also two long blankets. Why were we changing seats? And why were we sitting outside? At least the box had heat.

But then I thought back to the last few days. Anything. I'd do anything he asked. I changed into the skirt, folded my pants and put them in the bag. The blankets I shoved on top.

I looked at the ticket—middle level, if I guessed right.

I had. My new seat was on the first row on the middle level. And it was crowded. No one said anything as I took my seat. They didn't even look my way. Nathaniel joined me minutes later.

He draped an arm over my shoulders and drew me close. Drew circles on my shoulder. My heart pounded at his nearness.

He leaned over and whispered, "Do you know that three out of four people fantasize about having sex in public?"

Hot . . .

His tongue swirled in my ear. "The way I see it, why fantasize when you can experience it instead?"

Holy . . .

"I'm going to fuck you during the Super Bowl, Abigail." He bit down on my earlobe, and I sucked in a breath. "As long as you're quiet, no one will know."

Hell.

I grew wet just thinking about what he'd said. Looked around to the people beside us. Everyone was wrapped in blankets. I was starting to understand his plan.

Nathaniel was still drawing circles on my shoulder.

"I want you to stand up and wrap a blanket around yourself. Open in the back," he said. "Put one foot up on the railing in front of you."

I walked to the railing, my thighs growing slicker as I thought about what Nathaniel wanted to do. What Nathaniel *would* do. On the field below, someone intercepted a pass. The crowd around us cheered. I wrapped the blanket around myself—it was longer than I'd thought earlier. I couldn't even feel a draft.

The seconds ticked down on the field clock. Ten, nine, eight—Nathaniel came and stood behind me—five, four, three—the people around us stood—one. Everyone cheered as the players ran off the field.

Nathaniel wrapped another blanket around us. We were just any other couple snuggling. Nothing different going on. Except I could feel the difference pressed hot and hard against me.

Below us, men worked frantically to set up the stage. Nathaniel's hand shimmied its way up my shirt. I gasped as he rolled my nipple between his fingers.

"You have to be quiet," he warned.

He worked me into a frenzy underneath the blankets, his slow hands roaming under my shirt and his erection, hard as nails, behind me. And the entire time, he was murmuring in my ear, telling me how good I would feel, how he could barely wait, how hard I made him.

I knew what it was. It was payback for our tryst in the library when I made him play as I rode him. It was payback, and payback was hell. And heaven. It was hell and heaven pressed down, rolled together, and so intertwined you couldn't tell the difference between them anymore.

The lights dropped suddenly in the stadium. Nathaniel took a slight step backward, and I felt his hands undoing his pants.

"Lean over the rail just a little." He stepped closer.

I glanced to my right. Another couple was standing there at the rail, side by side. They weren't paying us any attention.

"No one knows," Nathaniel said, lifting the hem of my skirt up under the blankets. "People are so caught up in their own little worlds, they don't notice what's going on around them. The most life-altering event could be happening right next to them, and they'd miss it entirely." He slipped a finger inside me. "Of course, in this case, it's a good thing."

Someone appeared onstage and the crowd erupted in a thunder of noise and applause. Nathaniel thrust into me. My little shriek was drowned by the shouts of the audience.

Nathaniel moved in time with the music. We could have been dancing. I take that back—we *were* dancing. A slow, sultry, erotic dance. He wrapped his arms around me, pulling me close as he thrust inside again. I moved my legs farther apart and he slipped even deeper with his next thrust.

"All these people," he whispered in my ear, "and no one knows what we're doing." He went even deeper. "You could probably scream." He twisted a nipple and I bit my lip.

The song changed, and Nathaniel slowed down, taking his time, moving inconspicuously. But we were still connected and the feel of him inside me was divine. He slowed further, but it was enough. His speed didn't matter. What mattered was that he was still *there*. Still claiming me.

The next song was even slower. Again he was slow, but again he was there, and that was his point. He could be slow or he could be fast. He could take me against the door or in a stadium filled with thousands of people. Whatever he decided, he would do, but he was still there.

Finally the music picked up. Nathaniel dropped a hand and started circling my clit, his touch growing rougher with each pass. I feared for a second I'd fall over the rail. Or collapse in an incoherent blob. Around us, people swayed to the music, and under our blankets, his hand and body kept us dancing to our own beat.

I pushed back as he thrust forward, and he let out a small grunt. Faster and faster he worked me, thrusting and circling as the song reached its end. Lights flashed before me, or it might have been fireworks. Hard call. Seven strong staccato beats played out, punctuated by Nathaniel's deep thrusts.

"Come with me," he whispered as he thrust one last time, and we peaked together while the crowd roared with approval for the artist onstage.

We stayed there, against the rails, while the people around us calmed down. While our hearts calmed down. He stayed pressed against me, as he never had before, and I felt his heartbeat against my back. Felt it racing.

"Now, that," he said against my neck, "was an amazing halftime show."

Chapter Twenty-five

I sat on Nathaniel's lap for the entire third quarter. We just sat there, watching the game, wrapped in blankets. Occasionally, he'd run his fingers through my hair or trace the outline of my ear.

"We should head back to the box," he said as the quarter drew to a close.

Right, the game.

Who was winning?

I went to get up, but his arms wouldn't let me go.

"Do you know why we had to wait?" he asked.

Because you like me sitting on your lap.

Because you want to hold me.

Because you are fascinated by the tiny little details of my ear.

Because, as much as you try to deny it, you're feeling something.

Because, maybe, you love me.

"Because your face shows absolutely everything," he said. "You're an open book."

I laughed. *Okay, that too.*

We stood up. I still had a blanket wrapped around me.

"You better change," he said. "Felicia will have my head if she sees you in that skirt."

I had a feeling Felicia was going to have both of our heads anyway, but that hardly mattered at the moment.

After I changed, we walked back to the box. I overheard several ladies in the bathroom while I was changing—the Giants were winning. Good to know, since I'd be spending the rest of the game with people who'd probably watched the last quarter.

Felicia came right up to me as we reentered the box and drew me to the side. "Where have you been?" she asked quietly.

"We were busy." I tried to say it with a straight face, but apparently my expression gave me away.

"Damn, Abby. At the Super Bowl? Isn't that illegal?"

"Felicia," I said, putting a hand on her shoulder, "it should be illegal *not* to do what I've been up to."

"You are so going to get arrested one day."

"Prude."

"Perv."

The Giants won. After the clock wound down, Jackson ran to the middle of the field and looked up at our box. He blew a kiss in our direction. Everyone *ooh*ed and *ahh*ed.

Everyone except Nathaniel. He just shook his head and mumbled again about how much his cousin owed him. But I could tell he was happy for Jackson. Just the same way I was happy for Felicia.

We left the stadium after the trophy presentation. Nathaniel and Todd gave each other wary glances, but they finally came together in a friendly hug.

"Three weeks," I thought I heard Nathaniel whisper, but couldn't be sure.

Elaina pulled me into her arms. "If I find anything out, I'll call you."

Felicia was staying in Tampa with Jackson, but Nathaniel had to fly back, so I headed to the airport with him. The flight back home was much more subdued than our trip to Tampa. We spent our time in the leather captain's chairs.

"Did you make me an appointment for Wednesday?" Nathaniel asked. "Or were you just saying that to Linda?"

"I was hoping you would want to stop by," I said. Didn't he know by now I'd never lie to him?

"Wednesday, then." He smiled. "Research?"

"You do need help with your literature. If you try really hard, I'm sure you can do better than Mark Twain and Jane Austen next time."

"Really? Who would you suggest?"

"Shakespeare," I said, leaning back and closing my eyes.

I called and set up an appointment for waxing on Wednesday afternoon after work. I could have made it earlier, but I wanted to see if Nathaniel would say anything else about it when he showed up at one o'clock on Wednesday.

He didn't.

And let me say one word about being waxed.

Ohmygodithurtsofuckingbad.

But afterward—way, way, way afterward—I decided I rather liked it. It was neat, clean, and I could only imagine how sex would feel. It might actually make sex better, if such a thing were possible.

I also decided to give some thought to Nathaniel's idea of getting a car. On my own, of course. I talked Felicia into letting me borrow hers for the weekend. She rarely used it anyway.

Six o'clock Friday evening found me in the foyer of Nathaniel's house.

He pointed to my clothes. "Take them off. You'll get them back on Sunday."

I took my time undressing. I'd thought about the weekend all week, just as Nathaniel had planned, I'm sure. Wondered how I'd feel walking around completely naked. Crazy Abby was all for it and promised to keep Rational Abby occupied with new tax regulations or some such nonsense.

I hadn't forgotten what he'd said about Friday night, and when I stepped out of my pants—*look, Nathaniel, no panties*—the look in his eyes told me he wasn't joking about the Friday-night fiver. Matter of fact, he took me the first time right in the foyer.

And, uh, yeah. Sex *was* better.

I felt self-conscious at first, walking around without clothes, especially when doing something mundane like cooking. But as the weekend went on, I found myself growing confident. The way Nathaniel looked at me, the way his eyes followed my movements, it made me feel powerful. Again, probably his plan the entire time.

He was sitting at the kitchen table when I came down to cook breakfast Sunday.

"Go upstairs and put some clothes on," he said, very no-nonsense.

What was going on? I was so flustered, I didn't ask. I left the kitchen and went back to my room, where I fumbled my way into some jeans and a long-sleeved T-shirt before making my way back down the stairs.

"Have a seat," he said.

"Is everything okay?" I sat down, trying to figure out what would put such a . . . *guilty* look on his face.

"I'm sorry," he said, looking at me finally. His eyes were troubled. "I should have done a better job. Paid more attention."

"You're scaring me. What's wrong?"

He waved toward the window.

Shit.

Snow reached halfway up the glass pane, about four feet, and was still falling.

"I should have listened to the weather," he said. "Watched the news. Something."

"So what's the verdict?" I asked, still watching the snow. "How bad is it?"

He shook his head. "No one knows with any certainty. It could be days before you're able to leave. I'm sorry. I should have sent you home yesterday."

So I was stuck with Nathaniel for a few extra days. It beat being stuck inside the apartment—

"Felicia," I whispered. I had her car!

"She's with Jackson," Nathaniel said. "I talked with him not long ago—he picked her up yesterday. She'll be okay."

I nodded. Felicia was perfectly fine with Jackson, and I liked the idea of her being with him instead of holed up at the apartment.

"We need to discuss guidelines for the week," Nathaniel said. "I thought it would be easier to talk if you had clothes on."

That explained the kitchen table—he wanted my opinion.

"I thought we could split the meals up. I'll take one; you take the next." He looked at me, and I nodded. "I'll be working most of the time, so I want you to make yourself at home. The house is open to you except for my two rooms."

Guess that meant I wouldn't be sleeping in his bed.

"My rules stand," he continued. "You can use the gym and yoga DVDs. I expect you to call me 'sir,' but I don't expect anything from you sexually. I don't believe sleep will be an issue. You'll get your eight hours."

Snowed in with Nathaniel. Crazy Abby was turning cartwheels. Rational Abby had a nagging suspicion it might not be such a good idea.

"Do you have any questions?" he asked.

"Yes. You don't *expect* anything sexual, but you didn't say no sex. Does that mean there's a possibility of sex?"

"I thought we'd let things play out naturally, if that's okay with you."

Natural sex with Nathaniel? My face heated, and I felt the familiar ache of yearning tighten in my lower belly.

Be cool, Rational Abby said. *Don't let him know how much the idea excites you.*

Idiot, he knew that ages ago, Crazy Abby said.

Across the table, Nathaniel gave a knowing smile. Damn that Crazy Abby, she was right.

"I've been natural all weekend," I said, coolly. "Why stop now?"

He laughed. I hadn't heard him laugh very often—maybe being snowed in would be a good thing for us.

"Where do I sleep?" I asked.

He raised an eyebrow. "Your room."

Oh, well. It was worth a try.

"Okay," I said. "New rules start when?"

"Today at three." He looked at his watch. "You're mine for the next eight hours, so if you don't have any more questions, I want the clothes off while you cook breakfast."

You're wrong, I thought to myself as I went upstairs to undress. *I'm not yours for eight hours. I'm yours for always.*

Chapter Twenty-six

It was slow going on the natural plan. On Sunday afternoon, at three o'clock exactly, Nathaniel told me to go upstairs and get dressed. He said dinner was his responsibility since I had cooked breakfast and lunch.

We ate in the kitchen while watching the snow. It felt odd to have clothes on. Almost like I was hiding.

I called Felicia after dinner to make sure she was safe with Jackson. She acted a bit put out that I questioned her safety, but I knew how much it meant to her that I called. When I got off the phone, I made my way to my library and spent the evening alone. Nathaniel stayed in the living room. Though we spent the evening apart, I was surprised at how comfortable I felt in his house.

First thing on Monday morning, I called Martha on her cell phone and explained my predicament. She told me the library was closed due to the snow anyway, and she'd keep me posted. I refused to spend the day idle, so I used Nathaniel's treadmill after breakfast. I'd give him this much—he knew what he was doing when he set up my exercise plan. Already I could see improvements in my muscle tone, strength, and stamina. After just a few weeks, not only was I trim, but I was fit too.

Maybe it was the aftermath of spending the entire weekend naked, I wasn't sure, but I didn't immediately change out of my workout gear. Instead, I walked around downstairs while endorphins pumped through my body. I didn't feel like hanging out in my library again, so I decided to clean. Clearly, Nathaniel employed a housekeeper. One who wouldn't be able to come out due to the storm.

There was a supply closet off the kitchen, and I dug through it until I found what I was looking for—a feather duster. I glanced around—no Nathaniel in sight.

I walked to the living room, set my iPod on Nathaniel's player, and turned the volume up. I scrolled through my songs until I found one Felicia had downloaded for cleaning. We both agreed we didn't mind cleaning as long as we could dance at the same time.

When the music came on, I spun, twirled, and twisted. Around and around I went, wielding my duster, cleaning every surface in the room. At the end, I threw my head back and sang along.

Looking around the room with a self-satisfied nod, I turned to walk out. Nathaniel stood in the doorway, watching.

Gah.

"Abigail," he said, eyes shining with amusement. "What are you doing?"

I twirled the duster. "Dusting."

"I do employ a housekeeper for such tasks."

"Yes. But she won't be able to come this week, will she?"

"I suppose not. Although, if you insist on making yourself useful, you could wash the sheets on my bed." His eyes laughed at me. "Someone got them all messy this weekend."

"Really," I said in mock disbelief. "The nerve."

He turned, then stopped and looked over his shoulder. "By the way," he said, "I'm dropping yoga from your exercise routine."

Sweeter words have never been uttered.

"You are?" I asked.

"Yes. And adding dusting."

Nathaniel made chicken salad for lunch. "It's not as good as yours," he said, putting my plate on the kitchen table. "But it'll do."

I tilted my head. "You like my chicken salad?"

He sat down. "You are an excellent cook. You know that."

"It's nice to hear every once in a while," I teased.

"Yes." He smiled pointedly. "It is."

What?

I went over his words again.

Oh.

"You're an excellent cook as well," I said. Had I never told him before?

"Thank you. But you did compliment my chicken once before."

The mood was lighter after that, as if we'd crossed some hurdle simply by admitting that we liked each other's cooking.

"I was wondering," I said, in between bites, "if I could take Apollo outside this afternoon." It had stopped snowing, at least for the moment. Apollo sat beside Nathaniel and lifted his head at the sound of his name.

Nathaniel thought for a second. "I think that would be a good idea. He needs to get out, and he seems to like you."

"What's his story, if you don't mind me asking? Elaina mentioned something in Tampa that made me think he'd been sick."

"Apollo is a rescue," he said, reaching down and rubbing the dog's head. "I've had him for more than three years. He was abused as a puppy, and it made him hostile. Although he's never had a problem with you. Maybe he has some sort of sixth sense about people."

"And what about what Elaina said last weekend?"

"He gets anxious when he's away from me for extended periods of time." He gave Apollo's head another rub. "We're working on it."

"It must have been hard at first," I said.

"It was, but the payoff has been well worth the trouble."

"Hummph," I said, forking more salad. "There's a special place in hell for people who abuse animals."

"Why, Abigail, I never knew you had it in you to be so forceful."

"I'm not a big fan of dogs, other than Apollo, that is." I took a bite of chicken salad and chewed. Swallowed. "But for someone to cause harm to something helpless—well, I guess it brings out the worst in me."

"Or the best," he said, his smile saying he knew exactly how I felt. "I suppose that's why I decided to donate bone marrow. To help the helpless."

The bone marrow. "I wondered about that."

"It's Linda's pet project. She made us all sign the registry. I never thought I'd be a match for anyone. But when the call came in"—he shrugged—"what choice did I have? I had the power to save someone's life. There's not a lot of thought that had to go into that decision."

"Some people wouldn't feel the same."

"I like to think I have never been considered *some people*."

"Sorry, sir," I said, flustered. "I didn't mean . . ."

"I know you didn't," he said softly. "I was teasing."

I looked down at my plate. "It's hard to tell sometimes."

"Maybe I should wear a sign next time." He lifted my face with his finger. "I'd rather you not hide your eyes when you're talking to me. They're so expressive."

His gaze met mine, and for just one moment I almost felt I could read his thoughts. I wanted to swim in those deep green eyes. Fall in so deep, I'd never have to leave.

He dropped his hand, and we talked more about the boy who had received his bone marrow—Kyle. Nathaniel had grown close to him since the donation. He took him to baseball games in the summer and had hoped to take him to the Super Bowl.

"But he was sick and not able to go," Nathaniel said. "Maybe next year."

"Felicia said something about Jackson retiring. Will he play next year?"

"I think so, but it might be his last season. He's ready to settle down." He looked at me with the grin that always melted my heart. "If Felicia is amenable, that is."

"Are you ready to deal with Felicia as a member of the family?"

"I will for Jackson's sake," he said. "And she does have the most amazing best friend."

After lunch, I bundled up with some clothes stashed in the guest room and took Apollo outside. The snow had stopped and the wind had blown it in drifts that reached heights I'd never seen in all my years in New York. Apollo and I walked toward a large field. Or, I should say, I walked. Apollo ran.

I made a few snowballs and threw them, watching as he ran after them, shaking his head in disbelief as they shattered into nothing. I laughed, and Apollo looked at me and barked, wagging his tail, wanting more. I made more and threw them.

"You're confusing my dog," Nathaniel said, suddenly behind me.

"He loves it," I said, throwing another snowball. I giggled as Apollo bounced after it.

"I think he loves the person throwing them." Nathaniel balled snow together and threw one himself.

Apollo looked back and barked.

"You've stolen my game," I said, trying not to think about the fact that Nathaniel had just said *love*. No matter he was talking about his dog. I balled up more snow and threw it at Nathaniel. "Now he won't want to play with me."

My snowball missed.

"Oh, Abigail," he said, slinking toward me like a cat. "That was a big mistake."

Oops.

"You wouldn't happen to be wearing a sign, would you?" I asked.

"Not on your life," he said, tossing a snowball from hand to hand.

I backed away, holding my hands up.

"You threw a snowball at me." Still with the tossing. Back and forth. Watching me. Back and forth.

"I missed," I said.

"You still tried." He pulled his arm back to throw the snowball at me, but at the last minute he turned and threw it to Apollo.

I, of course, didn't see that and shrieked like a scared little girl. Turned and ran. Tripped over my boots and fell face-first into the snow.

Of all the . . .

"Are you okay?" he asked, coming to me and holding out a gloved hand.

"Nothing hurt but my pride." I was covered in snow and all wet. My body shook with the sudden chill. I took his hand and he helped me up.

"Time to go inside? Something warm by the fire?"

Fire. Warm. Nathaniel.

Count me in.

Chapter Twenty-seven

As always, Nathaniel thought of everything. A large fire burned in the library fireplace when we made it back inside, and the heat slowly permeated my wet clothes. Nathaniel went upstairs and returned with dry ones for me. As I changed, he poured us drinks.

I sat down and raised my eyebrow at the glass he handed me. "What is this?"

"Brandy. I thought about coffee, but decided this would warm us quicker."

"I see," I said, swirling the amber liquid in the glass. "You're trying to get me drunk."

"I don't, as a practice, *try* anything." He sipped his drink. "But it is more than forty percent alcohol, so you'd better have only the one glass."

Apollo ambled over and sat at Nathaniel's feet in front of the fire. Nathaniel stroked his head.

I was starting to realize that Nathaniel and I had different ideas on what "warming up" entailed. I was also beginning to wonder if "natural" was dom code for "never going to happen." It didn't make sense to me. He'd been happy to suspend our weekend agreement at other times—he came to visit me in the Rare Books Collection on Wednesdays, and twice we'd had sex in this very library, *my* library, here in his home, and we hadn't played by his usual rules. So why wouldn't he let anything happen between us now? Sometimes everything felt confusing. I loved the dom part of Nathaniel, the part that could make my knees weak and turn me to mush with a simple word. But I was starting to fall hard for this new weekday Nathaniel. If only there could be a way to combine the two. Was that even possible? Would he want that?

But if we weren't going to have smoking-hot sex in front of the fireplace, we were still in my library—and speaking of libraries . . .

"Did the library come with the house, or is it something you had added when you bought it?" I asked.

"I didn't buy this house. I inherited it."

"This was your parents' house? You grew up here?"

"Yes. I've made major renovations." He raised an eyebrow. "Like the playroom."

I scooted closer to him. "Has it been hard to live here?"

He shook his head. "I thought it would be, but I've redone so much, it doesn't resemble my childhood home anymore. The library is very much the same as it was then, though."

I looked around, taking in the vast number of books, and took a sip of brandy. It warmed my throat as I swallowed. "Your parents must have loved books."

"My parents were avid collectors. And they traveled frequently." He waved toward the section of the library that held maps and atlases. "Many of the books, they found overseas. Some had been in their families for generations."

"My mom liked to read, but mostly she just went for popular fiction." I hugged my knees to my chest, surprised he was talking about his parents, but not wanting him to feel pressured.

"There's a place for popular fiction in every library. After all, today's popular fiction may very well be tomorrow's classic."

I giggled. "This from the man who said no one reads classics."

"That wasn't me," he said, holding a hand to his chest. "That was Mark Twain. Just because I quoted him doesn't mean I agree with him."

The brandy worked its way through my body, making me feel all warm and relaxed. He was right—one glass did the trick.

"Tell me more about your parents," I said, feeling brave. Or maybe it was the brandy.

"The afternoon they died," he started, and I sat up straighter. I hadn't meant for him to tell me about *that*. "We were on our way home from the theater. It had been snowing. Dad was driving. Mom was laughing about something. It was very normal. I suppose it usually is."

He grew quiet then, and I tried not to make any sort of movement. I didn't want to do anything to impede his story.

"He swerved to miss a deer," he said softly. "The car went down an embankment and flipped"—he squinted—"I think it flipped. It was a long time ago, and I try not to think about it."

"It's okay. You don't have to tell me."

"No, I'm fine. It helps to talk. Todd's always told me to talk more."

The wood in the fireplace settled and shot sparks upward. Apollo rolled over onto his back. I wondered for a few minutes whether Nathaniel would continue or not.

"I don't remember everything," he said. "I remember the screaming. The shouts to make sure I was okay. Their moans.

The soft whispers they had for each other. A hand reached back to me." He stared into the fire. "And then nothing."

I blinked back tears, picturing it all too clearly in my mind. "I'm sorry. I'm so sorry."

"They used a crane to pull the car out. Mom and Dad had been gone for some time by then, but like I said, I don't remember it all."

I wanted to ask more questions. How long was he stuck in the car with them? Had he been hurt at all? But I felt so honored he had shared that much with me, I didn't want to push it.

"Linda's been wonderful. I owe her so much," he said.

I could only nod.

"She was very supportive. And growing up with Jackson helped." He smiled. "Todd, too. And Elaina, when she moved nearby."

I wanted to reach for his hand, to soothe him somehow, but I wasn't sure how it would be received, so I held still. "Your family's the best."

"They are more than I deserve," he said, standing. "You'll have to excuse me. I need to get back to my work now."

"And I need to start dinner." I reached for his glass. "I'll take that for you."

"Thank you," he said, looking deep into my eyes, and I knew he meant for more than taking his glass.

Over dinner, he asked about my parents and I filled him in on my mom and dad. I talked about Dad's work as a contractor. I watched Nathaniel's eyes closely as I talked about my mother, looking for some sign of recognition, but either he didn't remember her and the house or else he was a very good actor. He did look surprised when I mentioned her passing. For a second,

I thought he was going to ask me something, but he quickly changed the subject.

That night, I dreamed of Nathaniel playing the piano, but I knew where the music came from now and, in my dream, I ran to the library. He was there, sitting at the piano. When he saw me, he held out his hand and whispered, "Abby."

But he disappeared before I reached him.

On Tuesday, I decided I needed more of a plan. The snow had abated, but not enough for anyone to spend a lot of time outside. That meant another day stuck inside. I had dusted the house and washed the sheets the day before, and I really didn't feel like cleaning anymore.

Nathaniel cooked pancakes for breakfast, so I was up for lunch. Maybe I'd start lunch.

Lunch . . .

I walked into the kitchen and dug through the cabinets. Finding what I needed, I set out a cutting board and a few sauté pans.

I went back to the living room, where Nathaniel sat at his desk. He looked up as I entered.

"Yes?" he asked.

"Will you help me with lunch?"

"Can you give me ten minutes?"

"Ten minutes will be perfect."

Once I returned to the kitchen, I realized I'd forgotten the onions. I opened a far cabinet where I knew the onions were. I squatted down to find them.

What the . . . ?

When Nathaniel walked in later, he found me at the counter, head on top of my hands, looking at two label-less cans.

"Abigail?"

I stared at the cans. "I'm trying to decide what someone like you is doing with label-less cans in their kitchen."

"The small one is Italian peppers." He walked closer to me. "The larger one holds the remains of the last nosy submissive who bugged me about my label-less cans."

I looked up. "Sign?"

"Sign." He smiled.

"Seriously, what are you doing with label-less cans in your cabinets? Doesn't that break about a hundred different rules of yours?"

He picked up the larger can. "The small one really is peppers from Italy. The larger one should be tomatoes from the same company. I ordered them online."

"What happened to the labels?"

"They came that way." He set down the large can and picked up the smaller one. "They probably are peppers and tomatoes, but I've been hesitant to open them and never sent them back. What if they're pickled cow tongues? I don't have enough faith, I guess."

"All of life is faith. Just because something has a label doesn't mean it's always going to match the inside. Trust me. Sometimes it takes more faith to believe the label." I took the can from him and shook it. "Don't be afraid of what's on the inside. I can make a masterpiece with the insides."

He cupped my cheek, and I watched his eyes as another brick fell. "I bet you could," he said, then dropped his hand. "Now, what do you need my help with?"

I opened the box of arborio rice. "I want to do a mushroom risotto, but I can't stir the rice and cook everything else at the same time. Can you stir?"

"Mushroom risotto? I'd be happy to stir."

"You might want to take that sweater off. It'll probably get hot in here."

He raised an eyebrow, but shrugged out of his sweater. He wore a black T-shirt underneath.

Oh yes, much better. Thank you.

"I'll chop up the mushrooms and onions," I said. "You start the rice."

"Bossy little thing, aren't you?"

I put a hand on my hip. "It's my kitchen."

"No." He pushed me against the counter, a hand resting on either side of me. He rocked his hips, and I felt his erection through his jeans. "I said the kitchen table was yours. The remainder of the kitchen is *mine*."

Fuck. Me.

"Now," he said. "What was that about the rice?" He turned the burner on and poured extra virgin olive oil around the pan.

I stood still for several seconds until I could move my limbs again. I took two wineglasses and held up the white wine for Nathaniel to see.

"Yes, please," he said.

I poured us both a glass and got busy chopping the onions.

"You ready for this?" I said, once the onions were diced, but not really meaning the onions.

"I'm always ready."

I looked down and could tell he wasn't talking about onions either. His erection had grown another inch. And he was stuck stirring rice.

I wasn't.

Poor baby.

I leaned in close, pushed myself under his arm, and poured the onions into the pan. "There you go," I said, making sure my backside brushed against his groin.

I needed to dice the mushrooms, but I decided to be just a little evil. Okay, scratch that. I decided to be a lot evil.

"Want me to get that chicken stock for you?" I reached under his arm and grabbed the fresh stock. I poured a bit into the sauté pan, my arm knocking his biceps for the shortest second.

A line of sweat formed on his forehead, and he took a sip of wine.

My evil plan was working.

I slid over to the countertop and started on the mushrooms. Chopping them into little pieces, piling them up nice and neat. Taking an occasional sip from my own wineglass.

A mushroom *accidentally* fell to the floor. It rolled over to where Nathaniel was stuck at the stove. Stirring.

"Oops," I said. "Let me get that."

I strolled over to him and squeezed in between the stove and his body, noticing that time had not helped his little problem at all. I picked up the mushroom and grabbed on to Nathaniel's waist to help myself back up. The little brush to his groin was another *accident*.

What can I say? I'm very accident prone.

But I didn't say that because Nathaniel was trying really hard to concentrate on the risotto and, well, who needed words anyway?

I opened the oven and put in the chicken breasts. They would be ready the same time as the risotto, if everything went as planned. I passed the mushrooms to Nathaniel and took another sip of wine while leaning against the counter. My job was over, so I didn't have anything better to do than to enjoy Nathaniel's muscles working.

It really was getting a bit hot in the kitchen. So I stripped off my own sweater, revealing the little white tank top underneath. There was still a lot of chicken broth in the pitcher beside Nathaniel, but the risotto was coming along nicely. Almost done. I sneaked back between the stove and Nathaniel and lifted the pitcher.

"Need more?" I asked.

"Just a touch."

I poured a bit into the pan, but, oops, some got on me. White shirt. And double oops, I'd forgotten to put on a bra.

"Damn," I said. "Would you look at that?"

He was.

"I guess I need to take this off before the stain sets. It could be a problem." I turned around and went over to the sink, stripping off the shirt as I went.

The oven clicked off at the same time the stove burner did. I heard the sauté pan being moved, and the oven door swung open.

Two seconds later, Nathaniel grabbed me by the waist and swung me around. "I've got a bigger problem for you."

I looked down. Hell, yes, he did. Those jeans couldn't be comfortable.

He picked me up and set me on the counter near the stove, pushing cutting boards and cans out of the way. Something crashed to the floor.

He fumbled with the button on my pants and then pulled them roughly off, almost dragging me off the countertop. His eyes grew dark, because, oops, I'd forgotten panties. Again.

His jeans were on the floor in less than two seconds, and there he was, naked and magnificently erect.

"Is this what you want?" He came up to me, and I wrapped my legs around his waist.

I ran my hands up his shirt to get to his chest. "Yes."

He cupped my breast and rubbed my nipple with his thumb.

"Please," I said, drawing him closer. "Please. Now."

But it was his time to tease, and he ran his hands down my body, along my legs and back again.

"I didn't want . . . I didn't think . . ." he started, but I shut him up by nibbling on his neck, working up his jaw until I made it to his ear.

"You think too much," I whispered.

It was all he needed. He took my legs, and in one movement thrust inside and, damn, two days had been too long. I groaned as he pushed in deeper.

"Oh, hell, yes," I said as I took him inside. My eyes fluttered closed as he withdrew. "More. More, please."

He answered with the force of his body, thrusting into me once again. I bumped my head on an overhead cabinet and didn't even care.

"Harder," I said. "Please, harder."

"Fuck, Abigail." He took my ass with both hands and pulled me to him as he thrust, and we both moaned when his cock hit the back of my cervix.

"Again." I bit down on his ear. "Damn it. Again."

We scraped and clawed and bit, him trying to get farther inside and me trying to take more of him. I hit his ass with my heels and he sucked on my neck.

Deeper. We both wanted deeper.

"Yes," I said when he hit my G-spot. "Right there."

"Here?" he asked, thrusting again. "Here?"

I whimpered as he drove himself into me over and over. His fingers reached between us, and he brushed my clit. My orgasm was building, and I felt his cock twitch inside me.

"Harder," I said. "Almost there."

His fingers rubbed harder and his cock pounded into me.

"I . . . I . . . I . . ." I stuttered, my belly tightening.

I fell apart. He thrust deeply one last time and held still as he released into me.

"Damn," he said, once he could talk again. "That was . . ."

"I know," I said. "I agree."

He lifted me from the countertop and made sure I could stand before grabbing a towel and cleaning me. "That beats mushroom risotto any day."

Chapter Twenty-eight

Nathaniel cooked dinner. Usually when he cooked, I stayed in the living room or library, but I decided to sit in the kitchen with him that night. So, he cooked while I sat at the table and drank a glass of red wine. Enjoying the view, if you will.

I think he was cooking a marinara. At least, I suspected that was why he had the large label-less can out. He took out the can opener, and I got up to peek over his shoulder.

"Just checking," I said.

He smiled and hummed as the can opened. With a tentative finger, he lifted the lid. We both held our breath.

"Tomatoes," we said in unison.

"Drat," I said. "I was hoping for pickled cow tongue or some incriminating body parts."

"Rather anticlimactic, don't you think?" he asked, lifting a tomato out with a fork.

"No. It's better to know."

"You're right, and it's going to make us a delicious supper."

He dumped the tomatoes into a sauté pan that already contained onions and garlic.

"Smells good," I said, standing on my tiptoes to look over his shoulder. I took a big whiff as I did. Not so much to smell dinner, but to smell Nathaniel. Light musk and a hint of cedar. Yum.

"Go sit down," he said. "I'd like to have one hot meal today."

"Breakfast was hot," I protested. "And lunch was hot. At least the part before lunch was hot."

"Abigail."

"I'm sitting. I'm sitting," I said, walking toward the table.

I sat down and took a sip of wine. "You know, you had a breakthrough today," I said.

His shoulders hitched slightly. "What was that?"

"You opened one of your label-less cans. I think that calls for a celebration."

He relaxed. "What did you have in mind?"

"Naked picnic in the library?"

"That's your idea of a celebration?" he asked, setting a large pot of water to boil.

"I should have made bread for dinner," I said.

"You've done quite enough for one day."

I raised an eyebrow and tried not to giggle. "Yes, it is my idea of a celebration."

"Okay." He sighed, as if he were agreeing to something horrid. "Naked picnic in the library. Thirty minutes."

"I'll go set up," I said, getting up from the table.

"Extra blankets are in the linen closet," he called over his shoulder.

Twenty minutes later, I'd set out several blankets and started a fire in the library fireplace. Four plump pillows completed my impromptu picnic setup.

I checked the clock. Ten minutes to spare. I stripped and piled my clothes on one of the chairs.

Nathaniel came in carrying dinner on a large tray. He was already undressed.

"Do you need any help?" I asked, feasting on the sight of him.

"No. I'm fine. Let me set this down and I'll get our drinks. More wine?"

"Please."

He returned with two wineglasses and a bottle of red wine. I wondered if he had a wine cellar. Surely he did. Might have to check that out later.

The marinara was delicious. Of course, I expected nothing less from Nathaniel.

"This is superb," I said after a few bites. "My compliments to the chef."

"To label-less cans," he said, lifting a forkful of pasta.

"To label-less cans," I said. I went to twirl more pasta, but when I lifted my fork, I did it too fast and some sauce flew off. And landed on Nathaniel's . . . uh . . . you know.

He looked down in disbelief. "You got marinara on my cock."

"Oops."

"Get. It. Off."

I was fairly certain he wasn't wearing a sign. I leaned over and took the plate from him. "Lay back."

"Abigail."

"You want me to use a napkin?" I pushed down on his shoulders.

He didn't answer, so I took that as a "no." He put his head on one of the pillows and I ran my hands down his chest.

"The marinara, Abigail," he said.

My fingers breezed across his nipples. "I'm getting there."

"Get there. Faster."

I licked down his chest. Yum. He tasted good all over. I took a nibble of his lower belly, and he gasped in response. Mmmm. Nathaniel was much better than marinara. Even marinara made from label-less cans.

I dipped lower, blowing across the tip of his cock. He twitched. Ahh, yes, there it was. *Hello, marinara. Sorry I was so clumsy.*

Okay, that was a lie. There wasn't a sorry bone in my body.

I cleaned the sauce off with one lick. But like I said, he tasted good all over. So until he told me to stop, I decided to stay right where I was. I rolled the tip of him around my mouth, teasing. Occasionally, I would deep throat and take him all the way in, but for the most part, I just played with him. I used my hands, stroking him, holding his cock like it was a lollipop, licking the very tip. A drop or two leaked out, and I sucked it right off.

He drew a deep breath in through his teeth. "Fuck."

"I can stop," I said, but I wasn't sure I could.

"Hell, no. Swing those legs up here. I want to taste that sweet pussy."

I shifted my body, moving us into a sixty-nine position.

He wrapped his arms around my thighs, locking me to him. He wiggled his tongue inside me and gave a lick, ending at my clit.

"Mmmmm," he said. "Sweeter than the finest wine." He licked again. "And I'm going to drink from you until there's not a drop left."

I took his whole cock in my mouth—two could play that game—and sucked him hard.

He started a rhythm, matching his licks and nibbles to mine. I took him deep in my throat, and he rammed his tongue inside me. My teeth scraped his length and his grazed my clit.

My hips started moving of their own will, and before too long, he was thrusting into my mouth.

We rolled to our sides, kept the rhythm going, getting more leverage as he fucked my face with his cock and fucked my pussy with his tongue.

He added his fingers, thrusting three up inside me while his tongue moved to my clit. I cupped his balls and ran a finger from his sac to his ass. His cock twitched in my mouth, and he thrust harder. Doubled the tempo with his fingers.

As his cock hit the back of my throat, he sucked my clit into his mouth. Our movements became more intense, and we both hovered on the edge.

My lower body started to tingle, and I moved my head to meet his thrusts, wanting him to come with me. I groaned. I couldn't help it. It felt so intense, having him in *my* mouth while *his* mouth worked me. I came, my body shattering. He bit my clit, and I came again as he thrust into my mouth, releasing in several strong streams. I swallowed frantically, not wanting a drop to escape.

He pulled me up his chest, and I tucked my head under his neck.

"Dinner's cold," I said, snuggling into his arms.

"Screw dinner."

We eventually got back to eating—propped up on pillows, lazy and relaxed.

I took a bite of cold pasta. It wasn't so bad. "How long have you been a dom?"

He swirled his own pasta. "Nearly ten years."

"Have you had a lot of subs?"

"I suppose that depends on your definition of 'a lot.' "

I rolled my eyes. "You know what I mean."

He sat his fork down. "I don't mind having this conversation, Abigail. This is your library. But keep in mind that just because you ask a question doesn't mean I'll answer it."

I swallowed the bite of pasta in my mouth. "Fair enough."

"Then ask away."

"Have you ever been a sub?"

He nodded. "Yes. But not for any extended period of time, only for a scene or two."

Okay, that was interesting. I'd put that aside for later. "Have you ever had a sub use her safe word before?"

He watched me carefully as he answered. "No."

"Never?"

"Never, Abigail."

I looked down at the plate.

"Look at me," he said, and all traces of weekday Nathaniel were gone. I was talking with Dom Nathaniel. "I know how new you are to this, and I ask you, have I ever come close to pushing you beyond what you could handle?"

"No," I said honestly.

"Have I been gentle and patient and caring?" he asked. "Anticipated your *every* need?"

"Yes."

"Do you not think I would have been gentle and patient and caring with my past subs? Anticipated their *every* need?"

Of course he would have. "Oh."

"I am starting you out slowly, because I see this as a long-term relationship, but there are so many things we can do together." He ran a finger down my arm. "So many things your body is capable of that you don't even know yet. And just as you have to learn to trust me, I have to learn your body."

I might as well have rolled over and died right there. I was done.

"I have to learn your limits, so I'm working you slowly. But there are many, many areas we have yet to explore." His touch grew rougher. "And I want to explore them all." His hand dropped. "Does that answer your question?"

"Yes," I whispered, wanting to explore them all as well.

"Any other questions?"

"If your other subs didn't use their safe word, how did the relationships end?"

"They ended as any relationship ends. We grew apart and went our separate ways."

Okay, that made sense. "Have you ever had a romantic relationship with a woman who wasn't your sub?"

He shifted a bit. "Yes."

"How did that go?" I asked, wondering if I was walking into Melanie territory.

"You're here now." He cocked an eyebrow at me. "Was that a rhetorical question?"

Obviously, it hadn't gone well. But I just couldn't let it go. "Melanie?"

"What did Elaina tell you?" he asked instead of answering.

Caught. "That Melanie wasn't your submissive."

He sighed. "I would prefer my past relationships remain in the past. What Melanie and I did or did not do has no bearing on you and me."

I picked at the uneaten pasta on my plate, still not sure I felt any better about Melanie.

"Abigail," he said, and I looked up to meet his eyes. "If I wanted to be with Melanie, I would be with Melanie. I'm here with you."

My eyes roamed his fabulous body. "Did you ever have a naked picnic with Melanie?"

He smiled. "No, never."

I'm not sure why that made me feel better, but it did.

Chapter Twenty-nine

I woke on Wednesday with the crazy notion I should look out the window. I felt like an idiot, checking to make sure there was still snow outside, but I did it anyway. I pushed back the curtains and, sure enough, there was the snow. Maybe a bit less than the day before, but still there. Still no plow anywhere in sight.

I let the curtain fall back into place. I wouldn't be going home today. Tomorrow? Maybe, but what was the point if I'd just be returning on Friday? I might as well stay at his place for the rest of the week. Martha had texted to tell me the library wouldn't be reopening until Monday anyway.

I really didn't think Nathaniel would mind me staying, but decided to ask later and instead headed off to get breakfast started. I took a quick shower and skipped down the stairs. Once the coffee was bubbling in the coffeemaker, I focused my attention on the bacon and eggs. The frying pan heated up, and I did a quick two-step around the kitchen to the songs inside my head.

" 'I'll say she looks as clear as morning roses newly washed with dew,' " Nathaniel said, walking into the kitchen and leaning against the countertop.

Shakespeare?

He hadn't.

A grin covered his face.

Except he had.

I strolled back to the oven and flipped the bacon. " 'You have witchcraft in your lips.' "

He laughed, clearly enjoying himself.

> " 'All the world's a stage,
> And all the men and women merely players.' "

Okay. Fine. He had studied his Shakespeare. I could still outdo him.

> " 'Life's but a walking shadow, a poor player,
> That struts and frets his hour upon the stage,
> And then is heard no more.' "

He walked to the stove, held one hand to his chest and threw the other toward the open window.

> " 'But soft! what light through yonder window breaks?
> It is the east, and Juliet is the sun.
> Arise, fair sun, and kill the envious moon,
> Who is already sick and pale with grief
> That thou, her maid, art far more fair than she.' "

I giggled. I was such a sucker for Shakespeare. And no one had ever quoted *Romeo and Juliet* to me before. Still, best not to let him know how it affected me, although I'm sure he could tell.

" 'Asses are made to bear, and so are you,' " I said.

" 'Women are made to bear, and so are you,' " he quoted the next line.

Damn. He knew that one, too?

"'I have no other but a woman's reason: I think him so, because I think him so,'" I said.

He laughed. A deep, hearty laugh. "'O villain, villain, smiling, damned villain!'"

I looked at him in mock shock. "You called me a villain."

"You called me an ass."

I could hardly argue with that. "Draw?"

"This time," he said. "But I'd like the record to show that I'm gaining on you."

"Agreed. But speaking of gaining on me," I said, "I need to use your gym today. I have a few miles to log on the treadmill."

"I need to jog as well," he said, snatching a piece of bacon from the plate. "I have two treadmills. We could work out together."

Which was the only way jogging could possibly be fun.

After breakfast, I changed and headed to the gym. Nathaniel stood in the middle of the room, stretching. I joined him, slowly working the stiffness from my lower body. I spent a lot of time watching him, following his actions, because, damn it, if he ever decided to quit his day job, he could be a personal trainer. Or a chef. Or a literature professor. Or a lot of things.

When we made it to the treadmills, he kept pace with me. I thought it was awfully sweet—he could run me into the ground if he wanted to. Briefly, I thought ahead to spring, imagining running outside with Nathaniel and Apollo. Hadn't he said last night he saw us in a long-term relationship?

We jogged along together, there inside the gym, and my mind wandered. What would spring be like with Nathaniel? Would he even want to spend an afternoon jogging with me? I liked to think he would. Was that wishful thinking on my part?

The week had brought us closer so far. A few of his bricks had fallen, and even though there were many left to knock down, progress was progress.

Speaking of progress, I wondered how Felicia was doing. I couldn't remember the last time we'd gone so long without talking. How was her blizzard time with Jackson? Was she even more in love now than she had been? Was that possible?

Thoughts of Felicia and the blizzard took me to Linda and the lunch we were supposed to have had the day before. Maybe we'd be able to get together next week.

Then I wondered what Nathaniel and Todd had argued about in Tampa. Damn, I should have asked Nathaniel about that during our naked picnic. Not that he would have answered.

"Abigail?" Nathaniel asked, not even sounding winded. "Are you okay?"

I looked to my side. "Fine. My mind wanders while I jog." My mind *should* have been thinking about the delicious masculine specimen to my right, because who the hell cared about spring when you were snowed in with Nathaniel in February?

I made my way into the kitchen in the late afternoon, trying to decide what to cook for dinner. Maybe some fish? Shrimp? I tried to remember if he had any fish in the freezer. I glanced around the countertops. Maybe roasted potatoes to go with the fish? Something simple. My gaze hit on the cabinets, and I thought back to the day after the whipping bench. I never had explored the upper shelves.

I pulled a chair over to the cabinets and scrambled up to a standing position. I swayed a little bit and grabbed on to the shelf, telling myself to be careful. If I fell and broke something, how would I get to the hospital? Steadying myself, I peeked into the cabinet.

More cans. I smiled. With labels. I went through them, looking for something interesting to serve with fish, when my eyes fell on a large box at the very back.

I reached over the cans and pulled the box toward me, moving cans out of the way.

I held it in my hands in disbelief.

Chocolate bars?

Nathaniel had an entire box of candy bars in his cabinets. I thought back to the times we had eaten together. Only at the black-tie benefit and the family dinner during Super Bowl weekend had I ever noticed him eat sweets. And he had an entire box of candy bars in his cabinet? A box that had been opened?

It was golden.

The vague inklings of a plan formed in my head.

This was going to be fun.

Chapter Thirty

I walked into the library, the box of candy behind my back. Nathaniel sat at the small desk, thumbing through papers.

What happened next would end either very well or very badly.

"Nathaniel West."

His head shot up at my use of his full name. I realized that while I'd thought of him as Nathaniel in my head, I'd never used his first name. To him, at least.

His eyes narrowed. "I assume you will apologize for that slip, Abigail?"

"I'll do no such thing," I said with as much courage as I could muster. I pulled the box of chocolates out, hoping he'd see what I was doing. "What are these?"

He set the papers down and glared at me very intently.

Oh, dear. He is angry. Very angry. He wasn't seeing anything.

Or else he saw everything and wasn't amused.

Wasn't amused. At. All.

"They are chocolate bars, Abigail. It says so right on the box." He stood up.

Very badly. Odds were this was going to end very badly. "I know what they are, Nathaniel. What I want to know is, what are they doing in the kitchen?"

He crossed his arms. "What business of yours is it?" he asked in that you're-in-for-it-now voice.

Ouch, my backside hurt just thinking about the spanking I'd be getting. And it wasn't even the weekend. I had one more chance.

"It's my business," I said, shaking the box at him, "because these are not on your meal plan."

He blinked.

Understanding dawned in his eyes.

I stepped closer. "Do you think I put together a meal plan for you because I'm bored and have nothing better to do? Answer me."

His arms uncrossed. "No, Mistress."

Mistress. He understood. He was playing along.

I gave a dramatic sigh. "I had plans for today, but instead we'll have to spend the afternoon inside, working on your punishment."

His eyes darkened. "I'm sorry to disappoint you, Mistress," he said in that low, seductive voice.

"You'll be sorrier still when I'm finished with you. I'm going up to my room. You have ten minutes to join me there."

I spun and walked out of the library, then ran up the stairs to my room. I stripped my dress off and put on the silver robe Nathaniel had once complimented. Then I stood by the foot of my bed and waited.

He entered slowly. Quietly.

I crossed my arms and tapped my foot. "What do you have to say for yourself, Nathaniel?"

He hung his head. "Nothing, Mistress."

"Look at me," I commanded him. When he met my eyes, I continued. "I am not a mistress. I am a goddess." I pushed the robe from my shoulders. "I will be worshipped."

He stood for the span of five seconds, deep in thought. Then something snapped. He rushed forward, lifted me in his arms, and cradled me in his lap on the tiny bed.

His eyes searched mine, and a million unasked questions flicked across his face. He gently cupped my cheek. "Abby," he whispered. "Oh, Abby."

My heart twisted. *Abby*. He called me *Abby*.

He glanced down at my mouth, traced my lips with his thumb. " 'A kiss of desire . . .' "

" 'On the lips,' " I finished in a whisper.

His fingers shook. Ever so slowly, he leaned forward, and my eyes fluttered closed as he narrowed the space between us. His chest heaved in a shuddering breath. Then his lips pressed tenderly against mine.

Just a touch, but I felt the electricity spark between us. His lips came again, longer this time, but just as soft. Just as gentle.

Nothing more than a whisper.

I knew then that while Nathaniel knew many things and was right about most of them, he was completely wrong in this respect. Kissing on the lips wasn't unnecessary; it was the most necessary thing there was. I could live without air sooner than I could give up the feel of his lips on mine.

He sighed—a warrior's defeat at the end of a long-fought battle. Then he framed my face with both hands and kissed me again. Even longer. His tongue lightly traced my lips, and when I opened my mouth, he entered slowly, as if memorizing the feel, the very taste of me. I could have wept with the sweetness of it all.

I ran my fingers through his hair, pulling him to me, not ever wanting to let go. He groaned, and our tongues swept over each other's as the kiss deepened.

He broke away and stood to step out of his pants, looking deep in my eyes the entire time.

"Love me, Nathaniel," I said, holding my arms open to him.

"I always have, Abby," he said as he gently gathered me to him. "I always have."

Then he lowered me to the bed and his lips were on mine again for another long, slow, openmouthed kiss. And kissing Nathaniel was so much better than fantasizing about it. His lips were smooth and strong, and his tongue stroked mine with a passion and yearning that curled my toes.

And we weren't dom and sub; we weren't master and servant; we weren't even man and woman. We were lovers, and when he finally entered me, it was sweet and slow and tender.

And I'm not sure, but I think, somehow, in the seconds before he released into me, I felt a tear fall from his eyes.

Chapter Thirty-one

That was the first night I slept in Nathaniel's arms. Because the bed was small, he kept me on top of him with his arms around me, my head on his chest. We could have slept anywhere and I wouldn't have cared. His arms were the heaven I never wanted to leave.

I woke alone the next day, but I wasn't too surprised. Nathaniel never slept much, from what I'd seen. Still, it was a bit disappointing. The perfect ending to the night would have been waking up in his arms in the morning.

I jumped out of bed and threw on some clothes. Today we'd discuss how this would change our relationship. How to weave together the Dom Nathaniel and the Weekday Nathaniel. I was certain we could make it work.

I peeked into his bedroom, but it was empty. No one in the library, not even a fire. No sounds from the gym. I walked into the kitchen. The coffee was on, but no Nathaniel. At least he had been in there recently.

Whose turn was it to cook breakfast? I'd had dinner duty last night, but we'd never made it back downstairs for dinner. My mind wandered back to Nathaniel . . . the way his mouth fit mine . . .

Focus, Rational Abby shouted at me.

Right. Breakfast.

I decided it would only be fair if I cooked breakfast. After all, I had skipped my turn. Maybe after breakfast, we could go outside. Have a snowball fight. Quote more Shakespeare.

Kiss.

Where was he?

I stuck my head into the dining room and my jaw dropped.

There he was—reading a newspaper, for crying out loud.

What should I call him? "Nathaniel" seemed too casual for the dining room.

"Hello," I said instead.

That was better. Don't call him anything.

"There you are," he said, looking up. He wasn't smiling. Why wasn't he smiling? "I was just thinking that you should be able to make it home today."

"What?"

He set his paper down. "The roads are clear. You shouldn't have any trouble getting to your apartment."

I was confused. I didn't know how to properly address him. How to talk with him. Everything was so upside down. And why was he talking about going home? How could he think such things after the night before?

"But why would I go home? I'll just be back tomorrow night."

"About that," he said, looking at me with veiled eyes. "I'll be at the office most of the weekend, digging out from this storm. It would probably be best if you didn't come over this weekend."

Not come over? What?

"You have to come home at some point," I said.

"Not for any length of time . . . Abigail."

Abigail.

My heart sank. Something was wrong. Something was very, very wrong.

"Why did you call me that?" I whispered.

"I always call you Abigail." He sat completely still. I wasn't sure he was moving. Maybe he wasn't breathing.

"Last night you called me Abby."

He blinked. That was the only move he made. "It was the scene."

What the hell was he talking about? The scene? "What do you mean?"

"We switched. You wanted me to call you Abby."

"We didn't *switch*," I said as realization sank in. He was pretending it didn't mean anything. That last night was some sort of scene where he was the submissive.

"We did. It was what you wanted when you came into the library with the candy."

Damn, I couldn't think straight. Couldn't figure out what he was doing.

"That was my original intention," I said. "But then you kissed me. You called me Abby." I looked deep into his eyes, desperately searching for the man I loved. "You slept in my bed. All night."

His hands slipped off the table, and he took a deep breath. "And I have *never* invited you to sleep in mine."

Oh, no.

Oh, please God, no.

Tears prickled my eyes. This couldn't be happening. I shook my head. "Fuck it. Don't do this."

"Watch your language."

"Don't fucking tell me to watch my language when you're sitting there trying to pretend last night didn't mean anything." I clenched my fists. "Just because the dynamic changed doesn't make what happened bad. So we admitted a few things. So what? We move on. It'll make us better together."

"Have I ever lied to you, Abigail?"

There he went with the *Abigail* again. Damn it. I wiped my nose. "No."

"Then what makes you think I'm lying now?"

"Because you're scared. You love me and it's scaring you. But you know what? It's okay. I'm a little scared too."

"I'm not scared. I'm a coldhearted bastard." His head tilted. "I thought you knew that."

He wasn't going to back down. The wall was up. With reinforcements. We were right back to square one.

He sat, stiff as a board, with his hands in his lap and a discarded newspaper by his side. Watching me with eyes that offered no hope.

I closed my eyes and took a deep breath.

You had to have limits.

I'd told myself that once before. You had to know what your limits were. When to say, *Enough,* or *I'm finished.*

I thought through my options. If he was lying, he was doing an excellent job. If he was telling the truth, I couldn't bear it. So I thought through my options again, and for the first time ever, everyone was in agreement: Bad Abby and Good Abby, Rational Abby and Crazy Abby.

You had to have limits.

I'd hit mine.

I opened my eyes. Nathaniel waited.

I reached behind my neck, unlatched my collar, and placed it on the table. "Turpentine."

Chapter Thirty-two

Nathaniel stared at the collar, but I noticed he didn't look at all surprised.

"Very well, Abigail. If that's what you want." He could have been reciting numbers from the phone book. That was how dead he sounded.

"Yes," I said, my nails biting into my palms. "If you're going to pretend last night was nothing but a damn scene, this is what I want."

He nodded, a curt little movement of his head. "I know many dominants in the New York area. I would be more than happy to give you some names." He looked at me with blank eyes. "Or I could give them yours."

How dare he? I had noted on the application I sent that I was interested only in being Nathaniel's sub. Nathaniel knew that. He knew that and he was bringing up other doms to hurt me.

In that moment, I understood that love and hate were opposite sides of the same coin. For as much as I'd loved Nathaniel ten minutes ago, I hated him now.

"I'll keep that in mind," I said tersely.

He still didn't move. It was as if he were carved from ice.

"I'll go get my things." I left the dining room and went up the stairs to my room, where, mere hours ago, Nathaniel and I had made love so sweet that he'd cried.

He cried.

Last night, I thought he cried because of the feelings he had for me. Or perhaps the overwhelming emotions of his walls coming down. But what if he had cried because he knew what he would do hours later?

"Oh, Nathaniel," I whispered as the possibility washed over me. "Why?"

Why would he do that? What would have caused him to do such a thing?

Later, Rational Abby said. *Think about it later.*

Right. Later.

I changed into my own clothes and picked up my purse and iPod. I left the alarm clock. Maybe Nathaniel's next submissive would find it useful.

Nathaniel's next submissive . . .

He would find someone else. Move on. Explore pleasure and pain with someone else. Be gentle and patient and caring with someone else.

Oh, please, no.

But he would.

Later! Crazy Abby screamed.

I stifled a sob. Crazy Abby was right. I'd deal with it later.

I stood in the doorway of the room and bade goodbye to the place where I'd spent the most amazing night of my life.

Then I moved down the hall. Past the closed door of Nathaniel's playroom, where we hadn't spent near enough time. I stopped briefly at the door to his bedroom.

His words echoed in the still hallway while I stared at his perfectly made bed. *And I have never invited you to sleep in mine.*

Yes, Nathaniel had learned my body well. Very well. And my mind at the same time. For there were no other words that would have cut deeper.

Apollo met me in the foyer with his tail wagging. I dropped to my knees and put my arms around him.

"Oh, Apollo," I said, holding back tears once again. "You be a good boy." I dug my fingers into his fur as he licked my face. "I'm going to miss you."

I pulled back and looked in his eyes. Who knew? Maybe he could understand. "I can't stay here anymore, so I won't see you again. But you be good and . . . promise me you'll take care of Nathaniel, okay?"

He licked my face one more time. Maybe in agreement. Maybe in farewell.

I stood and left.

Well, I told myself as I drove back to my apartment, at least the day couldn't get any worse. There was something to be said for getting the bad stuff out of the way early. You had the rest of the day to try to make yourself feel better. Eat a few pints of ice cream. Down a few bottles of cheap wine.

Except I had to face Felicia.

Except Jackson might come over.

Except I would replay the morning over and over in my head.

And the night before.

Later, Good Abby reminded me. *Think about it later.*

Yes, I needed to keep my eyes on the road. How horrible would it be to crash now? To wind up at the hospital and have to explain to Linda why the kitchen staff wouldn't need to worry about Nathaniel this time.

I focused in front of me. The roads were safe; the road crews had done an excellent job in clearing them quickly. Only a few icy patches remained.

There you go. Focus on the road, on the pretty snowdrifts, on the way the sunlight bounces off the snow, on that car following you.

My eyes shot to the rearview mirror. I hadn't hit the highway yet, so traffic was light. And it wouldn't be out of the ordinary to meet other cars on this road.

Still.

I had a funny feeling . . .

I slowed down. So did the car behind me.

I tried to get a good look at the driver, but he was too far away. I couldn't even tell what kind of car it was.

I sped up. So did the car behind me.

I signaled to merge onto the highway. So did the car behind me.

Idiot, Rational Abby said. *You think it's Nathaniel? You think he's following you? Grow up.*

Right. That happened only in the movies. I ignored the car and turned my attention to the road.

I walked into the apartment and threw my purse on the couch, then went straight to the freezer and found my emergency stash of chocolate-chip-cookie-dough ice cream.

I ate half the pint before someone knocked on the door.

"Go away!"

"Abby!" Felicia shouted. "Let me in."

"No."

"Open the door, or I'll go get my key and let myself in."

I let her in and went back to sit down and finish the ice cream.

"You're home!" She trotted into the kitchen. "I was afraid you would stay on with Nathaniel and not come home. Guess what? It's the most amazing thing."

Her eyes flashed with excitement, her cheeks flushed a soft pink. She was the personification of a woman in love.

"I give up," I said, waving the spoon at her. "Tell me."

"Jackson proposed!" She spun around. "He got down on one knee and everything. We're going to pick out a ring this weekend. Isn't it romantic?"

Frankly, no. Romantic was the man knowing you so well, he could pick out the ring himself and have it with him when he proposed. But this was Felicia we were talking about, and Jackson had probably called it right by letting her pick out her own ring. Besides, it was Felicia's fairy tale, not mine.

Felicia's fairy tale.

Hell. Felicia and Jackson were getting married.

The day suddenly got worse.

"Damn, Abby, you could act a little bit excited."

Felicia and Jackson were getting married.

A sob broke free and tears slipped down my cheeks.

"Abby?" she said, really looking at me for the first time since walking into the kitchen. "What are you doing eating ice cream?" Her forehead wrinkled, and her voice dropped to a whisper. "Where's your collar?"

My spoon fell to the table. I put my head into my hands and cried.

"Ah, hell," she said. "What did he do? I'll kill him."

I cried harder.

She came to my side, bent down, and put her arms around me. "Abby," she whispered.

She waited until I had cried myself out. By then, she was in tears herself. She took my hand and walked with me to the couch.

"Will you tell me?" she asked, stroking my hair. "Can you talk?"

"It was the most wonderful thing," I said, when I got my voice back. "He finally kissed me and called me Abby and we made love . . ."

"*Finally* kissed you? He hasn't been kissing you?"

That only made me cry harder.

"Damn," she said. "Me and my mouth. I'm sorry. I won't say anything else."

Her phone rang. She ignored it.

"It's okay." I hiccuped. "But I don't want to talk about it right now."

When she wanted to and she took her mind off herself, Felicia could be very intuitive. Usually, it shocked the hell out of people—but when she put her mind to it, she could see anything.

"You love him," she said. "You really love him."

"I don't want to talk about it."

She stared at me dumbfounded. "You love the bastard. It's not just a kinky sex thing."

I nodded.

Her phone rang again. She looked at the display. "Hold on." She flipped the phone open. "Hey, baby," she said, walking into the kitchen. "Listen, tonight's not going to work."

Silence.

Her voice dropped. "Have you talked to Nathaniel?"

I groaned. It was my worst nightmare. The only problem was, it wasn't ever going to end.

"Let me tell you," she continued, "the only thing stopping me from butchering the worthless son of a bitch right now is that he's your cousin, and Abby might want to kill him herself someday. I'd hate to deny her the privilege."

Silence.

"Yeah, I know," she said. "Sounds great . . . I love you, too."

Shoot me. Please. Someone.

I pulled a throw pillow over my face.

———————

The entire first week, I was a zombie. I went to work, came home, and went to bed. I didn't sleep at all. I kept running my last week with Nathaniel around in my head. Wondering if I'd done something wrong. What I could have done differently. But I eventually decided I hadn't done anything wrong. It was all Nathaniel's fault.

I quit the gym and the meal plan. I spent my free time on the couch watching trash TV and downing entirely too much ice cream. But my body wasn't accustomed to downtime and junk food, so in the end I only felt like hell. And that was Nathaniel's fault too.

I went to work and remembered him walking into the library every Wednesday to visit the Rare Books Collection. I remembered sitting at the front desk, counting the hours until I would see him again.

My only point of solace the entire week was that my apartment was my own. My home was a Nathaniel-free zone. Not once had he ever ventured into my apartment, and I could enter any room and not see him standing there, climb into bed for another restless night and not feel his presence.

My only hope was that my presence had not left him. *Let him see me in the library*, I prayed. Let him not be able to play his piano without thinking of me in his lap. Let him make dinner in his kitchen and remember the way my legs felt wrapped around his waist. If there was a God in heaven, Nathaniel would think of me every time he turned around, every time he stepped outside, every time he rubbed Apollo's head, every time he ate a meal, every time he went to bed.

Every time he took a breath, I wanted my memory to haunt him with the knowledge that it was all his fault.

Chapter Thirty-three

Several things happened during the weeks following my split with Nathaniel.

First of all, I got off the couch and started my own exercise plan. I'd put a lot of hard work into my new body and I didn't want to see it all go to waste.

Second, Felicia and Jackson set a wedding date for the first of June. I was relieved—at least I had a time frame to work with. A June wedding meant four months before I would see Nathaniel again. In four months' time, I knew I'd be in a much happier place. In four months' time, I would be able to march down the aisle behind Felicia with my head held high and ignore the bastard.

That would be due to the third thing, Felicia asking me to be her maid of honor. Which I agreed to wholeheartedly. Perhaps, I thought in my more philosophical moments, the purpose of my entire relationship with Nathaniel had been to bring Felicia and Jackson together. In those philosophical moments, I felt like it had all been worth it to see Felicia happy. Felicia deserved happiness. Philosophical moments, however, were few and far between, especially because of item number four.

The fourth thing that happened? *People* magazine printed my name, albeit in a very small article. I'm sure Jackson's engagement to Felicia would have been overlooked by most people if it hadn't happened so quickly after the Super Bowl. But it did happen quickly, so there was my name in *People*: "Felicia Kelly's best friend, Abby King, has been linked romantically to Jackson's cousin, Nathaniel West."

Anyway. Moving on.

All this happened before item five—Linda decided to throw Felicia and Jackson an engagement party. In March.

Which meant I no longer had four months to prepare for seeing Nathaniel. I had one.

Elaina called me shortly after Felicia broke the news. I felt a little bad; I had ignored her after the break with Nathaniel.

"Hey, Elaina."

"Abby! Finally. I've wanted to talk to you so badly."

"I'm sorry." I sighed. "I just haven't . . . been ready."

"I understand," she said, and I knew she did. "I wanted to see how you're doing."

"I'm doing great." I sat down on the couch and tucked my legs underneath me. "Although I'm a bit pissed about this party."

"That was Linda," Elaina said. "She wanted to throw a big to-do for Felicia and Jackson. Especially since the wedding will be so small."

Felicia and Jackson would be getting married in June at Elaina and Todd's country estate. The bride and groom both wanted a small wedding.

"It's fine," I said. "I'll deal."

"He's a complete wreck," she said, switching gears completely. "I know you probably don't care and I don't blame you, but he's a wreck. He talked to Todd and asked for some names. He's getting help."

"Good," I said. "He needs help. He also needs a swift kick in the balls, but that's beside the point."

She laughed. "We all agree with you on that one. And as soon as you say the word, we'll be more than happy to help."

"I'll be sure to let you know," I said, and I smiled. It felt good to smile. "If you don't mind me asking, will you tell me what . . . Nathaniel and Todd argued about in Tampa?" There, I said his name, out loud even.

She sighed. "Todd still won't tell me. He says it's Nathaniel's story to tell." Her voice lowered. "And trust me, I tried to get it out of him."

I laughed and, damn, laughing felt good. "I'll bet you did."

I realized then how I'd missed feeling good—laughing, smiling. "What did Nathaniel say about our split?" See there? I told myself. Getting easier all the time.

"That you called it off. We don't believe him a bit. We know there's more to it than he's saying. He had to be a dickless prick to make you leave."

"Dickless prick?" I giggled. "Is that possible?"

She laughed. "It is when you're talking about Nathaniel."

From there we moved on to talking about other things. It felt normal.

And normal felt good.

Felicia and I argued when she came by on Valentine's Day with a ring.

"Do you ever think," I asked, after making the appropriate *ooh*s and *ahhh*s, "that you and Jackson are moving too fast?"

"This from the woman who . . ."

"Go ahead," I said, ready for the fight. "Go ahead and say it."

"No." She pursed her lips together.

"You want to," I said, pushing all her buttons. "You know you want to. Go ahead. Say it. This from the woman who let Nathaniel West fuck her up one side and down the other and then came running home crying because he finally fucked her too hard."

"Don't push me."

"Let it out. You'll feel better."

"Okay, then." She put her hands on her hips. "What the hell else did you think would happen? That he'd fall head over heels in love with you and everything would be just fine? That you were going to snap your fingers and he'd come running like a dog? If you loved him, really truly loved him, maybe you should have stayed and, I don't know"—she threw her hands up in the air—"talked about it. But no, you had to run home when it didn't go your way. You think Nathaniel has issues? Hell, we all have issues. Face them, damn it. Don't sit at home crying your eyes out and making everyone miserable in the process."

"Finished?"

"Not yet. I know this party will be hard for you. It's not going to be a piece of cake for anyone. You're my maid of honor and Nathaniel is the best man—"

"Nathaniel's the best man?"

"Yes. And it won't be easy for anyone involved. Jackson says Nathaniel's a shell of his former self. That he spent the first few days after you left drinking himself into a stupor. Linda's—"

"He did?"

"Yes. Linda's worrying herself sick over the whole thing and keeps asking Jackson to postpone the wedding. She thinks if we wait a few more months, you and Nathaniel can handle it better. But in the end, Jackson and I convinced her to throw this engagement party—"

"You convinced her?"

"Yes. Damn it all, stop interrupting me."

"Sorry."

"Jackson and I convinced her to throw it." She moved close to me. "And you're going to go and be nice and talk to the man, Abby. Understand me? And you'll talk to him in a civilized manner. I don't care if you tell him to eat shit and die as long as you're civil about it. Know why? Because I'm the bride, and I won't have you ruining my wedding."

Uh-huh, that was Felicia. But somewhere in there, I thought she might have made a few good points.

"Say something," she said.

"You're right," I said. "I should have stayed and talked. I took the coward's way out. I guess I thought he'd try and stop me."

"From what you've told me, he was keeping you at a safe distance from the beginning. Did it ever occur to you that you were doing exactly what he thought you would do?"

"Once or twice."

She put her hands on both of my shoulders. "I know you're mad at him. Hell, I'm mad at him. According to Jackson, Todd and Elaina are mad at him. But if you want him, talk to him." She shook me slightly. "But be willing to admit you made mistakes as well."

"That's asking a lot."

"Is he worth it?"

"I thought so once," I whispered.

"He's still the same man, and that means he's still worth it."

I wiped away a tear.

"But don't make it too easy. He has to own up to his mistakes. And his were a lot worse, in my book." She smiled. "And you and I both know that's the only book that matters."

The days before the party both dragged by and came out of no-where. One day I was looking at the calendar, thanking my lucky stars I still had two weeks before I saw Nathaniel, and the next thing I knew, I had two hours to get ready.

I wore a silver gown I found on the rack at a going-out-of-business sale. It was nowhere near as nice as the one Elaina offered me, but I turned her down. I wanted to do it all on my own. My way.

Felicia left early with Jackson the day of the party. I supposed that was to be expected, since she was the guest of honor. Jackson came by my apartment and hugged me before they left. I truly liked him. He didn't say anything, but his actions alone were enough. Jackson never talked too much about his cousin. I suppose he knew how uncomfortable it would make me.

My body shook as the cab took me to the Penthouse, the banquet facility where the party was being held. I tried to remember when I'd last felt as nervous and failed miserably.

Never. I had never felt this nervous.

Would he arrive first or would I? Would he speak to me first or would I make the first move?

How would he look? Had he changed at all in the last month? Would he look at me with the cold, dead eyes I remembered, or would his gaze be filled with regret?

Only for Felicia, I chanted as I walked up to the door. Only for Felicia would I do this.

Elaina waited for me inside. She took me and embraced me in a long hug.

"Oh, Abby," she said. "We can't ever go this long without seeing each other again. Promise."

"I promise," I said, and in that minute, I meant it.

She wiped her eyes. "He's not here yet."

"Good. I need a minute."

"Come and see Linda."

Linda was near tears when I found her. "Abby," she said. "Thank you for coming."

"I wouldn't miss it," I said, returning the big hug she gave me.

When I composed myself, I glanced around the room. The white walls looked creamy in the soft candlelight. A buffet of hors d'oeuvres lined one wall, right next to a bar, and the deejay stood in a corner, shuffling through songs. There was a hardwood dance floor and several draped tables and chairs.

"This is beautiful," I said.

"I couldn't think of a better place to celebrate Felicia joining the family." Linda laughed softly. "Jackson's counting the days until June."

"So is Felicia."

Conversation buzzed around us, low and steady like the gentle hum of bees. The hall filled slowly, the press of people somehow comforting. My gaze bounced around the room, landing seconds later on the person entering.

Nathaniel.

He looked good. I'd give him that much. His dark hair had that messy just-crawled-out-of-bed look and his black suit fit his body perfectly. He shook hands with several people as he entered, but he didn't appear to be paying much attention to any of them. His eyes were too busy scanning the crowd.

His smile faltered for just a second when he saw me.

He took a deep breath and made his way toward us. Linda discreetly moved away.

I wished I had a drink, something to keep my hands occupied. Instead, I intertwined my fingers, kept them down below my belly.

My heart thumped, and sweat broke out on my forehead.

He was almost by me.

I brushed a strand of hair away. Around us, people chattered brightly, laughing and clinking glasses.

Then he was there before me. Eyes soft and pleading.

"Hello, Abby," he whispered.

Abby.

"Nathaniel," I said, and I was proud my voice sounded steady.

"You look well." His eyes never left mine. I'd forgotten just how green they were.

"Thank you."

He stepped closer. "I wanted to tell—"

"There you are." A blonde interrupted us.

His head jerked to the left. "Melanie, this is not a good time." Melanie?

She was beautiful. Her off-white dress hugged her body and flaunted every curve. A delicate diamond necklace graced her neck, and flowing curls bounced to her shoulders.

She winked at me.

What?

"You must be Abby." She held out her hand. "It's nice to finally meet you."

I shook her hand, bewildered. What was happening? What was she doing? What was Nathaniel getting ready to say?

He was glaring at her. "Melanie, I—"

"Nathaniel!" An overweight, balding man walked up and slapped Nathaniel on the back. "Just the man I've been waiting for. Come with me. I need to introduce you to some people."

He allowed himself to be dragged away, but his eyes watched me from across the room even as he shook hands and made small talk.

"Whew," Melanie said. "That was close."

"You did that on purpose?"

She put her hand on my shoulder. "Honey, whatever Nathaniel was getting ready to say would have been too easy. If he wants you back, let him fight for you."

I stared at her in shock.

"I'm not so much of a vindictive bitch that I can't see when a man's in love." She squeezed my shoulder.

I giggled as she walked off.

Melanie was on my side.

Two hours later, it was obvious he wasn't going to fight for me. My path didn't cross Nathaniel's again. I told myself that was fine.

"I hate him," Elaina said, watching as Nathaniel talked to a large group of men. "I hate him. I hate him. I hate him."

"Elaina," I chided. "It's fine. It's gone well so far. You can't expect more than that."

"It's not fine. It hasn't gone well. And I can expect more than that."

A slow song started playing, and Jackson led Felicia out to the dance floor.

"It's for Felicia," I said. "All this is for Felicia."

Elaina crossed her arms.

I hugged her. "But I've had enough for one night. I'm going to leave. Let's get together soon, okay?"

She nodded.

I looked around the room one more time. Felicia and Jackson twirled on the dance floor. Linda talked with Melanie and Melanie's parents. Todd walked up to Elaina and put his arm around her, leaned over and whispered in her ear.

I didn't look for Nathaniel.

I was steps away from the front door when the music abruptly stopped. Conversation ceased. A microphone squealed.

"Don't leave me, Abby."

Nathaniel's voice echoed throughout the still banquet hall.

I spun around. He stood at the deejay's stand, microphone in hand.

"I let you leave once and it almost killed me. Please," he begged. "Please don't leave me."

Chapter Thirty-four

I felt torn.

Rational Abby was mortified Nathaniel had just begged me to stay in front of a crowd of people at Jackson and Felicia's engagement party and now everyone was staring at me. Crazy Abby was turning cartwheels inside because Nathaniel had just begged me to stay in front of a crowd of people at Jackson and Felicia's engagement party and she didn't care a bit that everyone was staring at me.

I forced my feet to move, to carry me across the dance floor. Couples stepped to either side, creating a path for me.

Felicia would kill me. For sure.

Right after she killed Nathaniel.

Nathaniel stood frozen, watching me. I jerked the microphone away from him and shoved it into the hands of the stunned deejay.

"What the hell do you think you're doing?" I asked. Obviously, Rational Abby had decided to speak her mind first.

He glanced around the room as if seeing the crowd for the first time. "I'm sorry, but I couldn't let you leave. It was wrong for me to go about it like this, though. Let me walk you to a cab." He held out a hand I refused to take. "I'm sorry," he apologized again, moving his hand away.

"I'm here now. You might as well go ahead and say what you wanted to."

"There's a small room in the——"

"Ladies and gentlemen," the deejay interrupted. "The best man and maid of honor—Nathaniel West and Abby King!"

The crowd erupted in polite applause as a piano concerto started to play.

Were we supposed to dance?

"Ah, hell," Nathaniel said.

Felicia stood beside the deejay, a knowing smirk on her face.

Yes. Yes, we were.

I hate you, I mouthed to her.

She blew me a kiss.

Nathaniel held out his arm. "Will you?"

I placed my hand on his bicep and he led me to the dance floor. He was tense. Around us, the crowd started murmuring again. We made it to the middle of the cleared floor and faced each other.

"I'm trying to decide how this could be more embarrassing and failing," Nathaniel said as I tentatively put my hand on his shoulder.

"I blame you completely," I said as his arm encircled my waist. "If you had just let me leave, this wouldn't have happened."

His gaze pierced my very soul. "I went about it all wrong, but if I had let you leave tonight, I'd never have forgiven myself."

Crazy Abby wanted me to tell him she loved the way he'd gone about it, but Rational Abby had other things she wanted to discuss.

"If you felt that strongly about it," I said, "then maybe you should have tried calling me sometime in the last month."

"I wasn't at the place I needed to be, Abby."

Every time he called me *Abby*, my heart skipped a beat.

"And you are now?" It felt odd to be in his arms again. Odd and strangely right. But I had questions—many, many questions for which I needed answers.

"No," he admitted. "But I'm coming closer."

The song continued, and we made our way around the dance floor. Other couples joined in.

"It was a mistake to think I could do this tonight." He stopped moving and we stood still, our arms around each other. "I have no reason to hope you'll agree, and I'll understand if you won't, but"—he searched my eyes—"will you meet me tomorrow afternoon? To talk? So I can explain?"

My heart gave a horrible lurch. He wanted to meet and talk? To explain? Was I ready?

"Okay," I said.

He smiled. His face lit with joy and excitement. "You will? Really?"

"Yes."

"Should I pick you up? Or would you feel more comfortable meeting me somewhere? Whatever you prefer." His words came out quickly, rushed.

He wanted to do what made me feel comfortable. That concession alone made me feel better. But I wasn't ready to be in a car with him. Or to have him in my apartment.

"The coffee shop on West Broadway?" I asked.

He nodded, the excitement growing in his eyes. "Yes. One o'clock tomorrow?"

"One o'clock will be fine," I said, as my heart threatened to beat right out of my chest. The song drifted slowly and simply to its ending.

"Thank you, Abby," he said, leading me off the dance floor. "Thank you for the dance and thank you for agreeing to meet me tomorrow."

When I finally made it home later that night, a package waited in front of my door.

I opened the note taped to the top and read the flowing script.

> To Abby,
>   For being right about the labels.
>
>   Nathaniel

I ripped the package open and giggled.

A pile of label-less cans filled the box.

He arrived at the coffee shop first the next day and was waiting for me at a corner table in the back. He jumped up when he saw me approach.

"Abby," he said, pulling my chair out. "Thank you for meeting me. Can I get you something to drink?"

"You're welcome, and no, I don't want anything to drink." I felt nervous enough as it was—if I drank anything, I'd probably throw it up.

He sat down. "I don't know where to start, really." He twisted a napkin in his hands. "I ran this through in my head a hundred times." He looked up and smiled. "I even wrote it down so I wouldn't forget anything. But now . . . I'm at a complete loss."

"Why don't you start at the beginning?" I said.

He took a deep breath and dropped the napkin. "First of all, I need to apologize for taking advantage of you."

I raised an eyebrow.

"I knew you had never been in a relationship like ours before, and I took advantage of you. The safe word, for example. I told you the truth when I said I'd never had a submissive use her safe word before, but beyond that, I didn't want you to leave. I thought if I made the safe word a relationship ender, you wouldn't leave me." He ran his fingers through his hair. "Of course, that backfired on me, didn't it?"

"It was your fault."

"Yes, it was." His eyes grew soft. "You gave me your trust. Your submission. Your love. And in return, I took your gifts and threw them back in your face."

I looked straight at him. I wanted to make sure he understood this point. "I handled everything you gave me physically. I would have handled anything you gave me physically, but emotionally"—I shook my head—"you broke me."

"I know," he whispered.

"Do you know how much that hurt? How it felt when you pretended that night meant nothing?" He winced at my words. "It was the most amazing night of my life, and you sat at that table and told me it was a scene. I'd have been better off if you'd plunged a knife in my heart."

"I know." A tear slipped down his cheek. "I'm sorry. So very sorry."

"I want to know why. Why did you do it? Why couldn't you just say, 'I need time to work this out,' or, 'We're moving too fast'? Anything would have been better than what you did."

"I was afraid. Once you found out . . ." He paused and focused on the window behind me.

"Once I found out what?"

"Our relationship was a house of cards I'd built. I should have known it wouldn't take much to bring it down."

What the hell was he talking about?

He took a deep breath. "It was a Wednesday. Almost eight years ago. I was—"

"What does eight years ago have to do with anything?"

"I'm trying to tell you," he said. "I was meeting Todd for lunch on campus. He wanted to meet at the library. I saw a woman running up the stairs. She tripped and fell, then looked around to see if anyone was watching. I went to help, but you made it to her first."

"Me?"

"Yes, it was you," he said. "You knew her, and you both laughed as you picked up her books. There were several people nearby, but you were the only one who helped." He picked the napkin back up and resumed his twisting. "I made sure you didn't see me, and I followed you into the library. You did a group reading of *Hamlet*. You read Ophelia."

Oh my word.

"I stayed and watched," he said. "I wanted more than anything to be your Hamlet. Am I making you uncomfortable?"

I shook my head. "Go on."

"I was late meeting Todd," he said. "He was upset. Then I told him I'd met someone. It was only a little lie."

"Why didn't you come up to me? Introduce yourself? Like a normal person would?"

"I was already living the lifestyle of a dom, Abby, and I thought you were a young, impressionable coed. In my mind, there was no way we would have worked. I had no idea of your submissive inclinations until your application crossed my desk. Even if I had known, I had a collared submissive at the time, and I am always monogamous once I collar a submissive."

"My submissive inclinations?" I asked.

He leaned across the table. "You're a sexual submissive,

Abby. You have to know that. Why do you think you hadn't had sex for three years before you were with me?"

"I hadn't found anyone who . . ." I trailed off as I realized where he was going.

"Who would dominate you the way you needed," he finished.

I squirmed in my seat. Was he right?

"Don't be embarrassed," he said. "It's nothing to be ashamed of."

"I'm not embarrassed. I just hadn't thought of it like that before."

"Of course you hadn't. Which is why you were so angry when I suggested other dominants for you."

"I hated you for that."

"I was very much afraid you would take me up on it. I searched my mind, trying to find someone I thought would suit you. But I just couldn't bring myself to imagine you with someone else." He looked sad. "I would have done it if you asked, though. I would have."

"You were thinking of me and what I needed when you suggested other dominants?"

"I knew you had asked specifically for me, but after actually being a submissive, I knew you would need to do it again. Then I saw how you reacted, so I'm sorry for that as well."

He was apologizing a lot. I wondered if he meant it all. But one look in his eyes told me he did. Nathaniel was still in pain.

And if I were honest, so was I. I hadn't moved so far on that I'd left all the pain behind. All the longing. The wanting.

Or, damn it all, the love.

"Jackson keeps saying you should have done more, tried harder to get through to me," he said, "but he doesn't know the details. What I did. It's easy for him to place blame. He doesn't understand there was nothing you could have done that would have changed my mind that morning. Nothing would have changed the outcome. Don't blame yourself."

"I pushed," I protested. "I shouldn't have expected so much so fast."

"Perhaps not, but you could have expected more than I was willing to give you. Instead, I shut you down completely."

I couldn't very well argue with that.

"But there's more," he said.

"Todd?" I asked.

"I didn't pursue you, but I couldn't let you slip away either," he said. "I would watch you at the library, hoping to catch a glimpse of you. He knew I was watching someone, but I told him I was working up the courage to speak to you."

"He believed you?"

"Probably not, but he knew I wouldn't do anything improper." He reached across the table and then pulled his hands back without waiting for mine. "And I didn't, Abby. I promise you. I saw you only at the library. I never attempted to find out any more about you. I never followed you."

"Except the morning I left you," I said, remembering the car behind me.

"It had been snowing and you were upset," he explained. "I had to make certain you were safe."

"So when you saved my mother's house—you knew who she was? You knew she was my mother?"

"Yes. I did it for you. I knew your name from the library. It was on the bank paperwork as well. You were the goddess I longed to worship. My unobtainable dream. The relationship I could never hope to have." He picked up the discarded napkin. "When we were in Tampa, after we played golf, Todd joked with me about the library girl from all those years ago. Dinner the night before had jogged his memory. I told him it was you, and he got angry."

It was that simple. Things were always simple when you got right down to them.

"A *relationship like yours demands complete truth and honesty*," Nathaniel said. "That's what Todd told me. And I was not being truthful in keeping my past knowledge of you a secret."

The story's end was close. I could feel it.

"He wanted me to tell you, and I agreed," he said. "I asked for three weeks. I thought that was enough time for me to plan how to tell you, and he thought that was reasonable."

"But we never made it to three weeks."

"No, we didn't. I would like to think that if we had, I would have told you. I had every intention of doing so. But then that night happened, and I was afraid you would think I had tricked you or somehow manipulated you."

"I might have."

"I've never felt for anyone the way I feel for you," he said, and I noticed he spoke in present tense. "I was scared. You were right about that. I thought it would be easier to let you go, but I was wrong."

While we had been talking, the coffee shop had grown quiet. The staff eyed us. We still hadn't ordered anything.

"I'm in therapy now." He smiled. "Twice a week. It feels strange saying that. I'm working through things. Your name comes up often."

I bet.

"I haven't allowed you a chance to get a word in," he said. "But you haven't run off screaming. Dare I hope any of what I've said makes a little bit of sense?"

He had just admitted he had known me for years, had admired me from afar. Had wanted me. Was scared of what he felt.

Did it make up for what he'd done? Or what he'd said? No, but I could understand.

Partly, anyway.

"I need to think," I said honestly.

"Yes," he said, standing as I did. "You need to think things through. It's more than I could hope for."

He took my hands. Kissed my knuckles. "Will you call me later this week? I want to talk more." He looked in my eyes as if gauging my reaction. "If you want to, that is."

The feel of his lips branded my skin. "I'll call you," I said. "I'll call you regardless."

Chapter Thirty-five

I spent much of the next two days thinking about what Nathaniel had told me. I replayed our conversation over and over, trying to decide how I felt about what he'd admitted.

That he'd watched me for years.

That he'd refused to approach me.

That he'd kept it from me.

And then I thought about me.

That I'd fantasized about him for years. That I followed him by way of the local paper. Was it any worse than if I had put myself in places where I knew he'd be? Would I have done the same thing if the situation had been reversed?

Hell and *Yes*.

And if you really thought about it, I was the one who'd taken the first step, because I'd contacted Mr. Godwin.

I called Nathaniel on Tuesday night.

"Hello," he said.

"Nathaniel. It's me."

"Abby," he said, and his voice held a note of restrained excitement.

"There's a sushi bar down the street from the library," I said. "Will you meet me there for lunch tomorrow?"

I made it a point to arrive first. I found a seat by quarter to twelve and waited for him.

My heart skipped a beat when he walked into the restaurant. His eyes scanned the tables, and he smiled when he saw me. And then, all gloriously male, six feet one inches of him walked straight to my table, completely ignorant of the female eyes following him.

This man, I thought. This man wanted me. Watched me. This one.

His eyes sparkled, and I knew in that moment I'd forgiven him.

"Abby," he said, sitting down, and I wondered if he said my name so often because he liked calling me Abby.

"Nathaniel." I delighted in the way his name slipped so easily from my lips now.

We ordered lunch and made small talk. The weather was getting warmer. I told him we had a poetry reading scheduled at the library. He asked about Felicia.

"Before we talk about anything else," he said, growing serious, "I need to tell you something."

I wondered what else he could possibly say that hadn't already been said. "Okay."

"I need you to understand that I am in therapy to work on my intimacy issues and my emotional well-being. Not my sexual needs."

I had a good idea where he was going.

"I am a dominant," he said. "And I will always be a dominant. I cannot and will not give that part of me up. That doesn't mean I can't enjoy other . . . flavors. On the contrary, other flavors make for good variety." He raised an eyebrow. "Does that make sense?"

"Yes," I said and hastened to add, "I would never expect you to give up that part of yourself. It would be like denying who you are."

"Right."

"Just like I can't deny my submissive nature."

"Exactly."

The waiter delivered our drinks, and I took a long sip of my tea.

"I've always wondered," Nathaniel said, "and you don't have to tell me, but how did you find out about me in the first place?"

Oh, boy.

My turn.

"Oh, please." I waved my hand. "Everyone knows about Nathaniel West."

"Maybe," he said, not missing a beat. "But not everyone knows he shackles women to his bed and works them over with a riding crop."

I choked on my tea.

His eyes danced. "You asked for it."

I dabbed my mouth with a napkin, thankful I hadn't spilled any tea on my shirt. "I did. Completely."

"Will you answer?"

"I first took real notice of you when you saved my mother's house. Until then you were only a man I read about in the society pages. A celebrity. But then you became more real."

Our sushi was delivered to the table. Spicy, crunchy tuna and unagi rolls for me. A nigirizushi variety for him.

I poured soy sauce into a bowl and mixed in wasabi. "Your picture was in the paper for something not long after that. I can't remember what for now." I frowned. "Anyway, my friend Samantha stopped by while I was reading the paper. I made some comment about how nice you looked and wondered what you were really like. She got all edgy and shifty."

"Samantha?"

"An old friend. I haven't talked to her in years." I popped a roll in my mouth, chewed, and swallowed it. "She went with her boyfriend to a party or a gathering or something—I'm not sure of the proper name—for dominants and submissives. They were dabblers."

"Ah," he said. "And I was there."

"Yes, and she told me you were a dominant. She said she shouldn't tell me and swore me to absolute secrecy, and I haven't told anyone—well, except for Felicia, when I had to. But Samantha didn't want me to get some romantic Prince Charming fantasy going with me as your Cinderella."

"Did you?"

"No, but I did fantasize about being shackled to your bed while you worked me over with a riding crop."

It was his turn to choke on tea.

"You asked for it," I said.

He laughed, drawing the attention of several tables. "I did. Completely."

I waited until everyone's attention returned to their own tables. "I didn't do anything but fantasize for a long time." I looked at my plate, not wanting to look at him. "Then I asked around. Several of Samantha's friends still live in the area, so it didn't take long to find Mr. Godwin. I held on to his name for months before I did anything. I eventually knew I had to call him, though—anything was better than . . ."

"Unfulfilled sex," he finished.

"Or just plain unfulfilled, in my case," I said, finally looking at him. "I couldn't have a normal relationship with a guy. I just . . . couldn't."

He smiled a knowing smile, like he knew exactly what I was talking about. "I believe there are varying degrees of *normal*, Abby. Who really gets to define what normal looks like anyway?"

"Frankly, I've done what's normal in the eyes of everyone else, and it's boring as hell," I said.

"Different flavors," he said, watching me carefully. "And they can all be delicious when tasted with the right person. But yes, one's natural tendencies do have a way of defining what one sees as normal."

"You tried a so-called normal relationship once," I said. "With Melanie."

"Yes." He took a bite. I watched as his jaw worked and he swallowed. "With Melanie. It was a miserable failure. We failed for several reasons—Melanie is not a natural submissive, and I couldn't repress my dominant nature." He sighed. "But she didn't want to admit we couldn't work. I never understood that."

"For what it's worth, she seems to be over you now."

"Thank God." He smiled. Then he grew serious again and lowered his voice. "Are you?"

Over him?

"No," I whispered.

"Thank God."

He reached across the table, across our plates, to take my hand. "Nor I, you."

We stayed like that for several seconds, holding hands, looking into each other's eyes.

"I'll do whatever it takes to earn your trust back, Abby, for however long it takes." His thumb ran across my knuckles. "Will you let me?"

I wanted to scream and jump into his arms, but I held back. "Yes," I answered simply.

He squeezed my hand before letting go. "Thank you."

The waiter came by to refresh our tea.

"Have you ever made sushi?" I asked Nathaniel, wanting to bring the conversation down to something lighter.

"No, I never have, but I've always wanted to learn."

"We have classes," the waiter said. "Next Thursday night. Seven o'clock."

I looked at Nathaniel. Should we try to have a date? To act like a "normal" couple? To see each other without expectation? To let him begin to earn my trust again?

Nathaniel raised an eyebrow—he wanted me to decide.

"Let's do it," I said.

As we were leaving the restaurant, he turned to me. "Kyle's in his school play. Opening night is Saturday and he asked me to attend. Will you come with me?"

Another date? Was I ready for this?

Yes, I was.

"What time?"

"I can pick you up at five—we could have dinner before the show?"

To be in the car with Nathaniel and to have him come by my apartment? It was a step in the right direction.

"Five it is."

I was nervous on Saturday. Felicia stopped by before leaving for Jackson's, and I had never been happier to see her go. Her sly little smiles, the absolute smugness of her expression, were more than I could take. She was very pleased with herself, as if she had orchestrated the entire thing.

Nathaniel arrived right at five o'clock and we were off. I didn't invite him into the apartment—I wasn't ready yet.

Dinner was all I'd hoped it would be. Nathaniel was a complete gentleman, and conversation flowed easily. I invited him to the poetry reading at the library and he accepted. We talked about Felicia and Jackson, Elaina and Todd, even Linda's non-profit.

I thoroughly enjoyed the play. Kyle didn't have a large part—he was in the chorus—but he put his whole heart into it. Every time he appeared onstage, Nathaniel's face lit up. I wondered how it would feel to save a life the way he had. How Nathaniel felt knowing Kyle was onstage only because of his gift.

Nathaniel kept his distance from me all night, making sure our elbows didn't touch while we watched the play and that our arms didn't accidentally brush as we walked. I knew he was doing his best to ensure I didn't feel rushed, and I appreciated his courtesy.

If there was a subtle undercurrent of electricity that still flowed between us, we both did a good job of ignoring it.

After the play, Nathaniel introduced me to Kyle and his parents. I suppressed a giggle at the worshipful eyes Kyle had for Nathaniel.

The only uncomfortable part of the evening came when Nathaniel walked me to my door.

"Thank you for inviting me," I said. "I had a really nice time." I wondered if he would try to kiss me.

"I was glad to have you with me. The evening wouldn't have been the same without you." He reached for my hand and gave it a gentle squeeze. "I'll see you Thursday night." He looked as if he wanted to say something, but instead he smiled and turned, started to walk away.

No, he wasn't going to kiss me.

Because he was letting me take the lead.

And I didn't want him to leave just yet.

"Nathaniel," I said. He turned and waited while I walked to him, his eyes dark and smoldering. I lifted a hand to his face and traced his cheekbone. I slipped my hand into his hair and pulled him toward me. "Kiss me," I whispered. "Kiss me and mean it."

"Oh, Abby," he said, his voice thick and husky. He placed his fingers under my chin, lifted my face, and lowered his lips to mine.

Softly and gently, we kissed. His lips were smooth and strong, exactly as I remembered. I took a step closer to him, and he wrapped his arms around me.

I teased the entrance of his mouth with my tongue. He sighed and pulled me tighter. Then he parted his lips and let me inside. And it was so sweet, so tender.

Then the kiss deepened, and he poured out his feelings for me.

It was all there in his kiss. His love. His remorse. His passion. His need.

It swept me right away. The feel of his arms around me, his fingers running lightly up my back. His mouth. His taste. His smell.

Him.

Chapter Thirty-six

We went out several times in the weeks to follow. The poetry reading at the library, sushi classes, and a double date with Felicia and Jackson that was nowhere near as awkward as I'd thought it would be.

Nathaniel and I were slowly weaving our lives back together, but our relationship was built on honesty this time. Open communication from both sides. He was still hesitant about doing anything physical beyond kissing, though. Not that kissing Nathaniel was anything to take lightly. He could make my heart pound by simply looking at me. And when he actually touched my lips with his own . . .

He came by the library one Thursday afternoon, three weeks after our theater date, to ask me to dinner the next night. At his house.

"To see Apollo," he added quickly. "He misses you, and when he smells you on me—"

I held up a hand. "I understand. I would love to come over for dinner and to see Apollo. I've missed him."

Nathaniel smiled and thanked me.

_____

Dinner wasn't as unsettling as I'd thought it might be. Apollo stood outside waiting for me, as if he knew I'd be coming. He nearly knocked me over when I stepped out of the car.

"Apollo, please," Nathaniel scolded, coming outside and wiping his hands on a towel. "You must forgive him, Abby. He's been excited all day."

"That makes two of us," I said, walking up the stairs to join Nathaniel. "What are you cooking?"

He leaned over, kissed me, and said with a glimmer in his eyes, "Honey-almond chicken."

"Mmm. My favorite."

"Come inside. It's nearly ready."

The chicken was just as tender and tasty as I remembered. Conversation flowed freely, and Apollo stayed by my side the entire time, often lying at my feet.

When we both finished eating, Nathaniel stood up to take our plates to the sink.

"Let me help," I said, hopping up.

"I can get it."

"But I don't mind."

So he washed and I dried. It reminded me of our snowed-in week—working together, laughing. I put the last dish away and eyed the countertop.

I turned to him. "Nathaniel—"

"Abby—" he said at the same time.

We laughed.

"You first," I said.

He walked over to me and took my hand. "I just wanted to say thank you for coming tonight. Apollo hasn't been so calm in months."

I pushed back from the counter. "Well, I'm glad for Apollo, but he's not the only reason I came over tonight."

"I know." His thumb stroked my knuckles.

I stepped closer to him. "Trust me. I'm a pretty selfish creature."

He lifted a hand to my face and traced my jaw with his index finger. "You're not. You're kind and loving and forgiving and—"

"*Nathaniel.*"

He put a finger on my lips. "Stop. Let me finish."

I took a deep breath and waited.

"You've brought my life so much joy. You've made me feel complete." His voice dropped. "I love you, Abby."

I couldn't breathe.

"Nathaniel," I said when I had my voice back. "I love you, too."

"Abby." He groaned and pulled me into his arms. His lips crushed mine, and he kissed me with all the pent-up longing of the last several weeks.

I snaked one hand down his back and pushed the fingers of the other into his hair. I tilted my head to better fit our mouths together.

His lips nibbled their way up my cheek to my ear. "Tell me to stop, Abby," he whispered, his breath hot against my skin. "Tell me to stop and I will."

"Don't." My eyes closed. "Don't stop."

He ran his hands down my arms, leaving a trail of gooseflesh in their wake. "I don't want you to think I brought you here for this." He bit on my earlobe. "I don't want you to think I'm pushing you."

I trusted him. If I told him to stop, I knew he would. He would pull away and we would continue talking. We would have a nice evening and he would kiss me soundly before I left for the night. Life would proceed the way it had for the last several weeks.

Or . . .

I pulled away from his embrace and smiled sweetly at him. He looked a bit shocked. He obviously hadn't expected me to pull back.

I held out my hand. "Follow me."

He took my hand and followed me as I walked up the stairs to his bedroom. I blinked back tears when I saw his bed, so many memories. But then again, so many memories still to make.

He lifted a hand to my face. "Abby," he said. "My beautiful, perfect Abby." He leaned down and kissed me—a long, passionate, openmouthed kiss. When the kiss became more urgent, he broke away.

"Let me love you." He lifted me onto the bed with one smooth sweep and pushed me so I was on my back. "I'll start with your mouth."

He nipped at my mouth playfully. Every so often, he dropped a small kiss on my lips. He took his time, slowly stoking the fire in me with his mouth alone. Knowing what I wanted, knowing what he wanted and making us both wait. But finally, he framed my face with his hands and kissed me. Really kissed me. His tongue moving with mine, his lips urgent.

After several long minutes, he pulled back. "I could kiss your lips for hours and never tire of your taste." His eyes swept over my body. "But the rest of you is so damn delectable."

Slow hands unbuttoned my shirt and pushed it from my shoulders. I arched my back, and seconds later the shirt was gone. His mouth went to my neck.

"I can feel your heart racing." He took my hand and brought it to his chest. "Feel mine."

I felt his heartbeat through his shirt. It was frantic.

I couldn't help it. I grabbed his shirt and slipped it over his head. I wanted to feel him. On top of me. Under me. In me.

Anywhere. Everywhere. My hands slid across his chest, and I reacquainted myself with his body. The firmness of his chest. The strength of his arms. The burning need of his expression. And, for the first time, the love shining in his eyes.

His lips continued their descent down my body. "An often neglected body part is right here," he said, lifting my arm to his mouth, "the crook of the elbow."

Then he peppered featherlight kisses right on that little space of sensitive skin. "It would be an unpardonable sin to overlook this tasty delicacy." He licked it, and my entire body broke out in gooseflesh. I didn't have time to recover before he bit me gently.

"Oh, God," I moaned.

He gave me an evil grin. "And I've only started."

He placed more kisses up my arm, across my collarbone, and down between my breasts. With nimble fingers, he removed my bra and threw it away from the bed.

"Your breasts are perfect. Just the right size. And when I do this"—he rubbed my nipple between his fingers—"your body shakes with anticipation."

He knew me so well.

"Do you know how sweet your breasts taste?"

"No," I whispered.

"A shame, really." He bent his head and sucked me into his mouth. Rolled the tip of his tongue around my nipple. I arched my back as he drew me deeper.

"More. Please," I begged as he bit me, the sharpness of his teeth sending shock waves through my body.

He moved to the other breast and blew. "Such responsive skin," he murmured before kissing around the base of my breast. He licked his way upward, stopping when he made it to the nipple. He palmed it with his hand. "And this one? Just as fucking sweet as the other." And with that, his teeth pulled my nipple. I grabbed his head and held him to me.

I lost track of time as he played with my breasts—nipping, teasing, sucking. At one point, I pulled him up to me and he groaned as I slipped my tongue into his mouth. I lifted my hips, desperate for friction. For something.

"Wait," he whispered against my lips. "I haven't gotten to the best parts."

His hands stroked my belly, igniting the fire under my skin. I ran my fingers through his hair and shifted my legs so they brushed against his hardness.

He pushed the waistband of my pants down, and his tongue circled my belly button, dipped into it. "Another overlooked body part," he said. "Do you know how many nerve endings are found here?"

No, but I knew he made every last one tingle.

With measured slowness, he unbuttoned my pants, drew them over my hips and down my legs. I kicked them from the bed and sat up.

"My turn." I pushed him onto his back and jerked his pants and boxers off. Then I spent time rediscovering his body—the toned muscles of his chest, the indentations of his stomach, the dusting of hair that led to . . .

"Abby." He sighed as my hands dipped lower and teased his cock.

"Roll over," I said, because I loved his back—his sharp shoulder blades with the sensitive skin in between and the two little dimples right above his tight ass. I kissed a path from the nape of his neck to the small of his back, delighting in the tremor that shook his body. I licked my way back up, hands stroking his utterly perfect body.

Mine.

He turned over and carried me with him, so he once again rested on top of me. "I forgot where I was. Now I have to start all over."

He began again with my mouth, kissing me until I couldn't think straight, his hands roaming down my arms. He pulled back. "We discussed your mouth." He kissed me softly. "And your neck." Another kiss. "Your overlooked elbows and belly button." He kissed my elbow and stroked my belly with his free hand. "And I definitely remember these." He dipped his head to my breasts for a long kiss. Or two.

Or six.

"Ah, yes, I remember now." He slid down my body. "Right"—he skirted my hips—"about"—he breezed past where I was swollen and achy—"here." He grabbed my knee.

My knee?

"The knee is an erogenous zone for many people," he said.

I had a feeling all my zones were erogenous where Nathaniel was concerned.

He tickled the top of my knee with soft kisses while he stroked the underside. Then he lifted my leg and kissed the delicate skin behind my knee. I never thought someone kissing my knee would be such a turn-on, but damn if it didn't make me groan as he switched to the other knee. And licked and kissed some more.

"Nathaniel." I moaned, lifting my hips off the bed. "Higher."

He ignored me and worked his way lower, stopping at my ankles and placing soft, simple kisses on the inside. Then he lifted first one foot and then the other, kissing the bottom of my feet.

"Now," he said, looking up at me with a smirk. "I feel like I forgot something. What was it?"

"You're a smart man. I'm sure it'll come to you." I bent my knees and spread them.

His growl was a deep, primal sound that sent vibrations up my spine. He crawled back up the bed, ripped my panties off, and slung both of my legs over his shoulders. His tongue stroked my slit gently and I lifted my hips again.

"Now, right here is an important spot, because this"—he licked me again—"is pure"—lick—"unadulterated"—lick—"Abby."

"Dear Lord."

"And after I spend hours kissing your mouth"—he spread me with his fingers—"I could spend hours kissing and licking and drinking from your sweet"—lick—"wet"—lick—"pussy." He put his mouth on me and pushed his tongue inside.

It had been too long, and he had spent too much time teasing me. My orgasm swept over me with the first thrust of his tongue.

He placed small kisses on my clit and stroked me with his fingers. Ever so gently, he took my legs down from his shoulders and laid them back on the bed.

He looked like a mountain lion as he crawled back up the bed to me. "Now," he said, his voice husky. "Let us continue."

I gave a sigh of relief as his body covered mine. His weight felt glorious. With one hand, he placed his cock at my entrance. Then he took both my hands and intertwined our fingers.

"Abby," he said, and I opened my eyes to see the love and yearning shining from his. "This is me, Nathaniel"—he pushed slightly into me—"and, you, Abby"—he pushed more—"nothing else."

"Nathaniel." His name was a sigh from my lips.

He leaned down and kissed me, slowly bringing our hands above my head. The kiss deepened and he pushed farther inside.

I groaned as he gave one final push and seated himself deep within me. He looked into my eyes as he withdrew and began a slow, drawn-out rhythm.

Oh, yes. My body remembered this.

The feeling of being stretched. Of him above me. Of the way we moved together as one.

His fingers squeezed mine as he pushed inside again. He was slow and careful, drawing out every thrust. Timing each one, pulling out and waiting until the very second he knew I couldn't stand the emptiness anymore and then surging inside me again, filling me completely.

I arched my back, wanting to drive him in farther. His muscles were tight and tense, his control betrayed by the sweat breaking out on his forehead.

"Nathaniel. Please."

He quickened his pace, driving faster, but still not fast enough. I pulled my fingers from his and jerked his head toward mine while wrapping my legs around his waist. I lifted my body with each thrust of his, and we both let out a moan as he slipped in deeper.

But he was still too slow.

I ran my nails down his back, scratching him. "Damn it, Nathaniel." I bit his ear. "Fuck me."

He growled, pulled back, and plunged into me. Pounding me over and over with each long, hard, deep thrust.

I felt my climax building again.

His chest heaved as he thrust forward. I threw my head back and dug my nails into his back.

"Oh, God, Abby!"

He continued his rhythm, slipping a hand between our bodies and slapping my clit in time with his hips.

"I'm . . . I'm . . . I'm . . ." I stuttered.

He thrust one more time, and my climax overtook me. I let out a scream as his cock plunged deeply again and again. Another climax shook my body, but he kept pounding away.

His cock twitched deep inside me. He thrust a few more times, then held perfectly still. He threw his head back and groaned. His release set off another orgasm for me.

He collapsed on top of me, chest heaving. I felt his heart pounding as he worked to catch his breath.

Then Nathaniel lifted his head and kissed me.

Later, when we could move again, he slid off the bed and walked to the dresser. I rolled to my side, the better to watch his naked self as he opened drawers and lit candles. Darkness had fallen, but the room slowly came to light as he lit one candle after another.

The candlelight played on his skin, casting shadows that flickered over his body. I rolled onto my back when he returned to the bed. He sat up a little and gathered me to him so my head rested on his chest.

"I didn't plan for this to happen tonight," he said, placing soft kisses on my forehead. "Truly, I didn't."

I snuggled down into his arms and sighed. "I'm glad it happened, though. Very glad."

His arms tightened around me. "Abby? I know you didn't bring anything, but would you stay with me tonight?" He pulled back and looked into my eyes. "Here, in my bed?"

In his bed.

A tear slipped down my cheek. "Nathaniel . . ."

He brushed the tear away. "Please. Sleep here. With me."

I sat up and kissed him. "Yes," I said in between kisses. "Yes,

I'll stay." I pushed him down onto the bed. "But we have hours before it's even remotely time to think about something as mundane as sleep. So for now"—I traced his lips with my fingertips—"let me start with your mouth."

He let out a low moan.

As we started moving together again, I knew two things:

Nathaniel loved me.

And someday, someday very soon, I would wear his collar again.

I woke to find someone trailing kisses across my collarbone. Soft lips wandered their way up my neck, across my cheekbone, up to my ear. It had been two weeks since I first spent the night in Nathaniel's bed, and whenever I slept over, he always woke me up in the most delightful ways.

"Good morning," Nathaniel whispered, his warm breath tickling me.

"Mm," I replied and rolled closer to him as his arms embraced me. Waking up to Nathaniel's kisses was my new favorite way to start the day.

"I brought breakfast," he said.

Okay, scratch that. Waking up to Nathaniel's kisses and having him bring me breakfast in bed was my new favorite way to start the day.

"What did you bring?" I asked, thinking about sitting up.

"Me." He kissed one cheek. "Me." He kissed the other. "And a side dish of me." He placed a soft kiss on my lips.

For as long as I lived, I'd never grow tired of Nathaniel kissing me. But today was a big day for us, for our relationship, and I felt a little playful . . .

I rolled away from him. "Well, if that's all you brought—"

His strong arms captured me, and I giggled as he rolled me back to him.

"Although," he said, "if you insist on proper nourishment, I did bring an omelet."

I ran both my hands over the expanse of his chest. "No, thanks. On second thought, I'll take the Nathaniel."

He sat up. "I better let you eat before it gets cold." He brought a tray from his dresser over to the bed and set it before me.

"For real? You're not going to join me?"

He leaned over and kissed me once more. "I ate already, and I really should get ready for work. You need to get ready, too."

I mock pouted as he walked off to the bathroom, watching as he stepped out of his pants on his way.

There were times I forgot how sensitive Nathaniel was. How he took everything so personally. Our relationship had grown by leaps and bounds during the last few weeks, but every once in a while, I caught glimpses of the fragile soul he was.

I took a bite of omelet. He needed to lighten up a bit. Learn to be more playful. As expected, the omelet was pure heaven on a plate—fluffy eggs, tangy sharp cheddar cheese—one decadent bite after another.

The sound of running water soon came from the bathroom. Nathaniel. Naked and in a hot shower.

Now, that was pure heaven. No plate needed.

I ate the rest of the omelet, drank the fresh orange juice, and set the tray back on his dresser before walking into his bathroom.

Nathaniel's bathroom was the size of my apartment, and he could host a small cocktail party in his shower. But even with all that, we'd never showered together.

He stood in the shower, obscured by steam. I knew from experience that two overhead and six side showerheads pounded his body. Whenever I used his shower, I never wanted to leave. Throw Nathaniel in the mix and I doubted either one of us would make it to work on time.

Oh, well . . .

I slipped the nightgown over my head and dropped it to the floor. Nathaniel had his back to me and couldn't hear anything over the running water.

I quickly brushed my teeth, then opened the shower door and stepped inside, breathing in the misty steam. He spun around at the click of the door. I walked to him wordlessly and slipped my arms around his neck. Our lips came together in a soft kiss.

"Good morning," I said against his mouth.

"Good morning. Was something wrong with breakfast?"

Yes, Nathaniel, I wanted to say. *I'm standing naked in your shower because I want to complain about breakfast.*

"Actually," I said. "There was something missing."

"Really? In the omelet?"

"Not the omelet per se, but I didn't get the you." I kissed one cheek. "You." I kissed the other. "Or the side dish of you." I kissed his lips.

"Can't have that, now, can we?"

"I should say not."

"Hmm." He pulled out my body wash from its place inside the shower and started soaping up his hands. Within minutes, I was covered in suds and I started washing my hair.

"I know we've discussed this at length," he said as the warm water washed away the soap and I rinsed my hair. "But I'm going to ask you to humor me one more time." He placed his hands on my shoulders and looked into my eyes. "We don't have to start anything this weekend."

"I know," I said, soaping my hands up and running them over his arms. "But I want to." I stopped, not knowing how to phrase what I felt. "I never thought it would be something I needed . . . something I craved so much. I still don't want to be with anyone other than you, but . . ." I forced myself to look into his eyes, to somehow convey to him how much I meant this. "I understand now why you thought it necessary to recommend other dominants for me."

He pulled me softly to his chest. "Thank you," he whispered into my hair.

And just like that, the last traces of doubt and guilt about our past fell away.

We stood like that for several seconds, feeling the past slip away, embracing our future. Slowly, he pulled back and lowered his head to mine. His tongue teased my lips, and I sighed as he slipped inside, losing myself to his masterful mouth. Giving myself to him. Allowing all the swirling emotions to take over.

It was almost too much.

"Damn," I said when the kiss ended.

"You feel it, too?"

I closed my eyes briefly and nodded. "Every. Single. Time."

The corner of his mouth lifted in a smirk. "Come here," he said and pulled me to the edge of the shower. He reached up and turned the overhead showerheads off so only the side ones sprayed us.

He took my right leg and set it on the tile-covered bench.

"Right here." He ran a hand between my legs. "You are very, very dirty."

Dirty?

What?

He noticed my shock. "Remember?" he whispered as his fingers grazed my wet entrance.

Oh . . .

He meant last night. I smiled as I thought back . . . Me straddling Nathaniel. Him above me, driving into me as I held on to the headboard.

I reached down and grabbed his hard cock. "Oh, yes. It's definitely starting to come back."

"Thank goodness. If you had already forgotten, I might have sunk into a deep, dark depression."

I tightened my grasp. "There's only one thing I want sinking deeply."

"Fuck, Abby," he said, working himself against my hand.

"Now, Nathaniel."

He stopped his hips. "Always so impatient, love. You need to learn to savor pleasure."

Damn incorrigible man. "I'll savor pleasure later. You're the one who said we needed to get ready for work."

He gave me a lazy smile. "That was before you joined me in the shower."

"We'll be late," I said, knowing full well my argument fell on deaf ears. No one cared if he was late—he owned and ran his own business.

He bent down and whispered in my ear, "I'll write you a note."

I turned my head to meet his lips. "Oh, yeah?"

"Mm," he said against my mouth. "Dear Martha, please excuse Abby's tardiness this morning—"

"Oh, no you don't."

He put his finger against my lips. "She was inadvertently detained, quite on purpose, mind, by a plumbing problem that arose inexplicably in my shower."

He started thrusting slowly in and out of my hand again.

"Your blatant attempt at sexual humor is quite juvenile," I said.

"Really?" he asked, stopping his hips. "I thought it was pretty good for something I made up on the spot. Besides, Martha and I are like this." He held up two entwined fingers.

"Just because Martha turns a blind eye to your Wednesday visits doesn't mean she's your best friend."

"On the contrary, I owe Martha a lot. I never would have left that rose if she hadn't found me with it."

I laughed, never having known how close I'd come to not getting the rose. "And it was Martha who explained the meaning to me."

"Remind me to send her a thank-you note," he said, thrusting again into my hand. "Later, though. Much, much later."

I slipped my other hand down to his groin, cupped his balls, and within seconds I'd forgotten all about Martha, work, and anything remotely pertaining to getting ready for anything except Nathaniel.

Our lips came together once more. Still softly, though, for both of us wanted to savor and prolong the moment.

He broke the kiss and cupped his hands under my breasts. "I've never been so jealous of water before." His fingers slid over my skin. "How it can touch you everywhere—all at once."

His head dipped to my nipple, and he lapped at the water there. I leaned my head against the shower wall, releasing him from my hand.

Pressing closer to where I stood, he slipped two fingers into me. I groaned and wrapped my leg around his waist. He quickened the movement of his fingers, adding his thumb into the mix, rubbing it softly against my clit.

And then, as if that weren't enough, he whispered:

" 'Shy one, shy one,
Shy one of my heart,
She moves in the firelight
Pensively apart.
She carries in the dishes,
And lays them in a row.
To an isle in the water
With her would I go.
She carries in the candles,
And lights the curtained room,
Shy in the doorway
And shy in the gloom;
As shy as a rabbit,
Helpful and shy.
To an isle in the water
With her would I fly.' "

His hands never stopped moving, gently working me into a frenzy so that when he reached the last line of Yeats's, I thought I would fly. My orgasm overtook me and shuddered throughout my body.

"I love watching you come." He stepped closer between my legs and moved his cock to my entrance. "It makes me so fucking hard."

His cock slipped easily into me, and I gasped as he thrust deeply inside. I didn't have a chance to come down before he was driving me toward another climax.

"Come with me, Abby," he said, thrusting over and over. "Take me with you this time."

I'd never grow tired of the way he felt inside me or the way our bodies moved together. I slipped my arms around him and dragged my nails across his back.

"Yes," he said in a low growl. "Fuck. Yes."

I tightened my grasp on him as my second climax began to build. He placed a hand on either side of my head and doubled his efforts, pounding into me.

"I never want to leave this shower," he said, thrusting. "Never want to leave you. 'Cause I'm never going to fucking get enough." My back slid against the wet tiles as he kept thrusting. "Never. Never. Never enough."

His teeth grazed my neck, and one hand came down between us to where we were joined. "Feel us. Feel me. So fucking good."

One of his fingers flicked my clit, and I felt my body tense. I let out a groan. He bent his legs, thrust again, and my release overtook me. With one last push, he held still deep inside and came hard.

He sagged against me as our breathing returned to normal and our hearts slowed. The drumming of the water slowly brought back the realities of the morning.

"Damn," he said, smiling against my shoulder.

"What?"

"I need another shower."

Chapter Thirty-seven

"Ms. King," the receptionist said, "Mr. West will see you now."

I stood and walked toward the dark wooden door. My heart really shouldn't have been beating as hard as it was. I knew exactly who waited for me behind the closed door. Knew him and loved him.

It was Friday night and I was at his office by my own request. Nathaniel hadn't seen the point of what I wanted to do at first, but he eventually went along with me.

I pushed the door open, stepped through, and took a quick peek at him. His head was down and he was typing. I shut the door behind me and walked to the middle of the room.

I stood exactly as I had months ago—feet spread the width of my shoulders, head down, arms at my sides.

He continued typing.

We had spent the last two weeks working out our new agreement. While sitting at his kitchen table, we discussed and negotiated what we both wanted. Explored our personal limits. Reworked safe words. Decided when and how to play. We agreed to have playtime from Friday evening to Sunday afternoon and to be like any other couple from Sunday afternoon to Friday evening.

Our first argument had been over how often I would wear

his collar. I had wanted it all the time, but Nathaniel felt differently.

"I wore it every day last time," I said, *not seeing the point in doing anything differently.*

"But things have changed."

"I'm not arguing with that, but by wearing it every day, I would keep that connection between us."

"I understand why you want to wear my collar every day, but will you listen to some advice? From someone who has more experience?"

"Are you going to play the experience card often?"

"Yes."

I huffed and leaned back in my seat.

"Abby, listen. Whether you admit it or not, the collar puts you in a certain frame of mind, and I don't want you in that frame of mind during the week. If I ask if you want peas or carrots for dinner on a Tuesday night, I want the answer to come from Abby, my lover, not Abigail, my submissive."

"I know, but . . ." I trailed off. He had a point.

"I'm not giving you a meal plan or an exercise routine or stipulating sleep, or——"

"Thank goodness for that, because insisting on eight hours of sleep would severely limit our weekday activities."

"Agreed, but to get back to what I was saying, if I want to have sex on a Wednesday and you're not in the mood, I want you to feel free to say so. The collar"—he shook his head—*"it will limit you. Even if you think it won't."*

So we agreed I would wear his collar on weekends only.

While it had been my idea to resubmit my application and meet him at his office, we hadn't discussed how the evening would progress. I stared at my feet and wondered if he had the collar here, in his office. I hadn't seen it since the morning I'd left it on his dining room table.

I listened to his steady typing and wondered what he was thinking. What he was planning.

I pushed aside my rambling thoughts and concentrated instead on my breathing. There was no need to wonder how the evening would play out. It would play out the way Nathaniel decided, and whatever he decided would be what was best for both of us.

I had no doubts.

He stopped typing.

"Abigail King."

I didn't start when he said my name. I expected it this time and kept my head down.

He pushed back from the desk and walked across the hardwood floor. I counted his steps.

Ten.

Ten steps and he stopped behind me. He lifted my hair, twisted it around his hand, and pulled. "I was easy on you last time," he said in a low, commanding voice.

My belly quivered with anticipation. Nathaniel the Dom was back.

I'd missed him.

He pulled my hair harder, and I forced myself to keep my head down.

"You told me once that you could handle anything I gave you physically," he said. "Do you remember?"

Yes, damn it. I remembered saying those exact words. I should have known they would come back to bite me in the ass.

He jerked my hair. "I'm going to test that theory, Abigail. We'll see just how much you're able to handle."

He let go of my hair, and I exhaled the breath I'd been holding.

"I'm going to train you," he said, walking to stand before me so that I stared at the top of his leather dress shoes. "Train you to service my every need, desire, and want. From now on when I give a command, I expect you to obey immediately and without question. Any hesitation, raised eyebrow, or disobedience will be dealt with on the spot. Is that understood?"

I waited.

"Look at me and answer," he said. "Do you understand?"

I looked up and into his steady green eyes. "Yes, Master."

"*Tsk, tsk, tsk,*" he scolded. "I thought you learned that lesson last time."

Last time? What?

"How do you address me before I collar you?"

Shit.

"Yes, sir."

"I let that mistake slide before," he said, walking to his desk. "But like I said, I won't be as lenient this time around."

My heart pounded. I really hadn't expected to mess up so soon.

"Lift your skirt and put your hands on top of my desk."

I walked to the front of his desk and lifted my skirt above my waist. Was his secretary still outside? Would she hear? I put my hands on his desk and braced myself.

"Three strokes. Count."

His hand swooshed through the air and landed with a slap on my backside. Ow.

"One," I said.

Again it came, landing on a different spot.

"Two."

Only one more. I clenched my teeth as he struck the third time.

"Three."

He stopped and rubbed my backside, soothing the pain away

with his expert hands. His touch felt good, and I had to force myself to remain still. He pulled my skirt down.

"Go stand where you were," he whispered.

I walked back to my spot in the middle of his office. In a way, I felt more at ease. I'd messed up and he'd dealt with it. We continued. Nothing to fear.

"Do you remember your safe words?" Nathaniel said from the side of his desk.

I thought back to that conversation.

We were at the kitchen table again.

"Two?" I asked. "You're giving me two safe words?"

"It's a commonly used system," he said, writing something down.

"But last time—"

He looked up. "I already explained my error in the way I set things up last time, Abby. I won't have you walk out on me again."

I reached across the table to take his hand. "I'm not leaving. I just don't know why I have to have two safe words."

"Because we'll be pushing your limits. If you say 'yellow,' I'll know I'm pushing, but can continue. 'Red' stops the scene completely."

It still seemed a bit much.

"But you've never had a sub use her safe word before," I said.

"I have now," he said, lifting my hand to his lips. "And I want you to feel completely safe and secure anytime you're with me. Even when I'm pushing you."

"Yes, sir," I said, snapping back to the present. "I remember the safe words."

"Good." He went back behind his desk, opened another drawer, and took out a box. Opened it.

My collar.

He lifted it up. "Are you ready, Abigail?"

"Yes, sir," I said, smiling.

He walked back to stand in front of me again. "Kneel."

I dropped to my knees. He slipped the necklace around my neck, fastened it in place. I felt complete again.

"I'll put this on you every Friday evening at six o'clock and take it off Sunday afternoons at three," he said, fingers trailing over my collarbone.

We had decided that would give us plenty of time to play on Friday night and plenty of time on Sundays to talk about our weekend and transition back to everyday behavior.

We had also decided what would happen immediately after he collared me every Friday night. But I waited for him to instruct me.

"Stand up," he said.

I stood, confused. This was not what we had agreed to.

His eyes shone with emotion. "You look so fucking good wearing my collar." He put a hand under my chin and kissed me. Hard.

I was lying in his arms the first morning after spending the night in his bed.

"The whole no-kissing rule," I said, running a hand down his chest. "Was that a rule with all subs or just me?"

He stroked my hair. "It was just you, Abby."

"Just me?" I lifted my head to look at him. "Why?"

"It was a way to distance myself. I thought if I didn't kiss you, I wouldn't feel as much. I'd be able to remind myself I was just your dom."

"You kissed your other subs," I mumbled, not liking the jealousy that coursed through my body.

"Yes."

"But not me."

He didn't say anything, probably afraid of how I would react. Of what I would say.

And part of me was angry he'd held back. That he'd denied us.

But the past was the past.

"You know what this means, don't you?" I asked, climbing up his body.

"No," he said hesitantly.

I put my lips near his. "You've got a lot of making up to do."

He gave me a soft kiss. "A lot?"

"Mmm," I said as he kissed me again. "With interest."

He smiled against my lips. "Interest?"

"Lots of interest. You'd better get started."

"Oh, Abby." He flipped me over and his body hovered over mine. "I always pay my debts."

He broke the kiss and pushed on my shoulders. "Back to your knees."

I knelt before him. His cock strained against the front of his pants, but he waited.

"Please, Master, may I have you in my mouth?"

"You may."

I unbuckled and unzipped him with quick fingers, ready for his taste. I slipped his pants and boxers down to his ankles and licked my lips at the sight of his massive erection.

He twisted his fingers in my hair as I took him in my mouth. I eased him in, but he didn't want slow and pushed himself all the way in with one hard thrust. He hit the back of my throat, and I quickly relaxed so I wouldn't gag.

He used his grip on my hair to thrust himself in and out. It felt so good, the sharp pull of my hair and the force of his cock battering my throat. I hoped it was as good for him. I sucked as he pulled out of my mouth and ran my tongue down his length as he pushed inside. I pulled my lips back so that my teeth grazed him.

"Fuck," he said.

A few more hard thrusts and he started to jerk inside my mouth. I brought my hands to his thighs in anticipation, ready for his climax. Wanting it.

He pushed in deeply and held still as his release filled my mouth. I swallowed it all, loving the salty taste that represented his pleasure.

His hands rubbed my scalp, gently massaging my head, easing away any remaining pain from his hair pulling. I held still and concentrated on the love in his touch.

"Buckle my pants, Abigail," he said, running his fingers through my hair one last time.

I brought his pants and boxers back up his body. Zipped him up and buckled his belt.

"Stand up," he commanded. He brought his hand to my chin once I stood and lifted my head to meet his eyes. "I'm going to work you hard tonight. I'm going to bring you to the edge of pleasure and leave you hanging. You will not release until I give you permission, and I will be very stingy with my permission. Do you understand? Answer me."

Dear, sweet, merciful heavens.

"Yes, Master."

His eyes danced with excitement. "I'll be home in an hour. I want you naked and waiting in the playroom."

To be continued . . .

Tara Sue Me wrote her first novel at the age of twelve. It would be twenty years before she picked up her pen to write the second.

After completing several traditional romances, she decided to try her hand at something spicier and started work on *The Submissive*. What began as a writing exercise quickly took on a life of its own, and the sequels *The Dominant* and *The Training* soon followed. Originally published online, the trilogy was a huge hit with readers around the world.

Tara kept her identity and her writing life secret, not even telling her husband what she was working on. To this day, only a handful of people know the truth (though she has told her husband). They live together in the southeastern United States with their two children.

Don't miss the next installment in

Tara Sue Me's trilogy,

The
Dominant

Coming in August 2013 from

New American Library in print and e-book.

The phone on my desk gave a low double beep.

I glanced at my watch. Four thirty. My administrative assistant had explicit instructions not to interrupt me unless one of two people called. It was too early for Yang Cai to call from China, so that left only one other person.

I hit the speakerphone button. "Yes, Sara?"

"Mr. Godwin on line one, sir."

Excellent.

"Did I receive a package from him today?" I asked.

Papers rustled in the background. "Yes, sir. Should I bring it in now?"

"I'll get it later." I disconnected and switched to the headset. "Godwin, I expected you to call earlier. Six days earlier." I'd been waiting for the package just as long.

"I'm sorry, Mr. West. You had a late application I wanted to include with this batch."

Very well. It wasn't like the women knew I had a deadline. That was something I would discuss with Godwin later.

"How many this time?" I asked.

"Four." He sounded relieved I'd moved on from his lateness. "Three experienced and one without any experience or references."

I leaned back in my chair and stretched my legs. We really shouldn't be having this conversation. Godwin knew my preferences by now. "You know my feelings on inexperienced submissives."

"I know, sir," he said, and I pictured him wiping the sweat from his brow. "But this one is different—she asked for you."

I stretched one leg and then the other. I needed a nice, long jog, but it would have to wait until later that evening. "They all ask for me." I wasn't being vain, just honest.

"Yes, sir, but this one only wants to service you. She's not interested in anyone else."

I sat up in the chair. "Really?"

"Her application specifically states she will sub for you and no one else."

I had rules about prior experience and references because, to be frank, I didn't have time to train a submissive. I preferred someone with experience, someone who would learn my ways quickly. Someone I could learn quickly. I always included a lengthy checklist in the application to ensure applicants knew exactly what they were getting themselves into.

"I assume she filled out the checklist properly. Didn't indicate she would do anything and everything." That had happened once. Godwin knew better now.

"Yes, sir."

"I suppose I could take a look at it."

"Last one in the pile, sir."

The one he'd held the package up for, then. "Thank you, Godwin." I hung up the phone and stepped outside my office. Sara handed me the package.

"Why don't you go home, Sara?" I tucked the envelope under my arm. "It should be quiet the rest of the evening."

She thanked me as I walked back into my office.

I got a bottle of water, set it on my desk, and opened the package.

I flipped my way through the first three applications. Nothing special. Nothing out of the ordinary. I could set up a test weekend with any of the three women and probably wouldn't be able to tell the difference between them.

I rubbed the back of my neck and sighed. Maybe I had been doing this too long. Maybe I should try again to settle down and be "normal." With someone who wasn't Melanie this time. The problem was, I needed my dom lifestyle. I just wanted something special to go along with it.

I took a long sip of water and looked at my watch. Five o'clock. It was highly doubtful I'd find my something special in the last application. Since the woman had no experience, it really wasn't even worth my time to review her paperwork. Without looking at it, I took the application and put it on top of my to-shred pile. The three remaining I placed side by side on top of my desk and read over the cover pages again.

Nothing. There was basically nothing separating the three women. I should just close my eyes and randomly pick one. The one in the middle would work.

But even as I looked over her information, my gaze drifted to the shred pile. The discarded application represented a woman who wanted to be my submissive. She'd taken the time to fill out my detailed paperwork, and Godwin had held up sending everything because of Miss I-have-no-experience-and-want-only-Nathaniel-West. The least I could do was respect that woman enough to read her information.

I picked up the discarded application and read the name.

Abigail King.

The papers slipped from my hand and fluttered to the ground.

I was a complete success in the eyes of the world.

I owned and ran my own international securities corporation. I employed hundreds of staff. I lived in a mansion that had graced the pages of *Architectural Digest*. I had a terrific family. Ninety-nine percent of the time, I was content with my life. But there was that one percent . . .

That one percent that told me I was an utter and complete failure.

That I was surrounded by hundreds of people, but known by very few.

That my lifestyle was not acceptable.

That I would never find someone I could love and who would love me in return.

I never regretted my decision to live the lifestyle of a dominant. I normally felt very fulfilled, and if there were times I did not, they were very few and far between.

I felt incomplete only when I made my way to the public library and caught a glimpse of Abby. Of course, until her application crossed my desk, I had no way of knowing if she even knew I existed. Until then, Abby had symbolized for me the missing one percent. Our worlds were so far apart, they could not and would not collide.

But if Abby was a submissive and wanted to be my submissive . . .

I allowed my mind to wander down pathways I'd closed off for years. Opened the gates of my imagination and let the images overtake me.

Abby naked and bound to my bed.

Abby on her knees before me.

Abby begging for my whip.

Oh, yes.

I picked her application up off the ground and started reading.

Name, address, phone number, and occupation, I skimmed over. I turned the page to her medical history—normal liver function tests and blood cell counts, HIV and hepatitis negative, negative urine drug screen. The only medication she took was the birth control pills I required.

I went to the next page, her completed checklist. Godwin had not lied when he said Abby had no experience. She had marked off only seven items on the list: vaginal sex, masturbation, blindfolds, spanking, swallowing semen, hand jobs, and sexual deprivation. In the comment field beside sexual deprivation, she had written, "Ha-ha. Not sure our definitions are the same." I smiled. She had a sense of humor.

Several items were marked "No, hard limit." I respected that—I had my own hard limits. Looking over the list, I discovered that several of them lined up with hers. Several of them did not. There was nothing wrong with that—limits changed, checklists changed. If we were together for the long term—

What was I thinking? Was I actually thinking about calling Abby in for a test?

Yes, damn it, I was.

But I knew, I knew, that if the application were from anyone other than Abby, I wouldn't even give it a second glance. I would shred it and forget it existed. I didn't train submissives.

But it was from Abby, and I didn't want to shred it. I wanted to pore over her application until I had it memorized. I wanted to make a list of what she had marked as "willing to try" and show her the pleasure of doing those things. I wanted to study her body until its contours were permanently etched in my mind. Until my hands knew and recognized her every response. I wanted to watch her give in to her true submissive nature.

I wanted to be her dom.

Could I do that? Could I put aside my thoughts of Abby, the fantasy I would never have, and instead have Abigail, the submissive?

Yes. Yes, I could.

Because I was Nathaniel West and Nathaniel West didn't fail.

And if Abby King no longer existed. Or if she was replaced by Abigail King . . .

I picked up the phone and dialed Godwin.

"Yes, sir, Mr. West," he said. "Have you decided?"

"Send Abigail King my personal checklist. If she's still interested after reviewing it, have her call Sara for an appointment next week."

Abby and Nathaniel's story continues in

the next installment

in Tara Sue Me's sensational trilogy,

The
Training

Coming in October 2013 from New American

Library in print and e-book.

The drive back to Nathaniel's house took longer than it should have. Or maybe it just felt like it took longer. Maybe it was nerves.

I tipped my head in thought.

Maybe not nerves, exactly. Maybe anticipation.

Anticipation that after weeks of talking, weeks of waiting, and weeks of planning, we were finally here.

Finally back.

I lifted my hand and touched the collar—Nathaniel's collar. My fingertips danced over the familiar lines and traced along the diamonds. I moved my head from side to side, reacquainting myself with the collar's feel.

There were no words to describe how I felt wearing Nathaniel's collar again. The closest I could come was to compare it to a puzzle. A puzzle with the last piece finally in place. Yes, for the last few weeks, Nathaniel and I had lived as lovers, but we'd both felt incomplete. His recollaring of me—his reclaiming of me—had been what was missing. It sounded odd, even to me, but I finally felt like I was his again.

The hired car eventually reached Nathaniel's house and pulled into his long drive. Lights flickered from the windows. He had set the timer, anticipating my arrival in the dark. Such a small gesture, but a touching one. One that showed, like much of what he did, how he kept me firmly at the forefront of his mind.

I jingled my keys as I walked up the drive to his front door. My keys. To his house. He'd given me a set of keys a week ago. I didn't live with him, but I spent a fair amount of time at his house. He said it only made sense for me to be able to let myself in or to lock up when I left.

Apollo, Nathaniel's golden retriever, rushed me when I opened the door. I rubbed his head and let him outside for a few minutes. I didn't keep him out for too long—I wasn't sure if Nathaniel would arrive home early, but if he did, I wanted to be in place. I wanted this weekend to be perfect.

"Stay," I told Apollo after stopping in the kitchen to refill his water bowl. Apollo obeyed all of Nathaniel's orders, but thankfully he listened to me this time. Normally, he would follow me up the stairs, and tonight that would be odd.

I quickly left the kitchen and made my way upstairs to my old room. The room that would be mine on weekends.

I undressed, placing my clothes in a neat pile on the edge of the twin bed. On this, Nathaniel and I had been in agreement. I would share his bed Sunday through Thursday nights, anytime I spent the night with him, but on Friday and Saturday nights, I would sleep in the room he reserved for his submissives.

Now that we had a more traditional relationship during the week, we both wanted to make sure we remained in the proper mind-set on weekends. That mind-set would be easier to maintain for both of us if we slept separately. For both of us, yes, but perhaps more so for Nathaniel. He rarely shared a bed with his submissives, and having a romantic relationship with one was completely new to him.

I stepped naked into the playroom. Nathaniel had led me around the room last weekend—explaining, discussing, and showing me things I'd never seen and several items I'd never heard of.

At its core, it was an unassuming room—hardwood floors, deep, dark brown paint, handsome cherry armoires, even a long table carved from rich wood. However, the chains and shackles, the padded leather bench and table, and the wooden whipping bench gave away the room's purpose.

A lone pillow waited for me below the hanging chains. I dropped to my knees on it, situating myself into the position Nathaniel explained I was to be in whenever I waited for him in the playroom—butt resting on my heels, back straight, right hand on top of my left in my lap, fingers not intertwined, and head down.

I got into position and waited.

Time inched forward.

I finally heard him enter through the front door.

"Apollo," he called, and while I knew he spoke Apollo's name so he could take him outside again, another reason was to alert me who it was that entered the house. To give me time to prepare myself. Perhaps for him to listen for footsteps from overhead. Footsteps that would tell him I wasn't prepared for his arrival. I felt proud he would hear nothing.

I closed my eyes. It wouldn't be long now. I imagined what Nathaniel was doing—taking Apollo outside, feeding him maybe. Would he undress downstairs? In his bedroom? Or would he enter the playroom wearing his suit and tie?

Doesn't matter, I told myself. Whatever Nathaniel has planned would be perfect.

I strained my ears—he was walking up the stairs now. Alone. No dog followed.

Somehow, the atmosphere of the room changed when he walked in. The air became charged and the space between us nearly hummed. In that moment, I understood—I was his, yes. I had been correct in that assumption. But even more so, even more important, perhaps, he was mine.

My heart raced.

"Very nice, Abigail," he said and walked to stand in front of me. His feet were bare, and I noted he had changed out of his suit and into a pair of black jeans.

I closed my eyes again. Cleared my mind. Focused inwardly. Forced myself to remain still under his scrutiny.

He walked to the table, and I heard a drawer open. For a minute, I tried to remember everything in the drawers, but I stopped myself and once again forced my mind to quiet itself.

He came back to stand at my side. Something firm and leather trailed down my spine.

Riding crop.

"Perfect posture," he said as the crop ran up my spine. "I expect you to be in this position whenever I tell you to enter this room."

I felt relieved he was satisfied with my posture. I wanted so much to please him tonight. To show him I was ready for this. That we were ready. He had been so worried.

Of course, not a bit of worry or doubt could be discerned now. Not in his voice. Not in his stance. His demeanor in the playroom was utter and complete control and confidence.

He dragged the riding crop down my stomach and then back up. Teasing.

Damn. I loved the riding crop.

I kept my head down even though I wanted to see his face. To meet his eyes. But I knew the best gift I could give him was my absolute trust and obedience, so I kept my head down with my eyes focused on the floor.

"Stand up."

I rose slowly to my feet, knowing I stood directly under the chains. Normally, he kept them up for storage, but they were lowered tonight.

"Friday night through Sunday afternoon, your body is mine," he said. "As we agreed, the kitchen table and library are still yours. There, and only there, are you to speak your mind. Respectfully, of course."

Both of his hands traced across my shoulders, down my arms. One hand slipped between my breasts and dropped to where I was wet and aching.

"This," he said, rubbing my outer lips, "is your responsibility. I want you waxed bare as often as possible. If I decide you have neglected this responsibility, you will be punished."

And again, we had agreed to this.

"In addition, it is your responsibility to ensure your waxer does an acceptable job. I will allow no excuses. Is that understood?"

I didn't say anything.

"You may answer," he said, and I heard the smile in his voice.

"Yes, Master."

He slipped a finger between my folds, and I felt his breath in my ear. "I like you bare." His finger swirled around my clit. "Slick and smooth. Nothing between your pussy and whatever I decide to do to it."

Fuck.

Then he moved behind me and cupped my ass. "Have you been using your plug?"

I waited.

"You may answer."

"Yes, Master."

His finger made its way back to the front of me, and I bit the inside of my cheek to keep from moaning.

"I won't ask you that again," he said. "From now on, it is your responsibility to prepare your body to accept my cock in any manner I decide to give it to you." He ran a finger around the rim of my ear. "If I want to fuck your ear, I expect your ear to be ready." He hooked his finger in my ear and pulled. I kept my head down. "Do you understand? Answer me."

"Yes, Master."

He lifted my arms above my head, buckling first one wrist and then the other to the chains at my side. "Do you remember this?" he asked, his warm breath tickling my hair. "From our first weekend?"

Again, I said nothing.

"Very nice, Abigail," he said. "Just so there's no misunderstanding, for the rest of the evening, or until I tell you differently, you may not speak or vocalize in any way. There are two exceptions—the first being the use of your safe words. You are to use them at any point you feel the need. No repercussions or consequences will ever follow the use of your safe words. Second, when I ask if you are okay, I expect an immediate and honest answer."

He didn't wait for a response, of course. I wasn't to give one. Without warning, his hands slipped back down to where I ached for him. Since my head was down, I watched one of his fingers slide inside me and I bit the inside of my cheek again to keep from moaning.

Shit, his hands felt good.

"How wet you are already." He pushed deeper and twisted his wrist. Fuck. "Usually, I would taste you myself, but tonight, I feel like sharing."

He removed himself and the emptiness was immediate, but before I could think much about it, I felt his slippery finger at my mouth. "Open, Abigail, and taste how ready you are for me." He trailed his finger around my open lips before easing it inside my mouth.

I'd tasted myself before, out of curiosity, but never so much at one time and never off of Nathaniel's finger. It felt so depraved, so feral.

Damn, it turned me on.

"Taste how sweet you are," he said as I licked myself off his finger.

I treated his finger as if it were his cock—running my tongue along it, sucking gently at first. I wanted him. Wanted him inside me. I sucked harder, imagining his cock in my mouth.

You will not release until I give you permission, and I will be very stingy with my permission. His words from the office floated through my mind, and I choked back a moan before it left my mouth. It would be a long night.

"I changed my mind," he said when I finished cleaning his finger. "I want a taste after all." He crushed his lips to mine and forced my mouth open. His lips were brutal—powerful and demanding in their quest to taste me.

Damn, I'd have a stroke if he kept that up.